COME BACK

SASKATOON PUBLIC LIBRARY **RM**
36001401567598
Come back

COME
BACK

Rudy Wiebe

ALFRED A. KNOPF CANADA

PUBLISHED BY ALFRED A. KNOPF CANADA

Copyright © 2014 Jackpine House Ltd.

All rights reserved under International and Pan-American Copyright
Conventions. No part of this book may be reproduced in any form or by any
electronic or mechanical means, including information storage and retrieval
systems, without permission in writing from the publisher, except by a
reviewer, who may quote brief passages in a review. Published in 2014
by Alfred A. Knopf Canada, a division of Random House of Canada Limited,
a Penguin Random House Company. Distributed in Canada by
Random House of Canada Limited, Toronto.

www.randomhouse.ca

Knopf Canada and colophon are registered trademarks.

*This book is a work of fiction. Names, characters, places and incidents either
are the product of the author's imagination or are used fictitiously. Any resemblance
to actual persons, living or dead, events or locales is entirely coincidental.*

Library and Archives Canada Cataloguing in Publication

Wiebe, Rudy, 1934–, author
Come back / Rudy Wiebe.

Issued in print and electronic formats.

ISBN 978-0-345-80885-1
eBook ISBN 978-0-345-80887-5

I. Title.

PS8545.I38C66 2014   C813'.54   C2014-902259-X

Book design by Terri Nimmo

Cover images: (letter) © Bruce Amos, (torn paper) © Robyn Mackenzie,
(bird) © Christos Georghiou, all Dreamstime.com

Text images: (bird) © Christos Georghiou / Dreamstime.com;
(feather) © Roman Malyshev / Shutterstock.com

Printed and bound in the United States of America

2 4 6 8 9 7 5 3 1

For my family,
and for
Robert Kroetsch (1927–2011)

For everyone will be salted with fire.

JESUS (Mark 9:49)

For now we look through a mirror into an enigma,
but then face to face.

PAUL (I Corinthians 13:12)

AUTHOR'S NOTE

The "Hal" in this fiction was a character in my first novel, *Peace Shall Destroy Many*, which was originally published in 1962; republished by Knopf Canada in 2001. The time then was 1944, and Hal was an eight-year-old boy in Wapiti, Saskatchewan, an isolated Mennonite community in the Canadian boreal forest.

R. W.

WEDNESDAY, APRIL 28, 2010

In bright spring snow a slim woman in a black hoodie walked by along Whyte Avenue leading three children barely higher than her knees. The children clutched mittened hands, strung out like little linked sausages as she hauled them along with her left arm, her right urging them *Come on! Come on!* towards the green "Walk."

From inside the coffee shop Hal watched them move across the window wall: blue, pink, purple stuffed parkas passing in a reflecting, streaky world. Could all those wriggly imps be hers? The pink little middle parka skipped twice, it began to shimmy within some body rhythm, tilting its hooded head back and tiny mouth open as if to catch snowflakes on its flickering tongue, and they reached the "Walk" corner at 104th Street with all three links infected by dance. Ignoring the huge Greyarrow bus roaring past them in the slanting snow, they pranced and wriggled south into the wave of pedestrians coming on the crosswalk. The woman's sharp face bent lower, scolding, but that only added more rhythm to the fling of their heads, their joined arms waving, their splotching feet.

April children dancing through a glassy world fallen brilliant white overnight: O Edmonton rejoice, all's right with your world.

They had sloshed themselves into disappearance, vanishing one by one past an ancient man bent over his walker wobbling through the snow, vanished completely behind a woman and man coming on. The woman's short red-denim jacket was flung open to a cream T-shirt, her breast declared in taut crimson: BORED DOE.

Hal laughed aloud. A lovely ironic woman in longing. And clearly not for the handsome oaf flapping his chin at her as they walked by; her perfect profile, it seemed, faced only distance as the right silver edge of the window cut them away.

Good passing show, momentarily better than usual. Hal leaned back in his Double Cup armchair. He considered the chair his, the drooping black leatherette fitting warm around his buttocks, he sat in it every morning except Sunday. If some coffee drinker was already seated there when he arrived, he simply waited him out, he had all the time there was, now, and if Owl came in before him, Owl took the companion chair across the shaky little table and told anyone glancing at the vacant chair that his friend would be along any minute, sorry. Hal lifted his cup, the silver Waterloo University mug he used on Wednesdays, and saw Owl lean forward in his chair: he was staring up at the left corner of the window wall.

There, beyond the double forks of the ash tree growing out of the sidewalk, perched a huge bird; bobbing on the arm of the streetlight. Pitch black in thin flying snow, with something white, large, clamped in its black beak. A raven . . . yes, that was it, he had never seen such a bird at a street intersection, not in all the years he lived in Edmonton. Its claws clinched tight on the snowy arm.

"She'll fly the circle," Owl said happily. "She was sitting on that southeast lamp over there by Kill for Chocolate and she flew straight across Whyte to the northeast post and sat there holding that white thing and then she come across 104th, across to here, and now she'll fly back over Whyte again, just wait, that southwest post—"

"That's no circle," Hal said. "If that's it, it's flying a square."

"Whiteman's circle." Hal could hear the grin in Owl's voice, "Yeah, there she goes . . . easy . . ."

The raven crouched, launched itself into the bright, slanting sky. Lifting over the turning barrel of a concrete truck and above six tight lanes of traffic to land, steady, on the arm of the opposite lamppost. It had flown the path of the dancing children. Where were they? Hal had neglected to look after them and now they were gone— silly, he'd been distracted as usual by any passing Bored Doe or bent geezer—but the raven sprang up, up to the roof edge of what he abruptly remembered was the Royal Bank building fifty-six years ago when he came to Edmonton to begin university—and a clump of snow dropped on the people waiting on Whyte for "Walk" as the raven scrabbled, flapping on the roof edge. It gained its balance, hesitated, leaning, then swung one, two, three hops past the crumbling chimney and was out of sight on the flat roof. Still holding that white thing in its beak, gone.

"It didn't complete your Whiteman circle."

"Come and gone," Owl said. "Good sign."

"Good for what?"

"Maybe . . . maybe bad. Hard to tell sometimes."

"I know," Hal said. "And you'll know which when it happens."

"Yeah, for sure. Something always happens."

They were both laughing a little, they splashed each other so often with their mutual skepticisms. Hope is the thing with feathers that perches . . . abruptly Hal gripped the arms of his chair, hoisted himself to his feet.

"I'm for refill."

But Owl's expression shifted; he seemed unwilling to let go. "You know," he said, "the first bird named in your Bible is a raven."

"What?" Momentarily Hal's memory was empty. "There's birds, lots in the creation stories . . ."

"Yeah, birds," Owl said, "but not named. Raven's named, the flood, he's in the ark and Noah shoves him out, go look for land."

"That's the first bird named in the Bible?"

"Yeah."

"How'd you know that?"

"Our priest, Fort Good Hope, he didn't like Raven. He told us that story all the time, raven never coming back, no message to help Noah."

"Yes, but the dove did, so they knew there was dry land again."

"So, for the priest bad black raven, good white dove."

Hal gestured outside, "Edmonton doves, they're grey."

Owl stood easily, laughing aloud. He pulled his worn toque down his brown forehead. "Time for hunting and gathering. Thanks again, coffee."

Hal picked up Owl's paper cup and his own mug. "Okay. Even when winter comes back end of April."

"Just a day. If it was gone too long we'd maybe forget it."

"Huh—Edmonton forget winter! How's it up north? You hear from your sister?"

"Not yet, this spring—but it won't be gone there, not yet. Deh-Cho River ice'll still be three feet thick, but real dangerous now, water under the snow on top."

"Safer hunting here, eh."

"For sure, just potholes." Owl pushed the door, snow twirled in on the draft, and then he was outside, waiting for the light to cross 104th Street. Yes, reverse the black raven. Hal turned and suddenly, as if a switch had flipped in his head, he heard the ceaseless sound of the coffee shop: something they called music these days thumping to a shriek or wail above the mutter of voices, he heard them but could easily refuse to listen, people sitting there forever repeating something, talking jokes or pleading sorrow, the music background actually less and less like any singing he had ever . . . but Becca was there, for once alone behind the counter lined with packaged food he never saw anyone buy.

Her hand accepted his mug. He groped in his jean pocket for the plastic card and a quarter, her face poised perfectly above her spring-green shirt and bare arms.

"A bit more. Need a hit."

Becca glanced up, and smiled. Always working, always silently lovely; an unwavering memory delight.

"On the house," she said. "Snow celebration."

"Hey, that's a good one."

"Only today, tomorrow it's all gone."

Hal laughed. "Just wait three days, there's still May," he said.

He seated himself with his warm mug. His everlasting northern streaky-white world beyond sheltering glass, today a wall of sloshing sidewalks and streets overlaid with the faint mirror of Double Cup space around him, silver mug and pale hand. He could see himself, dimly, a small, dark mound contemplating itself. The diaphanous window wall—so close if he leaned forward he would touch it—the shadows on the glass reflected him floor to ceiling, a mere spot on a faintly nurtured rubbing of the perfect coffee-shop gravestone—no—lifestone, so still, still but alive. Yes yes he was fine, just fine. Still alive ages after a Canadian bush boyhood and, miracle beyond miracle, an education none of his brothers or sisters could dream of and beautiful Yo and their three children—two . . . three—stop stupid, stop it. He was okay, his mind quick, sharp; he could concentrate on reading the endless passing bodies on the sidewalk empty and safe as a lifetime pushed behind him, more and more ignorable, forgotten—three boys walked right across the window wall, slouching past in furious talk, their jean pockets sagged barely above the backs of their knees—a lifetime may it please God forgiven.

And on Whyte Avenue light snow whirled in the wind following cars, was crunched into freezing slush by unknowable people and vehicles going and going, gone and sometimes coming back, thirty or forty thousand machines crossing this intersection—was that what they said?—and perhaps more humans every day and night in all directions, the traffic of street and sidewalk an instinctive, polite, thoughtless Canadian order.

A city bus sighed right across the window. Empty.

This unending scarf woven of movement, every van and pickup and bike and car and crew-cab and hatchback and wheelchair delivery truck different, every single human body moving, and unique, every day. And whenever he came every day it was here, human and different and empty and warm, he need do nothing but sit snug and look. Empty. Comforted because he needed none.

Orange. A brilliant orange jacket above blue jeans walked out of the right edge of the glass wall. Long strides passing left fast, thick downfill sewn in squares of taut seams, standing orange collar zipped up high over lower nose and ear, exposed forehead curved to a widow's peak of light-brown hair fluffed back with snow—ends curled! A moustache hidden by the collar?

Hal stared in stunned amazement: the tall, slender man with his half-hidden face gliding so fast across the mirrored glass to the trampled street corner and wheeling south into the crosswalk squished wet by cars, the long strides, the shift of shoulders inside the tight orange . . . there was . . . he was seeing, something, was it possible, a label, "The Down People of Canada / Michael S. Freed"—the tiny black label on the orange lining he had once found himself forced to remember beyond knowing, remember and remember until steadily, deliberately, he thought he had buried it forever into nothing—"6820 Size M Down 100%"—he saw that label he knew to be sewn inside that seamed orange jacket, that drift of light-brown hair curled at its edges above the crossing crowd—that high hairline of head turn! There would be a moustache—Hal exploded in a scream:

"Gabe!"

He leaped to his feet, rammed himself through the door and past the square pillar and across the slipping sidewalk, hit a waiting man's shoulder for balance and he stayed upright and was into Whyte Avenue, he was charging through sloppy slush right into the first wave of coming cars accelerating west at him across the intersection on their green light, he dodged into spaces between flashing, honking trunks and hoods though he was looking beyond them, beyond, he was waving his arms and screaming above the traffic,

"Gabe! Gabriel!"

as he floundered and fought the sliding street and the next wave of westbound cars reached him as he gained the third lane, their brakes squished as horns squalled but he was already across to the centre boulevard,

"Gabe!"

and a crash burst behind him, barely behind, and a hard-green pickup shuddered to a stop in front of him, horn blaring, as his shoulder—he just twisted to the side—slammed against the driver door—

"You stupid shit!" the driver shrieked out of her opening window.

"My son!" Hal yelled in her face and hurled himself around the front of the truck, hammered the hood with his right hand for balance as he leaped into the next lanes—at that instant the coming car was still two lengths away—and he was across on the south sidewalk even as he heard more brakes and horns squeal behind him, something else crush! and more plastic and glass break even louder but he was on the old Royal Bank sidewalk and running south as fast as his straining body could propel him through the splotching snow while just barely keeping balance—startled people at the bus stop jerked out of his path—he was already gasping, his legs so massively heavy he was leaning forward more and more as his head yearned for speed, he was squinting to see and his exhausted old body betrayed him, slammed him crooked against a wall at the corner of the alley opening onto 104th Street and he knew like a kick in his shuddering gut that—where was he running? He was gasping in sudden whiteness. The Orange Downfill could have gone in any direction, down either street or avenue, even east or west down these alleys, past—where was he running?

The raven scrabbled up there, disappeared west.

He stumbled west down the potholed alley, sliding and flapping his arms but somehow not falling, not even to his knees while staring into every crevice of building on both sides, around battered power poles. Why would a tall man in an orange jacket turn into this miserable back lane? No one was anywhere—a small woman in an apron stood beside a dumpster, her hand pulling a cigarette from her face—he could say nothing, not even gesture. His fingers and ears and arms and face were on fire with cold, his stomach heaving from that burst of running and screaming; he was barely in motion now and his right leg cramped, he found himself doubled over at the corner of a building. He could clutch, hold onto the wall and hide behind another dumpster and abruptly he heaved, convulsed into vomiting. He had not run in years, coffee and cereal and orange juice and sliced strawberries and more coffee like a smashed hose against the dumpster, *uggch*, get rid of it, he didn't need it, turn away quick, he was limping in the parking lane along the length of the TIBC bank. Spit and swallow and spit, spit out the taste, flex the useless right leg. He grabbed a handful of snow and swiped it over his face and the ice stunned him, get away. No parked bank cars, get away, he stumped north along the wall, balancing better now and he was at Whyte again still swallowing bile, fainter now, on the south side in the middle of the block rubbing at his wet face with his wet freezing hand, which way dearest God and loving Father lead me, O

lead me, Lord, lead me in Thy righteousness,
make Thy way plain before my . . .

the psalm soaked forever in his choir memory sang through him like radiance.

How could it be Gabriel? Gone a quarter of a century.

There were police flashers now at Whyte Avenue and 104th Street . . . and he sweating cold in shirtsleeves, his parka and beaver cap on that chair. His coffee mug.

A siren wailed long and low and longer to his left: out of the slanting snow a massive Fire Rescue truck lumbered past, lights aflame like a blazing bush.

Gabriel . . . my son my son, did I see my . . .

And an ambulance.

He realized he was tipped sideways, clutching the granite corner of his bank . . . credit card, chequing account, semi-annual RRIF . . . he groped along the front into the inset door, the shelter of the ATM vestibule. The yellow-vested guard stood beyond the inner door smiling as always, but suddenly his mouth fell open, staring. Hal turned to the farthest bank machine, forcing his frozen fingers to dig out his wallet. Why was he here? He would never find an orange downfill by glaring at his bank card, shoving it in the slot. The surveillance cameras were certainly reading him in shirt and snow so he deliberately coded in 6-1-8-5 and waited, counting in his mind by hundreds slowly, slowly, and then swiftly jabbed himself out again. He yanked the card free and wheeled, pushed through the door without glancing at the guard who would certainly remember him, he was always there smiling like any terminally retired idiot, out into colder snow.

Traffic lanes, the median trees on Whyte. Before him nothing moved. He had managed to empty six lanes on one of the busiest streets in Edmonton. As fast as he could he jay-walked across, shuddering, his arms were freezing and his wet feet staggering so badly his right leg hooked and very nearly sprawled him onto the median but he caught himself upright against a lean tree, panting, the Christmas lights wound there all year and then he was over, could tilt into the corner of Ten Thousand Villages where he volunteered one afternoon a week, thank God yesterday, could rest with only his stomach heaving empty down to the bile. His aching leg. Through the window the mahogany

Ganesha offered him incomprehensible wisdom—but he desperately needed—get away from here. If Yvonne looked out from behind the counter . . . step out, walk as calmly as any ridiculous old bare-headed-in-the-snow pedestrian past shops and the trackless alley—no one had walked there as far as he could see—back to the coffee shop at the corner of 104th. A cluster of people, silent, hunched profiles shifting, glinting faintly in patrol car and high Fire Rescue and ambulance colours. The inset door handle seemed frozen steel to his bare hands but he jerked it open without losing skin. Becca straightened up from the shaky coffee table. She was holding his silver mug.

To pick up his parka he had to steady a numb hand on her arm. She flinched, but turned into him. Her perfect arm, strong, so warm, to hold a body warm, a living body.

She said into his ear, "What about that?" and gestured outside.

"No! No . . . I don't want to be . . . no . . ."

"Okay." She was so calm; she had served him coffee for centuries. "I don't remember you here today."

"No," he said as softly, knowing what she meant, "No, don't—"

She took his hand and nudged it with her cheek. The shop was empty but for eternal Ben bent into his computer screen as if no whirling lights existed, his virtual genealogies never-unending in time and space. For an instant Becca's cheek brushed Hal again.

"You sometimes come in for coffee, sure, but no one will say," she said. "Nothing."

She was holding the other sleeve of his parka for him. He said, "They'll check your surveillance."

"They can't if we don't let them. It's our camera."

"Say nothing, okay, if you can, but if your boss—if something really bad . . ." he glanced towards the intersection. The lights swirling, the jacket backs of people. "Don't perjure yourself about me, please."

She touched his hand as he lifted his beaver cap, even as she turned away and gave him his mug, going. How could a teenage girl on minimum-wage boredom contain such gentilesse? God, you are good. He stuffed the cup in his parka pocket and walked out, shoved at the corner post to wheel himself north away from the crowd and the intersection heap of several crumpled—he wouldn't look. The ambulance whooped once, yowled, then roared away in the direction of the University Hospital. But he was past the women's boutique, the bar, across 83rd no matter what the light and lanes of idling cars, he forced himself to tramp on, his right side an agony at each step, good. And the funeral home squatting there—HOME—a grotesque word to nail on a dreadful necessity; the parking lot with its perfect hearse always waiting, waiting . . . never again, they would have to carry him in.

The world was covered white. Muttering with motionless cars and no snow falling.

Past the funeral building the air sifted gentle, almost warm against his face, snipping at spring suddenly. The tall stained glass of Blessed Redeemer Church where Owl stowed his stuff behind the lilac bush when it flowered in May against the brick wall and where he sometimes slept.

Home, he would get there, yes only one more intersection to get across, then railroad tracks, the alley, the giant boulevard ash trees flaring over his snow-lined apple tree trimmed no taller than he could reach and ready to bloom whiter than snow Lord wash me and I shall be, here, home.

He lay on his back on the kitchen floor. Breathing. He had managed to claw off his boots at the back door and toss aside his beaver cap and zip open his parka but that was it. The kitchen linoleum softened by the down parka. Blond cupboards all around over him, fridge starting with its tiny quiver. The house held him as it had for twenty-three years, precisely there, contained and complete in his mind to every space and shelf and door and stair-step, the main floor where he sprawled, the crowded basement, the second floor with the bedroom and long office and bath and sunroom and landing open to the stair and balcony rail and peaked ceiling of the third floor with the foam mat . . .

His mug was still hooked in his fingers.

On the floor. A presumably dignified middle-class seventy-five-year-old male laid out flat; an Emeritus Professor at "one of Canada's great universities" who had a few dozen mentions on Google, even a three-line bio in Wikipedia because he once edited an anthology of short stories that thousands of students were required to read, a world selection of thirty-five stories in English that included seven Canadian authors, such a brilliant 1967 idea to include Centennial Canadians in "the world" that wrote readable stories, at last, how many teachers thanked him. For a few years he had needed a business accountant to prepare his income tax and even wrestled with writing stories himself, three were actually published in very little magazines and he had occasionally thought he might be a "late-to-mature" writer, briefly laboured to convince himself. Flat on his kitchen floor tasting bile and his back held rigid above the ache, the right leg; white-hair and nose at the furnace vent below the sink. Warm air, breathing.

He should be lying on their ancient camper-foam mattress on the third floor where he napped every afternoon and awoke to the pine ceiling with its dark knots slanted together over him. He was certain that some day, ultimately, he would recognize those knot constellations fixed in pine as the patterns of unfathomable stars he saw when he stared into the night sky from the cabin deck at Aspen Creek. He searched and believed, certainly; some day, but never yet. Though the ceiling remained constant, and also the end wall of great arched windows where the winter sun was always sinking when he awoke.

Yolanda's arch. She had re-designed every detail so perfectly, the entire old house.

The floor hard through his parka. Owl lay in his parka every night, all year, somewhere hard, but he had four mattresses on four different floors where he could turn. Nurse oblivion.

Yolanda took over the house design when the architect annoyed her once too often . . . sweetest sweetest Yo, such a taker-over . . . 216 days, almost to the hour, gone. Their year of final knowing had at first seemed to wither timelessly: four weeks of travel and distant relatives who did not know what to say to them in England and Germany, and two weeks of a planned month on an "island paradise" of walking more slowly together along the golden beach and sitting under palm fronds and seeing the sea lick itself over the sand, so fully complete and forever unto itself, until they suddenly knew they must flee, home, back to Edmonton where daughter Miriam in Vancouver and son Dennis in Toronto could schedule quick flights, their lifetime of friends could call or visit any day if they wanted them. Then one morning Yo could not stand; she could not so much as sit up. So horrifyingly quicker than any doctor had the nerve to anticipate, a sudden skeleton under sheets in a palliative bed at the Grey Nuns despite every known technology and enormous needled monitoring machines. Shrinking. Bones. Gone.

The fear of death, the intensifying anticipation of death, the dread, the stiffening brutality, the relief . . . the guilt-ridden relief of unstoppable death. Nothing but massive memory to remember, to forget, and there it was, back, any time and there it is again, any forgotten and unforgivable weight of it, any fold or shrivel or loving . . . her strong arms pulling him tight, her open smile nuzzling moist into the bend of his neck. Their lifetime sleeping together in one tender bed.

Lying inert. Inertia. That inherent property by which matter will persist in a state of stillness until acted upon by some external force. The matter surrounding him so still . . . not a chair or sofa cushion had shifted its position since the last wailing ambulance took her. Not in the living room nor dining room nor kitchen, never had the lid of the Heintzman piano she played like a singing angel been lifted, and after the funeral he vowed nothing ever would until his back and balance staggered even more and he accidentally bumped something out of its place. When the cleaning people came, every two months, he drove his grey Celica to Aspen Creek or Drumheller or Lethbridge or Peace River for two days with nothing but landscape and sky and strangers and when he returned all was dusted and remained precisely where it belonged. He had so often teased her, As soon as I heard your name, I wanted to marry you because "yo" in Low German means "yes," so when I called you, "Yo! Yo! Yolanda!" I was already always agreeing with you.

But not even to hear her laughter could he say that to her at the last, their flat-footed loving silliness. Nor move her last novel or hairbrush on her night table, nor water a plant. After she was gone the sunroom she had nurtured in magnificent green slowly filled with the shrunken sweetness of dry rot. Her piano harmonies were fading to whispers, but for a time the scent of dying flowers sifted over him when he fell asleep in the bedroom and when he awoke it was his gentle first awareness, but now after seven months he needed to look into the sunroom when he passed to see how nothing in it was left alive. Not even smell.

But he remembered the smell. That memory would not leave him.

"Yolanda." He named her aloud flat on his back on the kitchen floor. Thinking to her: I've never watered your plants now shrivelled to heaps of dust nor opened a drawer in your dresser or shifted a blouse in the closet or fingered the keys of the piano you—Dennis disconnected the computer he taught you to use throughout his high school, it still sits there in your office full of everything you—I've never touched it, I've never touched one of those boxes on the basement shelves you packed and labelled GABRIEL in black felt pen. Yo, Yolanda, there's no evening flower smell, not one single beloved movement in this house you built, now. Only certain memory. And silent rot, Yo, Yo, all that lives rots.

But not he. Not yet. Sadly. Why? An eighth decade of life barely oriented by a daily coffee walk and CBC news and library books and an Oiler game on TV if he could endure their play. Empty pathetic.

The Orange Downfill walked into the window. One instant . . . one breathlessness. And he happened to be looking there.

He rolled sideways, heaved erect until he was on his knees shivering. The counter edge steadied him to haul himself to his feet. It was too fast: his head swirled, he was hanging on as his leg buckled for an instant and gorge roiled in his gut, okay, hold on there's nothing left to barf, barf nothing, here's the sink, better the sink than spraying a public alley and behind his clenched eyelids light split and shifted, white to black into flaming orange and his nothing control broke: he saw the day cracked wide open to that remorseless memory always poised to strike. It waited there exactly, enormous beyond fathoming and framed in the mirror of what would never be forgotten no matter how many day by days he forced himself to convince himself he had smashed and ground it to dust.

That day of irreducible remember.

Sunday, September 8, 1985, 1:30 p.m. And he was alone.

"I hear you have a grief in the family."

"What?"

His childhood friend Aaron's voice on the phone, from Toronto, no greeting just—

"Hal . . . you are home!"

"Yes, yes, just walked in, the house is empty, nobody's here—what 'grief'?"

"Hal . . . you just? . . . nobody's there?"

"Yes! Taxi straight from the airport, what are you saying?"

"Listen Hal," suddenly frozen calm, "you call Dave, you call him, I'll hang up right now and you call Dave right now."

"What're you saying!"

"God help you. Call Dave right now."

The phone goes dead and instantly he is pounding Yolanda's brother's numbers, his mind frozen, and nothing happens, what—a dial tone!—his crashing hand finally finds a dial tone and he hits the numbers again and Dave speaks at the first ring, like a whisper,

"Yes?"

"Dave, I'm home, what's happened, what?"

"We couldn't find you, we were phoning every—"

"There's nobody here! Yo—what happened!"

"The world has collapsed . . ."

Something breaks. "Gabriel."

"Yes. He's . . . gone . . . at the cabin he . . ."

Instantly he knows but he screams it anyway, "What do you mean 'gone'!"

"Hal, listen, listen," Dave's voice slowly hardens into his rigid strength, "Gabriel . . . we couldn't find you yesterday by phone or this morning and they all drove to the airport to meet your plane, don't move, I'm coming, just stay, stay put, I'll be right there," and the phone is dead again.

Gone. The wall above the phone table is not gone. It is there. It is stopping his forehead, pounding it harder and harder and he feels nothing that is what walls do, be there to pound you, pound, Gabriel spoke to him five days ago, Tuesday, his voice alive in the phone, not this phone, the cream phone in his apartment and Hal on the black one in the Edmonton Airport, they were talking together when Canadian Pacific began calling his Montreal flight and Gabe agreed, sure, okay, they could meet Sunday and there could be something good to talk about when he got back from business in Montreal, this coming Sunday, okay, sure, bye.

"I love you."

"Okay Dad, goodbye then."

He said that five days ago. "I love you." When had he actually said those words to his twenty-four-year-old son? But he had, yes he had. I love . . . Okay Dad. Goodbye then . . . On Tuesday.

He stands in the dining room bay window. Across the empty street the white boards of the community skating rink wait for winter ice. It is only September 8 but snow has fallen to hide the green grass sometime during the days he's been away, it is melting, dripping off the birch and poplar leaves of their corner trees, the elementary school still hidden behind their patchy gold and white and red flickering. The corner where little Dennis always turns to wave at Yolanda here in this window, every day, before crossing to school. But older Gabriel had never waved, had never looked back walking away.

I love you.

Goodbye then.

All of them had been trying to phone him, they all knew where he should be in Montreal and what he was doing there and who he was with and he had called Yolanda Friday evening from Montreal and she was fine, everything was fine; Gabe had come on Wednesday evening and borrowed the pickup to go shopping Thursday for shoes for Miriam's wedding, he only had his worn joggers, fine, that was okay, and Yo knew Hal's return flight on Sunday but oddly Gabriel hadn't brought back the truck yet and hadn't answered his phone, not yet, Friday—but now Dave said on Saturday, all day and evening Saturday and all this morning Sunday they had been calling everywhere they knew—even Aaron on the off chance that Hal had stopped in Toronto—but they couldn't find him.

Of course they couldn't. Nobody knew about Friday night and Saturday all day and Sunday morning, not even Yo was supposed to know, not yet.

And slowly, slowly he feels himself splitting. There is a crack in everything. That's how the night gets in.

But Dave said "Gone." "Gone" is not . . . maybe not O merciful sweet Jesus—

Dave's green Dodge is at the curb, it is there, he was staring right there but he hadn't seen it stop. How long can it possibly take for Yo's brother to lunge out, slam the door, run around the car and up the walk and jump the two steps and across the porch and through the door he yanks open, he has more than enough endless time to know what he need never say aloud but Dave has wrapped him in his arms, clasps him fiercely heads over shoulders, is a machine gun of words set on automatic fire against his chest:

". . . it was the blue cab of your pickup I saw it in the trees behind the shed at Aspen Creek, I come driving round the bend at the cabin Saturday morning and I saw Big Ed's van there already so he's working in the cabin and the sun glanced off something blue back behind the shed, in the trees there, everything was white, the trees hanging snow, it snowed Friday or maybe already Thursday night and the spruce still hanging—there were just Big Ed's van tracks on the road coming in but no tracks to the shed and what was your blue pickup, that must be it, it was that blue, what's it doing way back there in the trees, you never park there, you aren't even home, I wouldn't have seen it if the sun hadn't glanced off, so sharp just once as I drove in so I parked and walked towards the shed to look and I remembered Yo calling Thursday about going out Saturday to the cabin to make more plans for Miriam's wedding and I said I'd come too and she said Gabriel had borrowed your pickup Wednesday, but Thursday he wasn't answering his phone and I got a stranger and stranger feeling walking past the shed and towards that truck, it was your Chev pickup all right, the light-blue cab and the white canopy, why was it there, backed in there like that, I was getting sort of scared and thinking only pickup, it's backed so far into the little birches and poplars on that trail we cut to dig the root cellar, the small trees are so heavy and I shove past the hood, it's covered with snow and look inside the cab and it's empty, nothing on the seat. And the door's unlocked. I can open it, and then I see the key in the starter, it's turned on, all the way.

"So . . . I have to look in the back, into the canopy. Gabriel lying there, stretched out, face . . . staring up—"

"Dave! Dave!" He has to get him stopped, they are knee to knee on the living room couch and he has to hear him say it, "He's dead? Dead, in back of the pickup?"

Dave stares over him at the wall. "I didn't touch anything. Lying on his back. His eyes open. And that piece of hose from installing the dryer, it stuck into the canopy through the back window. I fell on my knees. It was taped . . . very neat, around the exhaust, duct tape . . . singed . . ."

They sit on the couch, crying face to face.

After a time Dave says, "I didn't know what to do. What is there? On my knees in wet snow, those snowy little trees hiding me against the truck tire, just stay down, down . . . I'm praying it's not true dearest God—and I remember Big Ed in the cabin and I get up and Gabriel's naked face—I ran back like crazy, Big Ed would know, something, to do, he was up the stepladder sanding the balcony railing and I yelled at him come down, and I told him Gabriel is lying in the back of the pickup in the trees behind the shed. Big Ed went white, he couldn't say a word and all I could say, 'What do we do, what do we do?' And then we hear the door, voices, Yo and Dennis and Miriam and her friends, someone laughing out loud at the silly snow, if it comes now there'll be none left next weekend for the wedding! Big Ed and I can't make a sound. But Yo sees us standing there, like that, and she comes so quick . . ."

"Yo . . . you told her?"

"What could I do?"

And the house door bangs open in the hall, the front door and Gabriel's mother is there, tall black-haired Yolanda who blessings be always knows what to do is striding into the house where their family of five has lived for fifteen years, and also Gabriel's older sister Miriam and younger brother Dennis and soon to be brother-in-law Leo; Leo closing the door very quietly while what's left of their little family swarms him, the missing father found at last: calling him, groaning, crying aloud together.

Slivered onions spat in the pan and he sliced in cooked potatoes to calm them. He got two eggs from the fridge. They spread out white and yellow quick, he stirred and shifted and flipped, then went back for a third egg, white as snow, wash me and I shall be whiter—cooking heat such a gentle sound, a soft reassurance. He sprinkled in chopped beer sausage, then shredded cheddar and slowly his random gestures melted into the fragrance of *Kaeseueberbacken*, cheese-baked-over, as they called it in the Marburg University student *Mensa*, though this was really *ueberbraten*—fried-over, his comfort food, his desperately seeking comfort. He could check his e-mail for whatever would never be there, he could surely call Miriam in Vancouver or Dennis in

Toronto and talk face to face, this was exactly why Dennis had insisted on setting up his Skype—but he had no words he could bear now, leave alone face faces, even electronic. This ruthless memory, he had buried it forever, he vowed so often, buried finally with his only Yolanda, enough, enough already! they had agreed together again and over again and then out of nowhere their beautiful son was between them again. Every relentless bit and scratch and word of him they could only rub against each other, concentrating and remembering and reminding, scraps and tag-ends streaming together while they scraped themselves even rawer, shred by shred they again talked their son into previously noticed and unnoticed existences; as if they would build a gigantic wall along the cliffs and ridges, over the tips of the highest most savagely broken mountains or the deepest river gorges and horizonless prairies of their past until they had again piled up every tiny grain of possible fact into an impregnable wall against every possible . . . and then her life stopped. She was gone too.

Blessed are you, Yolanda. Now you know.

Together over fifty years and gone. Gabriel only twenty-four and a half—though that was certainly enough, more than enough to need to remember. As Hal had watched Yo's final smoke vanish in blue sky he had vowed, on the memory of Gabriel's smoke and ashes, to wring every remembrance of Gabriel down tight into absolute refusal: NO MORE. Gabe would now be the black hole in his universe of memory. Not even sleep would betray him into one shard of dream, enough now, that past was completed and forever somewhere beyond this life and now Yo eternally knew all of it; he need only wait until he too was smoke and ashes and he too would know, he would not continue here like a stunned idiot pursued by these hounds of recall. Leave it. Think nothing.

And then today. Before he could defend himself memory walked past the Double Cup window. He had stared at it—stupidly. And he recognized he had been waiting to see that, sitting there over the months so deliberately blank and empty but actually waiting . . . now he stared down at the dark circle of cheese in the frying pan. There was a smell of something singed. Safe, the coffee shop had always seemed meaninglessly nothing, safe . . . but like a stupid shit—the screaming woman in the pickup named him all right—he jumped up and ran out after it. Why in God's name. How could he not.

"I changed my flight to—"

"You weren't on the plane, we were praying and paging and watching every exit and the Montreal plane landed and nothing, twenty minutes! not even your bag and then the RCMP came and said now he could tell me, your name wasn't on the Montreal passenger list, you—"

"No, it wasn't, I changed my flight."

"You never told me, Friday! We were phoning all over—"

"I came from Winnipeg, but Gabriel, tell me—"

"Winnipeg? What? We found Gabriel yesterday and you—"

"Tell me!" he bellows.

Their desperate hugs loosen, their sobbing sags. Young

Dennis ducks aside completely and Leo's aristocratic Argentinian face hardens into resolution—these words need distance—but Miriam pulls Hal harder into her tears as Yolanda stiffens in his arms.

"We ran," Yo says, "the path to the shed and past, when we looked we saw the blue cab easily through the leaves, we just hadn't looked there driving up, all the slippery snow and Denny and Miriam ran faster, they got there first and Denny stopped by the hood and didn't go any farther but Miriam shoved through the little trees and she screamed and yanked the canopy gate open, and I got there last and it was all open and I just crawled in beside him, he was lying on a mattress from the cabin with flowered sheets covering so smooth and his blue pillow and one blue blanket to his chin and his hands just lying by his side and his face . . . so peaceful, not . . . not . . . just quiet, like he would say when he didn't mean it, no problem, no problem at all . . . his face stone . . . oh Gabriel, Gabriel. This is so final . . ."

He is clutching Yo tight, they are all again clamped together crying aloud so hard they are staggering, and a thought breaks in him and he shoves himself loose among these beloved shoulders, arms that are still here:

"Where is he?"

They stare at him.

"Where!"

Behind him Dave says, "The police came—"

"Police?"

"Big Ed called 911, the RCMP came, and the ambulance and when the police finished the ambulance took him—"

"Finished!"

"They have to, come, to make sure—"

"He's in Leduc, in the hospital?"

Dave says very quietly, "No. The funeral people have him now."

"I have to see him! Before they smear all that makeup and—"

"Hal," Dave pulls at him, "they just got him today, noon, from the Medical Examiner."

"Medical Exam—"

"Any unexpected dea—"

"Yes, yes," Yo interrupts, "let's go to the undertakers, now, Dave, you drive us, c'mon."

And they are all at the house door. Strangely, there is now a crowd of people on the front lawn, and driveway, and along the sidewalk. Do all these people know? When did they come? Standing silently, looking, drawing back and some women reach out towards them, sobbing aloud, but Dave walks ahead, pushes past them gesturing, talking. The faces part and Hal recognizes them; more women and men are coming along the sidewalk, up the walk, but they step aside onto the grass, he recognizes friends from church, yes, from university and concert and theatre acquaintances, some neighbours he waves hi to when he sees them getting into their car, of course it is Sunday afternoon so everyone's called around and knows except he, he wasn't anywhere in Montreal or anywhere findable in Canada at any phone number they knew nor even on his scheduled plane from Montreal . . . they are driving. The usual street corners and merging lanes with cars and North Saskatchewan River valley and horses inside the rail fence and hills and stops and the bend around University Avenue onto Whyte and outside the car everything looks perfectly fall city normal, the trees over traces of snow are unchangeable evergreen or turning gold along the boulevard and the stop light . . . but Hal is not driving. It is not their car. Dave sits alone in front and Yo and Miriam clutch him tight in the back seat—

"Where's Dennis!"

Yo hugs him tighter, her cheek pressing his. It seems Denny is with Leo in their car following them. Miriam, he feels her tears on his hand, she is holding it against her face, it appears she has been talking, she is—

". . . the bathroom counter in the cabin, I saw a contact lens case right there by the sink, but Big Ed doesn't need glasses, what? Gabe's case? Whose else could it be? And I opened it and unscrewed the L and the R and there were lenses, floating in the fluid, they must be his, the case looked like his, we were so worried he didn't answer his apartment phone and he had the pickup—was he here—he drove to the creek alone so often for a day or two, why shouldn't he—there's no pickup outside but here's his contacts? Had he . . . how could he forget his—and I had this terrifying rush and I ran out the bathroom and Mom was coming towards me . . ."

Hal gets his right arm free of Yolanda and wraps it around Miriam as well, hard, her slender shuddering body, just hold that—his mind blank as an explosion—hold. After some stops and starts the car turns and through her hair he recognizes the great ash tree at the boulevard crosswalk on 104th Street. A few days ago, ten at most, he walked under it between Gabriel and Dennis walking so slim and tall on either side, laughing all together at the frothy Edmonton Festival play they had seen and Gabriel joking as they passed through the crowds crossing under the tree, "They play with the bigness of their littleness." Hal recognized the Kafka line and called him on it and they laughed again though Dennis didn't get the literary reference but did get the joke. They were all swinging along and he felt so good about Gabe's wit, it was amazing to walk so easily between his two tall, beautiful sons after a fun play, both already taller than he and laughing—and the corner sign twists above them as the car turns again: Strathcona Funeral Home.

Home. His body convulses. Long parking lanes and three doors, square brick pillars and three heavy and heavier doors sigh and there is Gabriel.

Not gone at all. On his back. In an ice-cold room. On a steel table. He is not gone, here he is, his feet bare, his blue-faded jeans and half a pale sheet and his favourite green woven-linen shirt, his slender hands laid over each other, his narrow face. His hair not quite so curly nor flying long around his shoulders as it did when he clanged that dazzling electric bass guitar, no, mussed and short, a lovely trim. His neat moustache, nostrils, full lips . . . somewhat shrunk, crushed against his beautiful teeth, but his skin clear, absolutely perfect after that endless year of swallowing pills and having to smear his face and neck down to his shoulders every night. Once, when Hal went into the basement, at that moment Gabe opened his bathroom door, Here, you want to see what it's like? His long face coated like glistening shellac, finger-painted dead white, forehead and cheeks and neck and circling his eyes and mouth and nostrils,

Every night a clown, see? Skin so perfect now and clear, nothing smeared, no clown left . . . but cold. His fingers, his cheek, his lips. He can dare to feel, hold every bit of him. Such a big man, so horribly hard. His gaunt ice feet.

"Cremation," he says aloud.

There have been various voices, for some time, talking very low, talking possible clothes and the church service for the funeral and Herbert the minister is there . . . his shoulders have certainly already been clasped hard and words, God give you . . . O . . . strength . . . comfort . . . what is there to say if not God . . . both extended families have already been phoned and they are all coming tomorrow. Margret and Ernst and ancient David from Vancouver and Saskatoon and Medicine Hat and the newspaper obit tomorrow, okay, Yo's sister Elaine won't come because of her heart but her husband will and her brother Joe, yes the funeral service could be late Tuesday afternoon at the church and the choice of coffin, a full range is available, all on view right here in our display room and the program and pallbearers and the organ music by William of course and the choir will sing and which cemetery, a plot can certainly be purchased in the Two Hills . . . any number of people glance at him and then quickly away; several he has never seen before.

In another room. Gabriel is not in it. Not lying flat on a stainless steel table and his eyes now shut. Only three polished desks with not a wisp of paper on them, one small computer not switched on. So he tells them exactly:

"He told me in August. We were wrapping poplars along the creek because of the beaver and he told me: 'I know nobody's ever done this in our family but if I'm ever dead, cremate me.'"

Their family is all together, alone, walking away through the funeral home lobby, when he breaks. He would have crumpled if Dennis had not been holding his arm, and Miriam quickly as well. He can only stagger, gesture. And they turn back, lurch back into the frozen steel room.

The glass of milk in his hand, Hal noticed, was half empty. The cheese-fried-over lingered in his mouth, it seemed to have tasted as good as always, golden and quietly salty. But nausea was nudging, bumping inside him again and he could not swallow anymore; let the pan cool for the fridge, there's always tomorrow. April evening sun blazed through the kitchen window, off the melting snow on the garage roof. There would be light till nine.

The Orange Downfill had ripped open what he locked down so carefully every day, every minute—Leo would call it a *barranca*. That was it, exactly, a violent chasm torn through the eroded mountains of his life. It had to be filled in again, fast, rammed solid with whatever concretion he could find to keep himself blank: fake TV virtuality, books, drugged sleep, *Globe and Mail* and *Journal* and *Herald* Sudoku and the world's endless, violent, banal facticity, movies, books, pretend to write stories page after page on the futile precision of computer screens that he never even printed on his ancient Lexmark and certainly no one would ever read *Deo juvante*, books, dig gulps of snow into barely unfrozen flowerbeds, listen again to Schubert's *String*

Quintet in C major, the adagio's lifting delight plucking away any possible thought, books by the thousand piled everywhere in the house and the public library just down the street . . .

Too vicious, too deep, that collar turn of orange *barranca*. The colour, the indelible walk, that fling of profile and shoulder disappearing.

He knew of course the only way he could fill it. Where he would find the hardest earthly stuff, more than enough, it was always there and had been for years, waiting, he needed to remember nothing to find it; if he dared. That secret day and a half in Winnipeg when he could not be found—when their son was dead—had twisted itself in and out of their larger pain; but his intentions for that disappearing, barely a second in any normal lifetime, had been so good! A marvellous surprise for the whole family, especially for Gabe whom he would phone the minute he got back home—the minute he walked in—to meet him immediately and tell him, tell him first, the others would wait, happily, if he told them it would make Gabe happy to know first—of the Winnipeg Film Board producer who had found Hal's short story "George Stewart" in a Manitoba school reader, about the ragged old bachelor on his boreal homestead who, simply because of his name, knew he was actually the true and rightful living King of England and the only way to get the world out of this stupid war with Hitler, real quick and easy, was just talk straight with him man to man, lay it on the line, praise the Lord and pass the conversation and we'll all be free! A short-short movie about the bushed old man and the boy who believes him and the producer would get Gabe on the film crew. Two weeks or three of Best Boy again and he would get more experience and make other connections, find more film jobs and get him working with something he loved already and could learn more and get him away from Edmonton and all the endless usual . . .

Hal was in his basement. Two, three stacked boxes in the shelves along one basement wall. HP 170, The University of Alberta Central Stores, 8 1/2 x 11–10 M, Paper for Use in Copy Machines. Labelled by Yolanda's thick black felt pen: GABRIEL.

She finally said, It has to be done. And she did it.

All he had done was heave them into place, here.

The boxes had no grips. He had to clutch the top one with both hands, and lift, and pull; he felt the muscle in his back tweak, almost heard it come apart. There were more boxes and also a full trunk in the cabin at Aspen Creek, clothes, bedding, not books, he had vanished them among his own—not the blue truck bedding . . . but here were the personal papers, piled envelopes and spiral notebooks and diaries—no, not the diaries yet—a small green-bordered book bound with plaited cord and "Gabriel" written above three tiny children: *Bible Lessons for Kindergarten Children, Year II*. Across the top of the book lay four yellow pages of black handwritten words. Labelled by Yo: "Rec'd Oct 6/85."

Dreaming of Gabriel

When I heard the news my first reaction was a powerful desire just to be with Gabriel one more time. I wanted to go somewhere . . . where? . . . and cry out to the sky,

demand that he be there. God! But as the news sank
in, and gradually became reality, I slowly accepted
more and more. So seeing Gabriel in a dream last
night came as a comforting surprise, lovely. Though
from the moment I awoke I have never been certain
how much was in the dream, how much was in
what-the-dream-meant-to-me, how much was
what-I-wanted-the-dream-to-be.

I was observing from the sidelines, and Gabriel
was being asked to show other people some gifts he
had received, and he was obliging. The gifts were
rings, jewellery. I felt like an outsider—not at all a
part of what I was witnessing.

Then Gabriel looked at me, smiled warmly, and
beckoned to me; he wanted to show me something.
I was surprised, and pleased, for this was the Gabriel I
knew, always considerate but he seemed happier
than I'd ever seen him. He said, "Come," we turned a
corner and we were alone.

He said, "Look at that," and gestured downward.
I looked and saw a coffee table covered with pamphlets
and books, magazines neatly arranged. And suddenly
I was grief-struck. The table was the shape of a coffin.

Gabriel continued, gently mocking me in my
hypocrisy (or so it seemed), "How can people say
that?" It seemed he referred to something written on the
cover of a magazine—but which one? His words did not
make sense to me. What suddenly made sense were my
thoughts in my grief, thoughts such as, *How could you
leave all this*, and, *How could you do that*, or just, *Why?*

Gently mocking my grief-thoughts for their irrationality.
Is grief rational? I looked at him to see his meaning.

His eyes seemed to say that things were better for
him now—but immediately the dream pulled itself
back to where it had been: "How can people say that?
What's the point of saying it?"

I tried to see the magazine on the dreadful table, to
respond to his questions, and I woke up.

After a time I found this dream somewhat comforting.

Oleg

Oleg, the one university friend Gabriel had still met for
the occasional coffee after three years, who studied gradu-
ate philosophy very hard while Gabriel avoided his university lit classes by repeating movies afternoon and evening.
One of six pallbearers.

Under "Dreaming of Gabriel" was a single folded sheet
lined with large looped handwriting: William's, superb
organist William.

GABRIEL W
Funeral Tuesday, Sept 10/85
Mennonite Church Edmonton

PRELUDE: .... CHORALE BACH (Intro. to B.)
Jesu Joy of Man's Desiring
Schmuecke dich, o liebe Seele .... Intro. to B.
(Soul Arise, Dispel Your Sadness) .... p. 6
(A tendentious translation; really: Adorn yourself,
o dear soul)

O "Suffer God," "Suffer little children to come . . ." suffer
indeed my soul, suffer O sufferer!—a multitudinous word
worthy to be included in Gabriel's long notebook columns
of definitions, necessary, he must surely have written it out
there, somewhere in his re-appearing lists of words with
his particular, selected and augmented meanings, ignoring
all others, lists he continued to extend as month by week
by day his handwriting twisted into steady illegibility—
indeed, here was one—

    Romantic - having no basis in fact, imaginary

                - impractical in conception or plan;
                  visionary

                - the imaginative or emotional appeal of
                  the heroic, adventurous, remote

                - mysterious

                - idealized beyond reality

Hal hunched down in the crowded basement with Yo's first large box uncovered. Suffer . . . peace . . . river so deep below that high . . . romantic . . . beyond reality. He had simply picked up the top papers, held them, and already ominous Gabe definitions glared at him—and on the instant another spike of memory leaped from a sheet lying there, nothing on it but a blue date:

Wednesday May 19, 1971

He hadn't so much as brushed a notebook and already that date stared at him, a birth date, like its incarnate "definition" written out again and again, he knew it would be, everywhere inside that opened box; he remembered it the instant Gabe's blue handwriting hit his eyes:

> Ailsa - from Ailsa Craig, Gaelic meaning
> Fairy (Elf), Rock or possibly
> Elizabeth's (Ealasaid's) Rock,
> an island between Scotland and
> Ireland off s. Ayrshire
> - Elizabeth—consecrated to God
> - Fairy / Elf—an imaginary being,
> ordinarily of small and graceful
> human form, capable of working
> good or ill to mankind

Working good or ill. Dearest God.

The definitions softly hummed the agonies of the funereal organ, suffer good or suffer ill, it is well with my

soul, which is imaginary and consecrated to suffer God
to guide me, O Ailsa. Suffer Ailsa.

> Suffer - to feel pain or distress
>   - to undergo punishment, especially to
>   the point of death
>   - to bear, endure

But to bear, endure, God's pain? Pain God endures, or
the pain/punishment that God hands out in "guiding"?

>   - to allow, to permit (obsolete)

The song sang easy as chimes in his memory. Seventy
years ago, when Hal was a child, their Mennonite congregation in Wapiti, Saskatchewan, sang the "Suffer God"
hymn often, always in its original German. Ancient Singer-
Heinrich's rising wail guided them so steadily into their
insatiable longing for reassurance:

Wer nur den lieben Gott laesst walten
> Whoever allows the dear God to rule over/
>   govern—control?—him as He pleases
Und hoffet auf Ihn allezeit
> and hopes in Him at all times . . .

For refugee families from Russia in Depression
Saskatchewan no seventeenth century prayer could ever be
obsolete. But the word was not really obsolete for Gabriel,
either. In the King James English he first heard, Jesus repeats

and repeats, "Suffer little children to come . . . come . . ." And had he . . . had he not . . . suffered, endured "the dear God" to do as He pleased—as he pleased? With Ailsa as good-or-ill fairy, with Ailsa as "Elizabeth" and consecrated to . . . what? Dearest Father in Heaven, in the top pages of this box there already were so many intersections of pain. How would he ever be able to endure all that was still piled below?

Okay okay, leave this one, lift the second box from the shelf, heavier, waiting—and don't think of those others stacked in the cabin above Aspen Creek—Yolanda O Yolanda, all this labelling, all this never throwing anything out and gone despite everything we agreed over and over about the past. Always this gathering and filing and piling into neat boxes and stacking one on top of the other to sit waiting forever and ever after devil damn it!

Have mercy on me.

A booklet: the Manitoba Golden Boy as if running with torch and wheat sheaf:

VINCENT VAN GOGH
VAN GOGH TREASURES COME TO MANITOBA
On behalf of the Winnipeg Art Gallery Association . . . We are greatly indebted to the Queen and Government of the Netherlands . . . The Golden Boys are happy to have assisted the Art Gallery in bringing this exquisite Van Gogh Art Exhibition to Manitoba December 20, 1960–January 31, 1961

A catalogue of 140 numbered pictures, oil, pen and ink, oil on canvas, on wood, on paper, pencil, charcoal (washed), watercolour, black chalk (washed), charcoal heightened with white, pencil and brush, reed-pen, black crayon on . . . The Hague, Nuenen, Arles, Saint-Rémy, Arles, Antwerp, Paris, Auvers-sur-Oise . . . Yolanda and he gazed in stunned amazement, at one after the other. Vincent van Gogh ablaze in the deepest Canadian prairie winter.

They had tried to consider, however impossible, each image very carefully, trying in one concentrated moment—there were so many viewers pressing them forward—to catch at least some flicker, comprehend some . . . it was the exhibit's last weekend, Friday, January 27, 1961. The strangely small pictures, like a thin line of flame seared at eye level around the blank walls of a government administration building. Yo gasped aloud, her hands clasped low around her abdomen. She was staring at—what? *Café Terrace at Night*? *The Peach Tree in Bloom*? *Road with Cypress and Star*? Several of the last magnificent 1890 paintings were there, *Fields and Blue Sky* and *Wheatfield with Crows*—no, not facing the crows. Where she gasped would have been #67, *Old Man in Sorrow*. The ancient body bent forward into the agony of a question mark, seated in an orange—*Orange*—chair, worn ragged in blue and thick fingers clawed into eyes. Also named *On the Threshold of Eternity*. Painted between seizures two weeks before Van Gogh killed himself. Yes, there, on the orange threshold.

Gabriel was born next morning. 5:27 a.m. in the Winnipeg General Hospital Women's Pavilion, ten days early.

Hal lay in their wide bed, the night table light on and two pillows, one doubled, under his head. He would read himself as always into sleep, he had two Van Gogh biographies and four massive picture albums beside him, if necessary he could insulate himself all night in desperate genius facticity, and against his knees his random hands opened one album not to any dazzling image but to words: theological, perhaps reasonable, words. Young Vincent as a Dutch Reformed Church lay pastor among the poorest coal miners of south Belgium writing his brother Theo:

> I must try, I will understand the real significance of what the great masters tell us in their masterpieces: that leads to God. One man tells it in a book, another in a picture.

O yeah Vincent, Hal thought, at age twenty-five you are able to write this, but within twelve years your own long-suffering masterpieces will lead you to the God of a botched bullet in your head—stay away from that! At twenty-five years of age, in January, 1961, Hal himself was studying theology at Winnipeg Mennonite College in order to become, perhaps, a Mennonite pastor, but also cuddling his second child in his arms while beautiful Yo and small Miriam talked to the crocuses blooming on her bedside table, and within twenty-five years that tiny sleeper—Gabe wasn't even twenty-five—don't go there, no, he will not allow that streak of Orange Downfill to break down—read something, anything—the funeral program that lay just below the Van Gogh catalogue in the second GABRIEL box, the folded paper he could not face in the basement, not standing, not endure the scrolled "Blessed are the poor in spirit: for theirs is . . ." But also incapable of letting it go, of dropping it once he had stupidly picked it up, he held it in his fingertips climbing two flights of stairs and managed to drop it on the bed so he need think of nothing in the bathroom, concentrate on doing: count the seconds to electric-brush each rock-solid tooth that remains in your head, fold and hang the towel exactly square above the toilet, seat yourself on the toilet and Kegel push to drain, you feel nothing but there's the tinkle clear as summer rain, drain every two hours, never more than two: twenty, so minimize the thin leakage that will now be there until the day you—

Blessed . . . Blessed . . . eight pale sandy Jesus blesseds. And inside, black words on greying white:

Funeral Service of
GABRIEL THOMAS WIENS
Mennonite Church Edmonton
Tuesday, September 10, 1985, 3:00 p.m.

. . . Following the service everyone is invited to a fellowship coffee in the church hall. Gabriel's wish was that his body be cremated and his ashes be scattered on Aspen Creek.

He was reading words he himself had once written and which Herbert, their pastor then, had spoken from the pulpit after the congregation sang "Children of the Heavenly Father"; reading very deliberately now, alone at night in their house on the last bed he and Yo had shared, seeing word after word distinctly and then he began to hear them, they were gradually growing louder between his ears, his mouth and face were contorting themselves into every necessary passage of his living breath, speaking aloud:

EULOGY

Gabriel Thomas Wiens was born in Winnipeg on January 28, 1961. The first flowers he saw were the purple crocuses standing beside his mother's bed. His sister Miriam, already two years old, quickly became his closest friend. He began kindergarten in Illinois, USA, and attended public school there, in Victoria, B.C., and three schools in Edmonton until he graduated in 1979. He further attended the Winnipeg Mennonite College for one year and the University of Alberta for almost three.

He enjoyed family travel: across Canada and the United States and to South America when he was five; there he examined the rock fortress of Machu Picchu and the feathers of a tame parrot in Paraguay with equal interest. At fifteen, with younger brother Dennis added to the family, the castles, cathedrals, rivers, highways and mountains from Italy . . . to the Netherlands and Scotland . . . *Scotland* . . . filled his eyes. In 1984 he made his own longer Europe trip, living for a time in Ath—

The words were gone. As if his voice, his mind had crashed black . . . . Hal realized his eyes were grimaced shut. When he forced them open, for an instant a new sentence uttered itself:

The image moving on a screen, or caught by the still camera: more and more his life was devoted to film. He saw over a thousand movies and wrote comments on—

But the words on the sandpaper would not hold; his eyes leaped to:

For music was another great love in his—

and the words were there but his voice staggered, broke completely on "love" . . . another . . . another . . . far beyond music as the "great love in his life," more like "love possessed," no no, "obssessed," his sudden sobs crumpled aloud into a rage of "desecrated, terminally infected by that little snit of a . . ." those words were not in the eulogy, they never would or could be. Only those other words that were possible to utter before family and friends. Spoken by a minister at a funeral, the rigid, controlled words that glared at him from the paper unchangeable as rock; his rage had laboured them together into control, weeping then too through that September night:

Music began with hymns and the Beatles, moved on into both heavy rock and classics. One great favourite was the *Miserere Mei* by Gregorio Allegri, Psalm 51:

> Have mercy on me, O God,
> in your great tenderness
> purify me from my sin,
> for I am very well aware of my fault.

This magnificent, heartbroken prayer would echo through his apartment—

Hal was blind, washed beyond words. A vehicle passed on the street, and another close behind, their lights arcing around the ceiling together like collisions waiting . . . a pickup and a long body, it couldn't really have been related to that thin child of a girl, let it go let it all go for tonight, how could you fault someone so young then, so unaware . . . could you ever wipe away—let it go, he would never be able to sleep. He had to stop this stupid, more than stu . . . he must go back to the street. Tomorrow. Sleep now, search tomorrow, tomorrow avoid the certain police and the certain consequences of his—no, not what he had started—no he had to watch and wait for something he could not now dare think he had to find to see . . . sleep now, avoid and search tomorrow, he was in the bathroom sitting on the toilet again, his urine seeping out. He felt only a kind of gentle aura radiating from the soothing trickle he could hear, he could clench it off without effort and start it again; all the exercises he had practiced for months after the operation where the blank hospital wall stared at him day and night while its enormous electric clock twitched at each, interminable, second. Yolanda force-rescued him after four days: longer time than his seventy years, those jerked seconds, Yo Yo sweetest love of my limp un-prostated life. Two more sleeping pills, not three more, no, that could over-reach into dream, nightmare. Two, temporary blank at least. Was death blank?

English had two words: dead and death, German only one: tod/Tod. The German meaning distinguishable only by the capital when written, but not when spoken. What did Rilke write—no, it was Nietzsche—*Gott ist tod* or *Gott ist Tod*?

Say it aloud: both.

The piano was playing. He could hear it with his better right ear snuggled in the pillow, Yo touching the keys gentle as dust:

Though he giveth and he taketh,
 God his children ne'er forsaketh.
'Tis his loving purpose solely
 To preserve them pure and holy.

THURSDAY, APRIL 29, 2010

The sun stood high over the square brick buildings, heating the north sidewalk of Whyte Avenue. Owl sat on his heels against the wall beside the Le Café door, one of his several places. The last clumps of shaded snow were melting over the curb into the gutters. Hal stopped in front of him.

"Hey. Have you eaten?"

"Not today."

Hal reached out; Owl took his hand and in one light motion was on his feet.

"May be good, frog legs today?" Owl asked deadpan. "Coming up to Frog Moon."

They were walking through the shop door. "That's Cree," Hal said.

"It's their land. All Edmonton."

"Okay. But just sad White stuff in here."

The glass food display counter they both knew, guitar/sax jazz quietly muttering; Breakfast Bagel Bacon Egg Gouda; Cheese Croissant; Breakfast Sandwich. The corner armchairs were empty and they sat down opposite each other, Hal making certain he faced the street intersection but then Owl never seemed to care, saw whatever he wanted to see no matter which way his chair faced; like the square-circle raven yesterday. Watching.

The endless drift of passing walkers, always there, going somewhere—or coming? What if none of them, every different shape and movement and skin and age and hair colour in the sunlight, were not going? What if everyone was coming back to somewhere? That slight teen with his quick, awkward steps, both hands thrust deep in his jean pockets, bleached in splotches, the waist as always belted below his buttocks and the crotch twitching almost between his knees . . . how . . . perhaps if he took out his hands the jeans would drop to his ankles. No one would care. He could be coming home.

The "Walk" light flicked green and a slender woman in a brief blue dress turned there; glancing around the intersection as the Whyte cars roared off. But she did not walk. She held a phone up to her perfect face with her right hand, talking, and with her left balanced two large Le Café coffee cups, one on top the other, upright against her talking chin. What a woman to have poised on a street corner, waiting for you. Her skirt hugged snug under her buttocks as she turned looking north up 104th Street, the black tights on her thighs flickered so beautifully with muscle. She shoved the phone into her hip pocket and plucked the top cup from under her chin: stir sticks protruded from both lids and she contemplated them one by one like a sudden mystery. Then she glanced up again and immediately ran across the bus lane so long-legged in heels, ran to the boulevard and a low black car easing to the curb, she ran in front of it into the traffic toward its opening door, the driver was leaning across and she ducked in and the car leaped ahead—the driver's profile strained forward, his blonde hair and shoulders black—nothing orange . . . gone.

He realized Owl had watched her run too, though he said nothing. He was tilted back and looking out, chewing a mouthful of Breakfast Egg-and-Bagel in serene Dene concentration.

Through the coffee shop window, the car window, the profile of the driver, every vehicle streaming past driven by someone, who could comprehend all the drivers in all the cars crossing here, crossing in Edmonton, all the near, the actual, accidents—no no—only one man walking, after twenty-five years . . . exactly fifty years after his conception, perhaps to the day . . . walking through the eulogy words Hal was finally unable to utter aloud last night but now not even numb-drugged sleep and morning sunlight could prevent them. When he broke down alone in their unchangeable bed he had glanced ahead, skimmed over those words forever unchangeably there and waiting, and now at the very thought he saw slivers of eulogy as if reading a book— have mercy on my visual mind—words he had written all night Monday, September 9, 1985, and long into Tuesday, read them word by malevolent word on the window shadows of Owl and himself shifting over Le Café glass:

. . . Such music and film made impossible demands on Gabriel's neophyte skill, tied to such a sensibility . . .

. . . filled scribblers with listed definitions quoted everyone from Heraclitus to Rilke . . .

. . . August 1985 he writes in despair: Why do I try to

scribble words? I have nothing to say, no courage for honesty . . . edited, lost somewhere between thought and hand . . .

. . . he is devastated by his growing inability to show love: he sees beauty in a glance, the touch of a finger, and yet he cannot . . .

. . . prayers lie scattered in his papers: I'm so selfish, I can never think of others . . . O God yes I'm sorry, I'm sorry, extremely sorry . . .

And then. Sometime between August 12 and 13: It's not that I don't want to live. It's that somehow I've lost the means. Has there ever been—

Owl's voice, across Hal's obsessive recall: "You're lucky. That's not who you're looking for."

"Lucky?" Hal could not comprehend the word.

"No chance, blond guy like that, a BMW."

Hal bit into his cheese croissant—"somehow I've lost the means . . ."—ahhh, the taste was salt and warm, almost as good as the memory of bake-over. But when he swallowed, bile thudded in his gut.

"That's not a joke, at my age."

"She don't mind us looking," Owl was still trying to grin, "running around like that."

"You know what I'm looking for."

"Yeah."

"Orange Downfill."

"That jacket, yeah. Good for spring snow. I was on that southeast corner, I saw that orange crossing Whyte from the Double Cu—"

"You saw it—yes!"

"Yes. Going for that opposite corner, it went through them others fast, there."

"But where did it go, after it crossed Whyte?"

"I never noticed nothing orange after, or on 104."

"Okay, but were you looking for it?"

Owl's black eyes, almost hidden in the folds of his brown face, were contemplating the air above him. The shop lights glinted in them like stars fixed in night sky.

"No," he said. "But I'd know if it come toward me."

"So it did go south?"

"Maybe . . . or maybe west, on that south sidewalk."

Hal stared at his friend. The Orange Downfill had gone wherever, in every direction the city lay around them in mazes of repetition. And then with a lurch he realized that the long-legged heel woman could be Ailsa, now! The classic black hair and narrow nose, that perfect chin holding one cup on the other in the ultimate elegance of balanced coffees, it could be Ailsa . . . where was she? Whatever Yo and his implacable memories had been, they hadn't seen Ailsa to remind them of anything since Grant—within two years after Gabriel—accepted that chair at the University of Victoria and silent distance could dry their tortured friendship into dust, none of them need ever meet to think about it. And Ailsa, she had married, years ago, wasn't she at one time living in Vancouver, or was it Montreal? So long gone, so long to forget; but Joan did remember. Obviously: she had sent a beautiful card for Yo's funeral. One of her brilliant abstract painting cards; there must have been an address on the envelope, if he could find it he

could write Joan and locate Ailsa, wherever she was, perhaps she *lived* here in Edmonton again! And finally have the
guts to ask her what, what had she . . . What would he ask?
The letter?

Owl said, "Maybe look different today."

"What?"

"Maybe too warm today for downfill."

"Okay . . ." Hal's thoughts broke slowly, "okay okay, but,
you're around all winter, you see everything here, all the
time, you ever see that jacket before?"

Owl looked into his eyes; the way no northern Dene
Hal had ever met looked at anyone.

"No," Owl said. "Not in fall, never in winter." His glance
shifted to the window. "But the way he moves, thin, strong,
head high, the turns . . ." he grinned slightly. "Hunters have
to know that stuff."

"You'd know him?"

"Oh yeah."

"You've seen him before?"

"Only yesterday."

"All the thousands of people on Whyte . . . ?"

"I think, yeah. I saw that orange crossing Whyte, with
all them others, to the old bank corner, and I never . . . but
then you run out there and I don't notice it just then, it was
you and all that—"

Hal followed Owl's abrupt look out. The Double Cup
sign was scrawled high and long across 104th Street and
through the traffic streaming below it the warning blinkers
of a white and imperial blue Edmonton Police car flickered.
Parked already. One, two figures, official hats, bending down,

still inside. His eyesight was too sharp, he could read the small words along the seam of their front fender: "Dedicated to Protect—Proud to Serve."

He clutched the arms of the chair and hauled himself up on his feet.

Owl did not move. He said flatly, "Always lots of people at The Coffee Shack, west on Whyte late afternoon. After four."

Hal nodded as he turned. He got himself between the crowded Le Café chairs, hardly stumbling, not bumping into anyone too badly, then he was out the door and turning left toward 103rd, Gateway Boulevard. The air was brilliant, barely warm but tanged with melting snow and intermittent people strolled on the sidewalk, men in tight T-shirts, teenagers anchored arm in arm, two women pushing baby strollers side by side and everyone talking, talking. A swirl of pigeons—could they be doves?— whipped a bluish-grey arabesque over the street and up the face of the Strathcona Hotel—the Holy Spirit descended upon him like a dove—Hal walked as nonchalantly as he could, as fast.

It had to be done: face Gabriel's writing. After years the complete diary again, 1984 words in blue pen forever unchangeable and waiting. And those heavy spiral notebooks with their practicing sentences, lists, letters juggled and edited and re-arranged and belaboured and never sent. Try and find the chronology—Yo would have placed it all in some order. The urtexts of that summer encounter in Europe of their two families—all of them except

Miriam preparing to trek her life into Spanish in South America that fall—intended as simply a few days of convivial travel together, it's what friends do: enjoy a few days of Europe together if places and dates can coincide. Yo and Dennis and Hal after two weeks in a rented VW beyond the Iron Curtain Wall in East Germany, as the world was divided in 1984, grey East Berlin and Buchenwald and architecturally ruined Dresden and Prague and Tabór and *Deo gratias* out to stucco-restored Vienna; drive autobahns to join Gabe in Frankfurt just arrived to start his months, however many, of Europe travel and maybe North Africa; and meet Grant and Joan and their two kids there at the same time—why? Whose idea was that? It seemed so easy, a three-day West Germany intersection of Edmonton friends on holiday, foreign enjoyment with a share of home, it's what friends do; it's obvious with Dennis and Colin such great buddies born within two months of each other, fifteen, and Ailsa always tagging along . . . just turned thirteen.

Face that all again, after twenty-five years. A girl two months a teen. Unimaginably dangerous.

GABRIEL, BOX #2

The bundle—bless you, Yo—of two daily planners, 1984 burgundy, 1985 black, and three tan spiral notebooks labelled by her pen 1, 2, 3. Hal held them tight, warm, such a heavy handful and his memory flickered into the night he first—no—nothing of that, just Gabriel writing, then— face it. He tugged the string open.

Everything was there in chronological order, as only Yo could arrange it: diaries and notebooks dated perfectly. All he had to do was lay them side by side, turn pages; dare to read.

UNIVERSITY OF ALBERTA DAILY PLANNER 1984
QUAECUMQUE VERA

What an irony: the university motto: "Whatsoever things are true"—so, finish Saint Paul's sentence: "think on these things." Yes. Today he would.

NAME: Gabriel Wiens
ADDRESS / TELEPHONE / SOCIAL INSURANCE NO.: (all blank)
BLOOD TYPE: Red
IN CASE OF ACCIDENT PLEASE NOTIFY: (blank)

Blank. Week 49, November Monday 28, 1983 to Week 29, July Monday 16, 1984: every date was blank. Then:

July Sunday 22
    'why would I want to phone you'

July Tuesday 24
    Leave Edmonton 3:30 p.m. In a.m. drop off book
    borrowed from Joan. Ailsa in shorts sitting on back steps,
    says they leave tomorrow for Frankfurt. Why am I flying
    to Holland alone, today?

July Wednesday 25

(Holland–W. Germany) Arrived Amsterdam 7:30 a.m.
went direct to train station, then bullet train to
"Terror in Frankfurt"

And there it was. On pages obviously torn out of a spiral notebook but kept doubled in the diary. Gabriel kept everything so close, always like Yo of blessed memory in his innate order; even when he threw it away in "File of Discards." But here two pages, four sides of words clawed, as seemed, off the ribs of Rilke's First Elegy days before Gabriel ever glimpsed Duino Castle brooding grey and cornered on a kink of the Adriatic: "For beauty is nothing but terror's beginning . . ." Tiny blue ballpoint letters gradually twisting themselves indecipherable: as he had lived them.

Terror in Frankfurt

I am about to stay up 40 hours straight. *Warum?* Because
I am so shy. However, I won't be the truly shy one unless I
do not tell anyone. Then, and only then would I be a
member of the truly shyest group of human beings.
Human beings so shy they hide their shyness. A shynik.
   Only blank paper
   I'm sitting outside the Central RR Station at Frankfurt
   train immediately and direct from Amsterdam, why?
what would I want here? No one's here yet
   again the mind moved into other ideas for a period of
time
   because I have been up 15 hours already

no, no, I have been up 29 hours already, waiting this out will change the grand total to approximately 50 hours. 50 hours I have to stay awake before I can go to sleep in a reserved and paid-for hotel. A whole day early

why did I fly a day early—to walk around Amsterdam—so why didn't I?

I haven't even eaten for six/seven hours, perhaps more, that plane breakfast

Let's think a bit

something new and different

I can't speak German; I'm already a person that doesn't even like to go into new entrances of malls he knows very well

shy compared to all Frankfurt, where I wait smiling with 5 bags of junk (with razors you can't plug in in Europe, a tent!) a place where you have to pay a quarter to take a shit or beat off in something. I stick out and someone is going to try me, an old guy, actually middle aged, 35, his acne skin don't I know it

he is just looking for a standout hick like me. What a WUSS, how can a person be such a travel asshole

pay a hundred bucks to be a day too early to sleep

all you want to do is sleep anyway. The man is eyeing me oh crap he moved and pulled off his jacket and sat down next to me. Ready for   Think I'll go get one of my bags I checked. I stand out writing. Just watch his body reactions, he is alone, looking around. Got to find a cool place. It is 6:41

6:51 p.m. *oder* 18:51 as the electric clocks run here and I have taken up a new spot. Damn cities there is never any

place just to sit always got to move. Sit in the places
where men, all the losers of the world seem to coagulate
    my joints ache
    my whole stupid body aches sleep, sleep if only never
to wake up and listen to the bullshit
    how the hell am I going to last for a year
away—travel!!!
    can't even stand forty hours. When I am alone I
absolutely fall apart
    I don't even care enough to write—writing takes time
    Writing = time
    thinking I suppose would equal time too but thinking
you don't have, get in part of your body, i.e. outside your
mind which, if you are being, experiencing, you don't
have to do anything extra. No work is needed to be
yourself, because you just are. What I mean is be in your
mind, you just are   what is being   human
    now to actually do something you have to put out
effort, however, isn't intent effort? Actually physical
effort—a day ago I was living in my parents' perfectly
lovely house that I didn't want to leave   all those plans
    but alas, when I wake up to myself I have hauled all
my junk and myself directly from the airport through
beautiful Amsterdam as fast as I can and I am in grey
smelly Frankfurt RR station. Here, I'm already sick of
walking around and I haven't even walked around yet.
I'm young, the good years they say   ugh   if only I could
climb into the box I stuffed my junk in
    and jerk the lid down tight. What junk. 7:04 another 13
0 yes 14 minutes 7:05 gone, now to the ex pursuer again.

I've noticed this was a louse, then how he went down the escalator

if he came back up I'd know

7:07 Idea—I could have taken my 6–7 thousand saved and just lived somewhere in Canada alone 9 or 10 months easy not a worry. Oh God another lone guy has come along, wants to get eye contact, for all I know I hit the homo pickup place to kill time on. How can anyone be so insane as to sit here—can you kill time? Maybe pass time—time till I can go collapse. I should go to that Burger King to eat something. No sense killing myself through the extremely primitive process of starvation. The man left but will he be back? You got to be rude to him. How could my personality ever get born in my family   who of them ever worries?

there need not be such pain put on people, why the

7:14 p.m. 16 hours and . . . 45 minutes left to kill before the reserved hotel across the street by time dragging on. My crossed legs

driving me insane. I should go to a film to kill time easy only thing is I do not know what the theatres look like and if they say the cost I will not know what it means need marks, and not understand a

7:20: my shoes are shiny, my parents and everybody thinks I'm in Edmonton till tomorrow but I left yesterday no   what day

in Frankfurt I am going nuts.

simple as that

For whatever good it is to him   he can have my body odour

God things are getting sick here   7:27 p.m.

got to move on. Drink   find somebody   peace
loving guy   just give him my bags, here   got to get
used to getting terror   why is the problem   7:29—
how much more time to kill, many thanks   oh   whip
a bun out of his bag   painfully killed time. There
probably are nice people in Frankfurt. But I'm here.
They went thanks be to

things can only get worse. 7:32 p.m. Should head for
Burger King. I could just sit here drinking till I die
what made me do it, here comes another one   bottle in
hand   off I go. 7:35. Do it.   This   I can't order anything
in German, this is worse than my shit trip to Toronto.
off off off I go. 7:37

8:00 why does it go on and on, self-inflicted. Dear God
where are you   Man and alone   both sets of parents
have cars   they must both be somewhere close   close
only counts in horseshoes   XH4U

5.30 DM *fuer* a Whopper and coffee

End this—

I can do it. To hell with money   here I go.

In bed by 9:45 p.m. Wednesday   o sweet sleep of the
dead   be dead

DAILY PLANNER 1984: *July Thursday 26*
Frankfurt   leaning on hotel balcony. And below me,
there's Denn's blond head! In lobby Mom, Dad, Denn
Colin & parents, then Ailsa

Then Ailsa.

They had so sensibly planned everything, coordinated the city, the day, the hotel, the day trips—Europe for Joan was art, art—Yo and Hal and Dennis would arrive in Frankfurt by rental car from Vienna, Grant and Joan and their two children by air from Edmonton, Gabriel by train after a day sightseeing in Amsterdam. And within an hour of the planned 15:00 everyone was there, Hotel Stein across from the Frankfurt train station; everyone except Gabriel. They waited in the hotel lobby, waited on the *Allee* jammed with travellers flooding around the enormous *Hauptbahnhof*. Finally they left a message at the desk and went to their rooms to clean up for dinner, and Denn went out on their balcony to watch the people swirling over the *Platz* and suddenly a familiar voice shouted his name from above. Gabriel! Leaning down over a higher balcony railing. Already there the night before! And so all was—should have been—well, the two families together as they were so often in Edmonton—but without Miriam's quick laugh calming everything—in a strange city surrounded by crowds of strangers, but easy, Hal thoughtlessly thought then, good home friends and easy, let Denn and Colin natter—

—"then Ailsa." Gabriel printed the words with blue ballpoint in his University of Alberta Planner 1984. After their loud dinner already filled with travel adventure (inevitable toilet?) stories—none from Gabriel, going back up to his Frankfurt hotel room alone for the second night; but then Denn moved in with him.

DAILY PLANNER 1984: *July Friday 27*

Frankfurt   saw Roman ruins, Drei Roemer, the ugly gaps still left from WWII.

A: Are you really going to stay away for a whole year?

G: I probably won't be able to stand it.

A: Good (quietly)

G: What?

A looking down, smiles. Scotland in her name. The great rock, "craig," in the sea off Ayr is called Ailsa. Joan told me, laughing like she does, they had so little contact with their Scottish relatives they at least gave their kids Scottish names.

Dinner after Goethe Haus—pasta, A beside me. She found my hand on my leg.

July Saturday 28

Drive early, Dad & Grant & boys to Marburg, his old Uni, and Mom, Joan, Ailsa & me to Mainz. The Chagall windows in St. Stephan, still rebuilding it from the war (40 years), a blue shimmer over the chancel. Joan entranced. But A whispers: "Why are you mean to me?" I couldn't answer. Evening, walk streets alone, too many others.

And same-day notes in the third tan notebook: unlimited space, for whatever he felt, and could write:

SPIRAL NOTEBOOK (3): *July 28, 1984*

I feel so terrible. Walking the Rheinufer/Gutenberg Museum in Mainz, Ailsa showed clearly she likes me, all I

ever wanted. And I couldn't talk to her. Felt like I was
chained shut. She doesn't /nobody/ knows how much I care
    <u>Hope</u>: feeling expectation and desire
           a person or thing giving cause for this
  Give me your hand again, anywhere, I'll kiss every one
of your thin fingers
   why can't we be alone no people no church no age just
all I ever wanted have mercy please one dream growing
three years—can it already be three?   so long so young
please forgive me for

DAILY PLANNER 1984: *July Sunday 29*
Heidelberg, after Castle hiked over bridge & Philosophen-
weg for view. A tries to put her arm in mine. "Are you mad
at me?" Meal (pasta again) in Altstadt, sit beside her. Her
hand again. "A year away, you'll forget me." Walking to cars
we find a girl (dope, valium?) curled on street cobblestones.
Scary and sad, we all just let her be. I drive our rental back
to Frkfrt, A in back like always with kibitzing boys, no touch
possible. But we have held hands twice.

SPIRAL NOTEBOOK (3): *July 29, 1984*
  Ailsa Helen: born May 19, 1971
          - Gaellic/Scot./English, Elsbeth/
           Elizabeth: consecrated to God
          - Greek/Helen: light, a torch—a flame, yes
  loves pasta perogies ice cream
  burns the outside of hot dogs before eating them
  hates garlic swimming pools has great marks in art
not phys. ed.

Dear Ailsa, Dearest Helen,

Consecrated, dedicated to all that is light and beautiful,
flame of my being. Forgive me for acting so cool, for
almost seeming mean/mad. It is absolutely not that
this is really the case—just that my feelings are so
strong I feel very awkward and apprehensive with both
our families always so close around. Your pretty thin
fingers, your lovely eyes are all that is beautiful in the
world. Your affection for me is beyond dream. Forgive
me if I at times seem standoffish, really that's NOT
what I mean, I care for you so deeply and do not want
to hurt you ever, in any way. Hopefully the future will
be better for us.

> *With all my hope, my love, Gabriel Thomas Wiens*

DAILY PLANNER 1984: *July Monday 30*
  (W. Germany–France–W. Germany) Had to leave Frkft.—
  but with great hope—they're driving to Paris. Parents,
  Denn, I drove to Alb. Schweitzer town Kayserberg, Fr.
  Good to concentrate on traffic, crowded Autobahn. Night
  in Freiburg Ger. hotel, ate pasta in memory   now more
  than dream!

July Tuesday 31
  Climbed Freiburg huge gothic spire, Denn hung out
  waving, scared Mom. Drove through Black Forest.
  Round hills, bent roads. Crazy laughs with Denn.
  Lonely

August Wednesday 1

Dostoevsky plaque at Baden-Baden, baths sulphur, high
castle ruins, mountains and forest. He never got over
being a gambler, but wrote—dare to be a gambler!

August Thursday 2

(W. Germany–France) lv. alone again, Strasbourg tr.
station, lots of strangers, evening 8:00: this, all this that
we love within us . . . the dried up riverbeds of ancient
mothers, the whole silent landscape under the clear
heavens—all this, my dearest girl, preceded you (Rilke)

August Friday 3

Nice, arrive 8 in the morning   small "Terror in Nice"
got it stopped walking, to Albert Hotel and there was
Fred, as planned   quiet Karen O is with him

Fred: *Deo gratias* for that year at Winnipeg College where
Gabe met young people from all over Canada—so why didn't
he meet a Karen too? He must have, there were dozens.

August Sunday 5

(France–Italia) Chagall Museum, Nice: whole Old
Testament floats for him, in blue, stunning. But the
thick erect snake and Eve with red apple, Adam groping.
O Joan mother mother. All 3 of us on evening train
to Milano

Dearest Ailsa,

I'm in Italia sitting on a rock embankment in the resort
town of Desenzano overlooking the lake called Lago
di Garda. It took an hour and a half by train to get here
from Milano. It is 10:30 in the morning and the big
French boys who were playing in the water near me,
making the usual beach sounds, have rented paddle-
boats and are disappearing into the hazy lake.

Since I cannot remember your family's art itinerary,
I can't place at this moment, August 7, 10:40 am, your
whereabouts. (Oh Ailsa, I do care, very much. Back in
Edmonton, if I hadn't had the opportunity to see you
for a while, I would drive past your house to see if
your bedroom light was on or off.) Here the only
closeness I can get, so much feebler, is by my meals.
I've eaten lasagna 3 times already, in memory of you
and your hands and Chagall blue. I saw an enormous
museum of his paintings in Nice, and every painting
had something of you and blue in it.

I would never deliberately be mean to you. There are
times, like in Mainz, when I've seen your sensitive soul,
at least I think I have. I would so much love to know
more about what goes on behind those green eyes.

Please, forgive me when I acted foolishly those few
days we had in Germany. I have nothing but tender
feelings towards you, Ailsa, it's that I felt extremely
awkward near you so long and together with our

parents and our always joking brothers; which is why I want to be alone with you, and we never have been, or were walking then, so I never felt I could explain what I am trying to do making this trip. You said so quietly in Frankfurt, "Good," when I confessed I probably couldn't stay away for a year. And believe me, I felt so good then, too.

Now I took a walk, got some things to eat at the market here, there are hundreds of sellers. And the thought struck me: I don't really want to be here, at this dull, supposed to be beautiful! lake—and it is, I can see that—in the middle of north Italy. But I am, far away from you, here, searching to try and say what is on my mind, but I don't really know where I could stand with you, or what I could explain. To show my feelings I tried to arrange some verses from the Song of Solomon that I was reading in Nice August 3, 4, in the Holy Bible (with pictures by Chagall too). I admit I've walked the streets of Nice and Milano trying to find you. Once in a while I found someone with eyes like yours, or very young with lovely shoulders, but of course they were never you. And those girls didn't care about me, or even noticed I was alive in front of them.

Yet, there are some places I want to see here in Europe. I must say that I will be back by at least Christmas, most likely a lot sooner.

But then what! This question was already on my mind on the street in Heidelberg, the night of the unconscious valium (?) girl. I was in a state of melancholia because I knew those few seconds walking

beside you were going to pass, so fast, everything goes.
Your affection and goodness . . . there, in Germany, I had
the opportunity to show you how I care for you, and
because I'm so shy and feel so awkward in front of the
others, because I (stupidly) keep thinking ahead to when
we won't be together, I couldn't show you. Only hide
my worry, think ahead and worry. Isn't that foolish?

So this letter is a declaration to you, a sensitive,
beautiful and very young lady.

I love you, Ailsa Helen, birthday Wednesday May 19,
1971. How I long for you to be here, to talk with me.
Please write me so I know you exist.

Even now, in this letter, I cannot express the feelings
and thoughts . . . there is so much we could say, but
never do, and so much we shouldn't say but barely do.
Here I don't know if I can even try to mail this letter.

DAILY PLANNER 1984: *August Thursday 9*
Can $1 = 1330 liras

At 10 o'clock walked from Monfalcone, Hotel Excelsior
#15 to Duino, arrived 12:30. Everyone friendly—found
zimmer across from Duino Castle, Albergo Susy #7,
walked to Sustiana   met Yugoslav family, invited us to
their place—tried to get into Duino Castle—no luck,
closed—that's me every time

August Friday 10

Long wonderful shower—off to write some letters home
here in Duino. Found out stuff on Castle, took pictures in
the grey rain, the sea, the white cliffs snarled with trees,

the castle roofs and thick towers—perfect for elegy and longing. Re-write, re-copy letter to A   Long after midnight, still rain.

SPIRAL NOTEBOOK (3): *August 10, 1984*

Duino, Italia

My dearest Ailsa,

As I write this letter, one of many drafts, you are still in Europe. Since I was not told your family's exact itinerary, I can't place your whereabouts. However, when you receive this letter in Edmonton you will obviously be at home, a place I remember very well. I helped your family move into that house when you bought it, and I put your bed together in the bedroom you chose. Remember?

I started ~~one, many~~ a number of letters; ~~August 3 in Nice, France, on August 7 another in Desenzano, Italy~~ but have mailed none. Now in Duino, a small town overlooking the Gulf of Trieste; Trieste is a city located 50 km south of Duino, I write what will hopefully be the final draft of a letter which will be mailed.

~~Oh, I will write you and write you, Ailsa, I will never forget you~~

The main problem in writing this letter ~~was~~ has been the choice of <u>motif</u>. The ~~mo~~ theme chosen has been the ~~declar~~ confession. A person can never reveal everything that is on his/her mind, especially if it is complex, and even more so if it has to be told in a short letter.

~~First off I want to tell you why I came to Duino~~

I came to Duino, Italy, because a great German poet, Rainer Maria Rilke (a male), stayed at the castle, the high grey structure on the cliff in the postcard picture enclosed, on invitation from the Princess who lived there in 1912. At the Duino Castello he started what were later called *The Duino Elegies*—his greatest poems. Here are a few lines from the 7th Elegy, translated from the German (not by me):

Nowhere, beloved, can the world exist but within us.
　　　Our life is spent in changing. And ever lessening,
The outer world disappears.

That's what I feel here, the world changing in me. Presently Prince Raimondo della Torre e Tasso owns the Castle, and when the flag is flying, which you can see on the tip of the tallest tower, the Prince is at home. The flag is flying as I write, so no visitors are allowed inside. My luck as usual.

I have been debating whether to include a poem here that was written in one peak of despair in a Nice hotel [August 3], selecting and changing a few words from a Holy Bible version of Song of Solomon. It's kind of contradictory, both lament and joy, but that seems the way things are now:

Sorrow

Whither is my beloved gone,
O thou fairest among young women?

Thou hast ravished my heart, my beauty, my rose;
Thou hast ravished my heart with both of thine eyes,
and with just one of thy looks.

How fair is thy love, my beauty, my rose;
How much better thy love than wine,
and the presence of thy being beyond all others.
I will rise now, and go about the city,
and in the streets I will seek her whom my soul loves:
I sought her, but I found her not.

Whether is my beloved gone,
O thou fairest among women?

Ailsa, ~~I do care~~ I love you. You are the most beautiful
young lady in the world. I would never be deliberately
mean to you. I will never, never, forget you. ~~I'll be back
before Christmas.~~

I've been entranced with you ever since I ~~first
noticed~~ first really became aware of your existence.
This occurred at the 1980 church Sunday School
Christmas program. You, Ailsa, were nine years old
and in the children's choir, and you were not singing.
You just stood there in the front row while the other
children joyfully sang, including your brother and

mine, but you with a ~~pained~~ sad face and a silent gaze into the congregation. I was enchanted. Then for one song you did begin to sing. In the song there was a pause, most likely a verse change. Well, you started singing before the rest of the choir. You immediately noticed your mistake and stopped but some children beside you looked at you and laughed and your cheeks flushed, you scuffed your arms in extreme embarrassment. And you never did sing again, not any song that entire evening.

~~At that moment, and at many other times in the three and a half years since, I have felt that I could see into your inner being. Perhaps it is just that as I am an extremely sensitive and shy person, and I feel other people's pain, but esp. yours~~

I felt very sorry for you, a sensitive and shy person, because I too know the pain of extreme embarrassment. I also felt that I could see into your inner self ~~something that one does rarely with most people~~ which I have had a number of opportunities since then to witness

~~??????? Bullshit confusing !!!!!! and horrible transition~~

Ailsa, speaking of embarrassment—(better awkwardness—no one with any sensitivity would ever be embarrassed with you wanting to be close to them) in Germany I felt very awkward with our family members always around and so I outwardly showed little affection ~~for~~ to you. You were so very kind and tender, I didn't mean to be mean or cold: I just didn't know what to do, where to look. But you are so brave, you talk right out loud.

On the viewpoint over Heidelberg when you asked
me what was on my mind, what I was thinking was
our being together would not last. So silly! I've been
longing for you to enjoy my company, and here you
were showing great tenderness and I due to shyness
~~apprehension the future the others~~ could not
respond. The sadness I felt was that my chance to
show you how much I do care for you was being
wasted, just like that poor girl curled together on the
street that evening. The whole world walking those
cobblestones after our beautiful meal was suddenly so
helpless, so sad.

~~Why did I waste that moment? Always apprehen-~~
~~sive, about what's coming —~~

Ailsa, this is my confession today: I love you. How
this will be experienced in the future, just as how this
letter works, I don't know. Please forgive me for
seeming cold and silent in the near past, it was not
meant against you. Better—think of the Chagall blue
heavens in Mainz, and I'll think of his Nice paintings:
of the great ladder going up into blue heaven and
those winged people like flying flowers everywhere.
That's a way we can hope together.

I am presently with Fred and his friend Karen O,
and we are hostelling/camping our way to Athens,
Greece. I intend to be in Greece till the end August,
maybe a week longer. Please answer, mail your letter
to me at the Canadian Embassy, Athens, Greece,
address on the back of this letter. Please—answer.

With all my love, Gabriel Thomas Wiens

DAILY PLANNER 1984: *August Saturday 11*
    Parents/Denn back in Canada today   **<u>mailed
recopied letter to A</u> **
    mailed postcard to parents from Duino, did laundry
Venice tomorrow, @ 4 hrs.

SPIRAL NOTEBOOK (3): *August 10, 1984*

                        Panorama Di Duino (Trieste)
Dear family,

I've been staying in Duino since Thursday noon,
we will be leaving Sunday morning for Trieste and
perhaps a short day trip into Yugoslavia. The Castello
(centre of picture) is still owned by relatives of the
Princess who invited Rilke to stay here in 1912 and he
worked on his Elegies. Presently Prince Raimondo
lives there, and it is strictly a private place and nobody
can get in to see the rooms where Rilke stayed when
he's home. Right now as I write it is raining quite
heavily, and my laundry which I hung out to dry is
getting a second rinse. I plan to be in Italy/Greece for
the rest of August.
                    Love you all—Gabe (X marks my hotel room)

DAILY PLANNER 1984: *August Monday 13*
    Spent 3:00 a.m.–7:00 a.m. Fred, Karen, I stuck in Florence
train station   yuk ABC #5 tiny inner courtyard. Phoned
home, Mom answered, they got home and all fine as

usual. 2 minutes, can't ask anything re A and she of course says nothing.1,500 lire.

SPIRAL NOTEBOOK (3): *August 13, 1984*

Started with $1400, now $930 / 25 days $470 spent / enough to end of Sept?

Firenze, San Lorenzo, Tombo in Marmo per Berta Moltke di Giovanni Dupre (1817–82) Young lady on left side of marble mausoleum with a little boy in front of her. Muscular yet finely feminine arms, long, straight nose, smallish mouth and exposed breast. When looked at from the side you see this perfectly shaped breast, truly marvellous: with the young Lady's sad, melancholic stare into nowhere. She stares year after year, for a century, always down and away. Lady of marble, why am I . . . you aren't even alive. This shape of female, not seemingly obscure but—what is the object of desire? I'm a foolish person, can't touch

What the hell's my problem, I continue to look, even walking away I grab one more look. What is this, obsession? Do I really like it or does it control me. I just can't seem to help it, my mind and gut take over my spine. Too much passion. Always the same type too, so obvious. Some very young girl—this one is a bit older   good grief   pathetic person to the nth degree

always that obscure Object of Desire

Obscure - dark, indistinct, not easily understood
Object - something solid that can be touched

>   Desire - feeling one would get pleasure, satisfaction
>   from (touching?)

. . . Walked streets alone. People everywhere sitting together at café tables, beautiful. Laughing as if they were happy.

. . . In front of the Uffizi Gallery near the river (where our family went 8 years ago and little (then) Denn saw a dog in a painting and yapped about getting one the rest of the trip) I'm thinking how useless all the pictures I have taken today are. When 20,000 people go around and basically take the same pictures as you, I feel so cynical, so stupidly average. Thousands of cameras have taken this view, right where I sit. What does taking it too give me. Proof I was here—so? Luckily I'm off to see an art lecture tonight so I can get my mind onto something else. The question is whether I actually do <u>have</u> a mind. Hnnnn

DAILY PLANNER 1984: *August Wednesday 15*
Slept in late, everything closed, holiday in Italy. Karen gave me a haircut, feels good   Mass at St. Salvatore in Ognissanti—Amerigo Vespucci tomb, name oddly attached to all the Americas   Midnight walk to Ponte Vecchio   Karen said pure obsession, and said that's okay, that's okay

So you said something about your feelings to Karen? Gabe, that's good—very good—how much did you dare say? A warm, sympathetic, non-threatening listener. Did Fred mind? Did he know? Surely there was a world of understanding possible, especially for travelling young people, sitting around, waiting for the next bus, train—talk, impulse talk.

DAILY PLANNER 1984: *August Thursday 16*
(We 3 now 13 days together) Uffizi Gallery Young lady tomb again You could stand and stare at it forever, remains the same, stone, constant Karen followed her plan, left for Naples south today (hnnnn) we guys on train east, Florence to Rome/Tagliacozzo evening walk with Fred town people

SPIRAL NOTEBOOK (3): *August 18, 1984*

> Pure - not mixed with any other substance,
> free from evil, chaste
> Chaste - virgin, not sexually immoral, simple
> in style
> Virgin - person who has never had sexual
> intercourse, undefiled, not used—not yet . . .

I am sitting here on a beach in Italia. Oh, I suppose I am conscious of it, thereby proving I am alive, but what will I do. Like Tolstoy wrote: "What then <u>must</u> we do?"

August 20/84

Dearest Ailsa,

I am sitting on rocks on a beach along the Adriatic Sea in Termoli, Italia. My Canadian friend Fred and I have been camping in my tent (some use for it at last) on the sand. The water is warm, bluer than sky. It is about 7:00 p.m., so back in Edmonton it would be 11:00 a.m., are you up, fixing your room with things you bought in Europe, perhaps listening to records? Right behind our tent there are rocks and train tracks.

My feelings at present are neutral; not up or down. I would love to have you here to talk to. However, what would we talk about. Let's face it, is there anything we really have in common, you a girl barely 13 and I a man 23 and a half. So.

A boat is crossing the water going north. Sound. The traffic on the road behind me. Sound. The waves barely making one continuous rush. The sun sinks.

I am alone. By my own doing, but I do so feel I need someone. If only you had not acted so affectionately in Germany I might have forgotten you, or at least . . . now I think of nothing but you. I must get your letter [[so stupid !!! blaming her]]

The sun is bright red, and low. I hope, hope with the hope of a fool that you

There is nothing to say. My body is cold, the waves continue to come on the sea, the sun ever deeper red sinking into the hills. A short train rushes past. End of day.

DAILY PLANNER 1984: *August Wednesday 22*
(Greece) Our Adriatic ferry made two stops, did not get to Patrai from Brindisi till 5:00 p.m. 20+ hours on that dumb ship. Try to see Hitchcock *The Birds*,

still on marquee, but theatre closed for summer.
Supper: spaghetti + meatballs + tomato salad +
memories

August Thursday 23

Spend another day in Patrai, leave tomorrow, Athens.
Read Van Gogh book and walk around looking   food a
lot cheaper than It   big shaded squares where you can sit
and drink   Retsina great

August Friday 24

1:30 train standing room only—crowded into bar train car
with no windows open, loud American in bar   sweaty
people crammed together   Embassy p.m. already closed
for weekend   find cheap hotel easily

August Saturday 25

Saw Theatre of Dionysus and climbed up to Acropolis
ugly heat up there, boiling   took a number of usual
tourist shots   it was after we had the Athens room I
found out the name, Hotel Orpheus, o great story for
me, make it all the way to hell and one big mistake and
come back still alone. Start reading *Love*, Stendhal

SPIRAL NOTEBOOK (3): *August 25, 1984*

4:00 just woke from a short nap. Had a wonderful
dream, a dream like one has in high school. There is
such pleasure while you are dreaming then but upon
waking up everything overwhelms you because the
dream will not carry on. The real over the imagined,

Yes!!! Such awesome hope I have, tremendously
imagine, never ending!

Sunday August 26, 1984

(Athens)

Dearest Ailsa:

I walked up the Acropolis today again   on top of high
hill   white rock   very hot and on this famous place
I think of nothing but you   see young women walking around, I follow them, watch their habits, body
movements for traces of you but no matter how
slender they are, how long their thighs, what graceful
very young   Naturally if this is the truth—I want to
kiss you, I do, even, especially to get over you to go on
to something else   this is ridicu—

August 26, 1984

Sorrow   I have been making a major mistake these past
days. I have gone under the assumption that Ailsa cares
for only me. This is a ridiculous and selfish stance to take.
Except for one evening, three unforgettable days and one
goodbye morning in Germany I have hardly seen her over
the past two years, my moments in her presence would
come monthly, not even weekly, they are barely glimpses
of her if I go to church, and then at a distance over heads
in the lobby or down the stairs in the teens room surrounded by giggling girls. Or sometimes she tags along
with whatever Denn and her brother do. Ever a word?
A glance? It's really been pathetic on my part. And just

because I get back to Edm. doesn't mean anything will change, why should it. So I remain faithful to something that doesn't really exist, and I'm a fool for blabbering on about it, and on.

<u>I don't want to travel</u>   this is sick. Who cares about ancient rock piles and millions of camera tourists. I've been a fool. One can't expect anything. Oh, one can hope, but one cannot expect anything

A few hours later: triple fool

Not sorrow but faith. Orpheus had to <u>have faith</u> not to turn around. I will have faith, not necessarily in any particular future but faith that to remain as I am is a good and worthy thing. Things <u>will</u> work out, life goes on. Caring love survives.

DAILY PLANNER 1984: *August Monday 27*

Can. Embassy first thing, only one long letter, Mom. Good excuse, phoned home about business, I am really healthy, doing fine, Mom said she got my Duino pc—so A must have got my letter, sent same day. She mentioned A's family's back, and all I could dare was, "They okay?" and she just said yes—to be so close but   Right after I got my plane ticket booked for Rome Sept. 15   scout more book stores   movie tonight *Who's Afraid of Virginia Woolf?* Hotel, read *Tess*. I miss home so much.

August Friday 31

Two separate letters, Mom and Miriam, lovely with all the ordinary family news; nothing else for Canadian Citizen Gabriel T. Wiens. Mir packing for South Amer.

study, and of course laughing at the mess of it. Got
money from bank. Fred leaves to join Karen in Italy,
return to Canada with her   I am completely alone
moved to narrow HOrpheus Rm #7   make notes on *Tess*
in my favourite secluded spot in National Gardens   Brits
play cricket in heat   by pool Greek mother, grand-
mother, great-grandmother with three little children
running. Beautiful bodies all.

September Tuesday 4

Never mail—almost a month. Where are those hands that
reached and touched me   I need people around me
Athens good grief I'm in world-renowned Athens Greece
of all places, alone   don't know a soul don't know a word
don't move don't want to be here / Mail is the only reason
I sit here but can't go to Embassy every   nothing

Ach Gabriel: the telephone! Okay, the personal computer
and e-mail and Facebook and Twitter and cellphones and
iPads and all that instantaneous tech grabbing everyone
together anywhere in the world didn't exist in 1984, but
you air-mailed that one and only "Confession" letter on
August 11—twenty-four days—how often in your days of
sitting, watching, walking in the dead heat of Athens did
you pass a public telephone? A post office where the booths
stand row on row, lift the receiver and operators are ready
with Greek and instant English? You must have looked.
And agonized. You phoned us in Edmonton—always
during the day when you knew I wasn't home?—each time

you made a full page of notebook notes of what to say: I'm healthy . . . doing fine . . . I got the money . . . got Mir's lovely letter . . . won't be too long in Italy, after 10th don't mail Marseilles, mail to Paris embassy. You explained everything so carefully to Yo—and the entire world was waiting in those booths of coded numbers, waiting for the one number you certainly knew, by heart. That white phone with the long flexible cord hanging on the wall just outside her room, the smaller room she deliberately chose because the phone cord was long enough to reach in and close the door—if one of her parents answer, fine, they're your friends, just to say hello—what were you thinking when you always had to see all those telephones? Of course there was none in your tiny Hotel Orpheus room, but even in the lobby—

Hello? And then you would have to speak. Say something.

Abruptly Hal recognized the ordered basement shelves standing over him. So neatly built by their Argentinian son-in-law Leo; filled with a lifetime of stacked file boxes. Yo's and his, ordered and labelled, such unimaginably comfortable lives made possible by the desperate refugee flights of their Mennonite parents from Stalin's devastating Soviet paradise on the edge of Europe and Asia; so both of them could be born in Canada and given every humane Canadian right: they always had enough to eat and could grow and learn to trust in God and work and pray and dream and develop themselves however they pleased in whatever community they pleased until their last living day. And so now he could sit here, alone on his own basement floor among the paper remains of his son's freely chosen "world travel," that unsuspected beginning of the end in Europe,

July 24 to October 18, 1984—ach, never a "memory hole" possible there—a few months hinted at in bare words of places, times, movies, a rare flip of something seen or a moment's contemplation of history, but overwhelmingly nailed down into that emotional laceration by those quick days in Germany. Gabriel alone and living only, as it seemed, every solitary repetition of night and day with pen and paper in hand and writing, writing mostly the same, words.

My son: could you not move? That exquisite Mediterranean world—move!

As if you had been sentenced to motionless life by a girl barely thirteen.

DAILY PLANNER 1984: *September Wednesday 5*
I woke up in HOrph #7 bed thinking of Ailsa   of kissing her long thin fingers, of the soft skin just below the neck in the back, of her eyes, her beautiful teeth. Will she ever care for me again? What are those fingers doing do you still sleep in the bed I put together for you when your family   escape to movie *Cannonball Run*   ugggh

September Friday 7
Mir leaves for Lima. Letter—not A—from Mom, she mentions Joan told her A had received a long letter from me—oh heaven and earth and hell what are they talking about me   how stupid did I sound in that
     My letters   I'm working on the next, I need to be more dignified, more   not to regret again what I wrote when I come back to Edm.

SPIRAL NOTEBOOK (3): *September 7, 1984*

(postcard rehearsal)

Dear Big Ed: This is the old pile of rocks that makes
Athens famous. (There would obviously be lots of
work for you here). If man-made things here are not
thousands of years old, they invariably take on the
other extreme, as you can see. I sit downtown having
tea surrounded by the other (brutal) extreme. Cheers.

Reading notebook entries: am I too much, only, my
narrow self? Writing the same trivial things over and
over in the same childish way? Note, objective fact:
there are millions of mosquitoes in Athens. I have
dozens of bites. So. Good night.

Sept 6, 7, 8, 9, 10 1984

<u>Letter rewritten—Athens</u>

If my Duino letter was a confession of love, this
letter will be a confession that I do not really know
you, what goes on in your mind on a late Friday
evening when you can't fall asleep—why do you haunt
me so? The most simple answer probably holds most
of the truth: you are a dream to hope for, but, once
obtained, would fall away. Naturally if this is the
truth—but I do want to kiss you   I do, even, especially, to get over you, to go on to something
    —this is already truly ridiculous—

Ailsa my Love
    If ever any beauty I did see, which I desired and
        sought (got)
    'Twas but a dream of thee.
                    (John Donne, "The Good-Morrow")
                If ever any beauty I do see,
                    That I desire, and seek, it's but a dream
                        of thee.

            —nothing double here, just me—

Psalm 102
Turn your ear to me, O Lord,
    when I am in dark distress.
        Listen to my voice, dearest.
            Let my cry come to you.

September 9, 1984

I wake up and it is 2:00 a.m. How all this sounds so
contrived, so artificial. And why should you care anyway?
I think I have a slight fever. To think that we are all dying.
The instant one is born you start to die and nothing ever
seems to get done or said the way one feels it should
happen. You once said aloud at our Aspen Creek cabin,
"Who would want to live out here!" I would, and have,
and it's very good there. One reason I went to the cabin
so often was to get away, actually to forget you among
trees and running water, in four steps one has disappeared
into nature, every look up at a night sky carries one away
into space, nobody anywhere, except God, maybe—I

realize this sounds silly because I hardly ever saw you in Edmonton, not even weekly, barely monthly when I went to church, and always when I did you were with the boys and/or your parents and as an adult I could really speak only to them and act cool. So much so that maybe you remember you once asked me, "I don't even know if you like me." But that kind of close yet untalkable distance is dangerous, a seeming possible that can hardly be endured while doing nothing. And here, far away in Europe where I can't possibly talk to you, I write words words to/about you like some kind of fool. If you or anybody laughs, you have good reason. But remember we are all dying, and a hundred years from now who will care what I have felt or even acted. Yeah, but I live now. Life goes on and people continue to lay their living room carpets

ATHENS LETTERS IN ADDRESSED BUT UNSTAMPED AIRMAIL ENVELOPES

I have before me a hundred blank pages. I have in my hand a ballpoint pen full of blue ink. I sit at a desk covered with repeating letters, only to stop and begin them again in the very same way, until my thoughts, my writing becomes unreadable. My room, Number 7, Hotel Orpheus, 58 Chalkokondyli Athens, Attica, 104 32, Hellas, is littered with letter attempts, books with quotations ready and under-lined, laundry drying on the line I've strung up, and food. I have basically stayed in this narrow room since Thursday Sept 6—it is now Tuesday 11. Six days in solitary trying to write the perfect letter to you. Emotionally I have gone full circle so often I have reached my present state: resignation

. . . The time here in Athens, Hellas is 8:50 in the evening of the 11th day of September 1984 (19 days in Athens, a whole 31-day month since my   ) and therefore according to my second watch, the one always set on Edmonton time, you will shortly be walking home from Rowand School for lunch. Last May one day I deliberately drove past your house. It was getting close to noon and at the school intersection I saw you walking on the wide sidewalk towards the lights. You adjusted the Walkman on your head as you walked home alone for lunch. As soon as I could I turned around and followed you home at a careful distance—now in Athens I follow you home again down the same streets in my mind with the same care. I follow you past the church, past the corner store, past the walk-ups, past the patch of intersection lawn, around every corner and across every intersection—Look both ways!—towards your house. You enter through the back door and run so easily up the four steps into your kitchen where you slide your slim body into the nook and read this very letter. Perhaps one day this will, in fact, happen.

Ailsa, I love and miss you. (I kiss every one of your fingers that touched me so briefly in the Mainz restaurant) (No, confirm love not kiss—restraint) I quote Stendhal's novel *De l'Amour* (the core of this book is Stendhal's obsession with Mathilde Viscontini Dembowski—no—cut that—just quote):

"I am trying extremely hard to be dry. My heart has so much to say, but I try to keep it quiet. I am continually beset by the fear that I may have expressed only a sigh when I thought I was stating a truth."

The other day, Sunday 9th, I went to the National Gardens, Areos Park, frequented by less tourists—I didn't come to Greece to watch Germans drink beer—my favourite place to sit is the X on the enclosed pc map—and I saw in the distance—the O on the map—a slender girl in a white dress coming towards me. As she drew nearer I made out facial features and easy body movements that were strikingly similar to yours. She even had lively green eyes that looked straight at me. But she was not you. She walked past me so easily . . .

A couple near me is having a tender moment. They sit on the bench backwards, facing the hedge, however I can see their heads tilted together. The girl is crying and talking and the man is comforting her. He is comforting her with physical tenderness, no words. I sit under great trees in famous Athens

. . . In my Duino letter I said the theme was my confession of <u>love</u>. Here, in Athens, I need to declare that my feelings are much stronger: I am obsessed with you. The only thing that gives me the courage to say so now is the very distance and time that separates us. Mind you, sometimes when I was out at Aspen Creek and you in Edmonton I would go through a similar experience, except there, in Canada just facing it, I felt I was <u>too close</u> to even write down words. Only drive past your house, remember every detail of your family moving in . . .

. . . your actions in Germany caught me by surprise, the Ailsa who tried to slip her arm around my waist, who twice placed her hand on mine in the restaurant. But what does Ailsa Helen think, now, on late Monday nights when she can't sleep, what does she dream now when she's bored already in her Social Studies classes . . . o sun of my soul! Write to me, so I know you exist, that you feel. I'll go to London to seek your response, please write to the Canadian High Commission, London address below. Please, don't laugh at this awkwardly written letter, if you want to, burn it, but please write a letter now saying you have done this.

    Turn your ear to me, Ailsa,

        let my cry for help come to you   — ugggh —

"Gabriel called today."

   "Oh, good. Where is he? Is he okay?"

   "He sounded okay . . . I think . . . he mostly asked about us, you know how he—"

   "And you always tell him, every detail."

   "Well, he misses us."

   "Good—so what's he doing?"

   "He's still in Athens."

   "Athens? He's been there since the middle of August!"

   "August twenty-fourth actually—"

   "Over three weeks, he's supposedly travelling, what's he doing holed up in—"

   "'Holed up?' There's plenty to explore in Athens, he's probably taking day trips, Olympus, the Islands, old Sparta, there's lots—"

   "Did he tell you that?"

   "Don't yell!"

   "Okay, okay . . ."

"We didn't talk too long, he's okay for money, he says he's healthy and happy. Fred's left now, to go to Karen in Italy and then back to Canada, but Gabe said he's fine. Alone he can just go easy, see what he wants."

"One postcard and two quick calls . . . he's not telling us much."

"He supposed to report? When I talked to Joan, she said Ailsa got a long letter from him, a few weeks ago."

"Ailsa? Why would he—what'd he tell her?"

"She didn't say."

"Didn't you ask?"

"She just said it was a pretty thick letter. She wouldn't read her kids' mail."

"Good grief! Ailsa's barely twelve, why wouldn't she know?"

"Ailsa's over thirteen. So, ask Joan—she's your friend too."

"But you didn't."

"No. And she didn't offer."

"Hunnn . . . did you notice anything, in Germany? With Ailsa?"

"Ailsa? They walked together, a few times . . . we all did."

"I think they sat beside each other to eat, once or twice. In Heidelberg . . ."

"Yes . . . and in Mainz, when you guys went to Marburg, Joan was so enraptured by the Chagall windows she told me about his whole tangled life on the river walk, and Gabe and Ailsa walked behind us, quite a while . . ."

"She's just a little kid . . ."

"But thoughtful and pretty, and so serious all the— remember how he watched that tiny gymnast who never smiled, even when she won all the gold medals, remember?"

"Yeah, Montreal Olympics—that was just a little boy crush."

"He was fifteen."

"A teen, it happens all the time and lasts fifteen minutes."

"He wasn't 'just a little boy.' And he didn't get over that girl in fifteen minutes—you remember the letter he wrote us about her?"

"Oh yeah, you're right . . . yeah . . ."

ATHENS "AKROPOLIS BY NIGHT" POSTCARD

Sept. 11/84

Dear Mother, Father, Brother and (world-travelling) Sister,

It is nine in the evening. I sit on my balcony and experience the city. A writer across the street two floors up is working as usual. He is a very big-bellied, bearded man who is at his typewriter every evening except Sundays. Such discipline. In the hotel beside his apart. two floors down are three men getting ready for a night on the town. Most likely going to Syntagma Square, the local pickup place. I've just finished having a snack of one 7up and a roasted corn on the cob. Venders roast and sell them on street corners all over. 50c–$1.00 depending on size. Somebody is playing a

sax, somewhere. Last night, or rather, early this
morning that sax was also being played. And everyone
yelled when it got too loud. However, it's all Greek to
me. It's a cloudless night, but then it always is here. It
is so dry, jeans dry in one night. I am feeling very good
this evening, it's been awhile but . . . I trust that all you
people, whom I so dearly love, are doing extremely
fine. I miss you.

Love, Gabe

DAILY PLANNER 1984: *September Wednesday 12*
I have decided <u>not</u> to send any of my A letters. She is 13 +
not yet 4 months—in no position to understand my
writing. Thank you Lord for letting me not make a bigger
fool of myself than I already am and for not letting me
hurt her with such an obsessive letter of despair   what
to do today   open the door   walk out of this room

September Friday 14
Countdown. My sentence in the Athens wilderness is
done—no letter, not a word, but that should not matter
just say you love her. What to do finally today   kill time.
Go to Areos Gardens, my habitual retreat, sit, watch. So
many people, so much doing, hurry hurry it has to be
done! Why God why do I have to feel things so intensely
I need   always a movie somewhere   *The Getaway* Sam
Peckinpah
     Evening: extreme loneliness   when I call, oh, answer me
     —off tomorrow, ROMA

Paris, France

Sept.21/84

Dearest Ailsa,

I'll write a quick note before I leave Paris for London. I
waited in Athens ~~27 days~~ for a letter from you, any
small note or card, I want very much to hear from you;
that is, if you care to write.

I mailed you one letter (Saturday, August 11 from
Duino, Italy), but have actually started dozens more to
you, in many different countries; I cannot mail them.
They are too extreme in their loneliness to send.
Unfortunately, in many ways I find myself too extreme,
too intense in my feelings and moods. I have learned to
keep them to myself so others will never know what I
go through. Besides, no one where I am knows me.

Ailsa, I have gone to many different places but my
heart is not in it right now. I see Athens—beautiful
ancient rocks, but lots of shoddy mod city buildings
too, then back through Rome, Florence—the only
thing that made me feel good in Flor. this time was a
young man from Poland a little older than me,
Przemyslaw P. He was in the hostel bunk next to mine
and speaks perfect English, he studied in England over
10 years and earned the money to now travel around
by selling ice cream on the street in London. There are
many interesting people travelling but he and I actually

hit it off, he's the only one I would want to talk to, we may meet in London in October / I didn't go through southern France, Arles to see the van Gogh places but travelled by train through Bologna, Italia and Montreux, Switzerland—saw the Palace Hotel where Vladimir Nabokov lived his last years (1961–77) writing his books on cards while lying in bed, very classy place, and am now here in Paris which is beautiful—but I can't really care much for anything I see because you are never there.

Oh, this all may sound quite strange, and I don't mean to hurt you or make you feel guilty. It's just that I'm completely alone in Europe. I am not in any way embarrassed of my love for you, but I do have major problems admitting that I need other people. All my life I have been alone, even with my family that I love, and now I am alone in Paris.

Rainer Maria Rilke wrote the poem *"Einsamkeit"*— "Loneliness"—here, but for me it's a lot stronger than that, I'd call it ~~Being All Alone~~ "Aloneness." He wrote the poem in Paris while walking these rainy streets September 21, 1902. Well here it is 82 years later, after midnight exact to the day, and I walk Paris streets with rain falling on my bare head, so I changed a few words of one translation (underlined) to show my feelings. I have no reason to inflict you with my sadness, but here, now in this rain under blue streetlamps is just the right distance that gives me the courage to think that perhaps you care:

Aloneness

<u>Aloneness</u> is like a rain.
It climbs up from the sea to meet the evening,
it climbs up from the world's far distant prairie
towards heaven, which has it forever.
And only then, from heaven, does it fall upon the city.
    Rains o so gently in those barren hours
when all streets bend themselves to search for dawn;
and when those bodies, which have still found nothing,
bereft and disappointed, <u>let despair fill their souls</u>;
and when these people who can only hate <u>themselves</u>,
must <u>each sleep alone in one solitary bed</u>:
    <u>aloneness</u> then moves onward with the rivers . . .

I've just read this letter over and it doesn't make any
sense
    Some black men on the crowded night subway were
singing, "Everythin's gonna be all right now." Singing
together like crazy, no thinking visible, whole big body
sing

DAILY PLANNER 1984: *September Friday 21*
No forward from Athens at Can. Embassy, nothing.
Walked. Saw *Paris, Texas*. Watched it again at a different
theatre half hour later—my God N Kinski is so beautiful,
the child become woman—in morning I started and quit
another letter to A   Train Paris Nord 10:40 p.m. boat
overnight Dover, arr. London 8 a.m. 22, F19.50
    (France–England)

September Saturday 22

London. Guest house, Movie House Guide. Find
Przemyslaw P . . . Polish hostel? I can hear again!
Afternoon and evening with Prz.   walk and talk and
eat and talk

September Monday 24

No Can. House mail. See Herzog films: 1) *Signs of Life*
2) *Fata Morgana* 3) *Even Dwarfs Started Small,* evening
4) *Spring Symphony (1983)* N Kinski does a lot of the same
stuff but the scene with her when she is first being kissed
is marvelous

September Tuesday 25

Phoned home—all okay of course loving Mom—saw
Paris, Texas (great, after x 2 in Paris, France!) "That's not
her, just her in a movie." Got bus ticket—65 pds. London
return to Ayr/Girvan, Scotland—o the sea the sea north
to the sea of Ailsa Craig. Bus leaves Victoria Sta. 7:30 p.m.

Paper like layered snow all over the basement floor. It
never melted, never ran away leaving barely a stain.

". . . all my life I have always been alone, even with my
family . . ." Gabriel, you wrote that. Did I know? Or Yo—
did she know that? Of course we knew, how could we not?
You were a solitary kid, okay, often very quiet and by yourself—but *always alone*? Not as a child tumbling around and
so happy playing "Pretend" with Miriam, and then Denn—
where was your aloneness? When did it come? How can

your young memory hold only that? ". . . even with my family that I love . . ."

Hal lay on his back. The thick rug on the basement floor, once a bachelor apartment living room before he and Yolanda bought the house and rebuilt it; but the apartment kitchen cupboards were still there, the square outlet for an electric stove visible between boxes on the new storage shelves. Solid rug/wood floor on concrete, good for lying on your back, flat. Who was the Karen O travelling with Fred? Had she ever been in Edmonton? She cut Gabe's hair, told him "Pure obsession"—ha, pure as untouchable stars—they must have talked some, why not more?—she left for Naples . . . ran perhaps . . . if only . . . obviously she had been travelling with Fred—was she still? A wife now, Karen and Fred kiddies, children that could be over twenty—avoid that, avoid.

Alone. With Rilke's Paris "Einsamkeit." What an implacable determination to everywhere, in every way, find not only "loneliness," then deliberately change it to starker "aloneness." And no fumbling Robert Bly translation either: where did Gabe find that beautifully direct "Aloneness [not quite the rhythmic 'loneliness'] is like a rain . . . it climbs up from the world's far distant prairie"— "*Ebene*" in Bly are plodding "flat places." Must be Canadian, driving the long land and a narrow black rain comes on over the western horizon. And Ailsa, always—well, her child's thundering silence. But even before any of that obsession the July 21 "Terror in Frankfurt," and after that a smaller "Terror in Nice" August 2—those terrifying Rilke angels at train station arrivals, always alone? Was it the echoing din of terminals, the slimy washrooms? People rushing nowhere? But not a hint of that (deliberate?) in later arrivals at Rome, Florence, Bologna, skipping Marseilles and obsessed Van Gogh's Arles for obsessive Nabokov's Montreux (was it *Lolita*? Never a mention), then Paris, the train and boat and train to London, no terrifying angels when he arrived in London? Walked the streets, Hyde Park . . . avoided?

Hyde Park, 1976. Gabe was fifteen . . . just days before the Montreal Olympics. Could that have been the first time?

Hal's eyes had been open for a long time, the basement ceiling was pale stippled stucco; Gabriel probably often walked by this old house as it was then between Whyte Avenue and the North Saskatchewan River valley, though he was certainly never in it. After him they could not endure Riverbend where they had all lived together fifteen years with the outdoor hockey rink across the street, they had to move, away—in this basement ceiling there seemed to be the random pattern of a pool in the stucco trowel marks, a pool with edges swirled like the wading pool in Hyde Park, July 1976: Dennis dances along the concrete edge shouting at the top of his lungs, at last! space to bellow his everlasting Grade 2 song that has together driven them all both laughing and crazy south and north across Europe:

> Down in the bushes, beside the pool!
> The frogs are having a singing school!
> Old frogs, tadpoles . . .

And slim Miriam, seventeen, sways behind him, her arms and body in supple rhythm with his celebration at one more release from their "cozy," really "cramped," English Commer camper, five of them squeezed together for 12,000 kilometres from London south to Paris and east down the Rhine and on south to baking Florence and Rome and Naples and back north to Ravenna and Zermatt and Marburg and Harlingen and Ayr and again to London, that astounding family journey with not one yelling confrontation from anyone:

. . . and sang, "Ko-kak! Ko-kak! Ko-kak!"

Denn brays while Miriam dances. Yolanda is tracking them with her slide camera—"Watch the cobblestones!"—and Hal thinks, You've already taken a hundred with his mouth wide open and that crazy song! the air so English-London-park blue, sweet and cool as poet daffodils; but through the park trees he is watching something else: the squat bunker among the flowers and bushes where Gabriel has disappeared into the MEN. Behind the wall that shields the entrance. Gabe just said he needed to go, so why does he feel such growing apprehension, watching it?

But he was, Hal remembered that clear as the ceiling over him. And Gabriel suddenly emerges there, but does not come towards them, does not look towards the wading pool where he certainly knows they are all waiting for him, no, he walks very fast and angled away from Denn's "Ko-kak! Ko-kak!" walks away as if none of them exist. He sees Gabriel so clearly at that instant, walking, that he jerked erect to sit on the basement rug. In Hyde Park he is on his feet and walking too, but not too fast, not looking at the MEN or Gabriel, just staring between them and keeping them both at the farthest periphery of his sight, walks faster and faster so he has gotten between them when he abruptly meets Gabriel face-to-face, panting behind a high bush.

"Gabe! What happened?"

His tall son seems shrunken; does not look at him. He says, more softly,

"What?"

"A man was looking at me."

"You didn't use a cubicle?"

"He was in the next one, with a mirror."

"Mirror!"

"I saw it, it poked under the wall, and drew back, twice, I . . ."

"Did you see him, a face?"

"His hand, and I stood up and pulled up my pants quiet and jerked the toilet paper loud and the mirror came again and I kicked it so hard, his hand, he yelled and I ran out . . ."

Sitting on the basement floor, Hal remembered. Heavy as the file boxes and lamps and worn hats and brief cases and discarded computers piled around him, heavier than his avoided but merciless memory, he felt the whispered beauty of his lost son: slender, light-brown hair curly but not yet shoulder length as it would be, no moustache yet above the perfect part between his perfect teeth; fifteen, and within the year fully as tall as he.

. . . his shoes were neatly placed together . . . he was lying with
his right foot crossed over his left ankle and his hands . . .

No need to hide his weeping. There was no one here to touch him, to attempt a stupid comforting word. He could wail, scream, howl, laugh—what thundering angel would hear him? God, that eternally suffering Rilke! Gabriel bought the *Duino Elegies* in July 1984 to take on his journey—*always alone even with my family*—a journey he gradually grew to disdain as deeply as the life he would return to without hope in suburban Edmonton, on October 18. Within the first four elegiac lines:

> For the beautiful is simply
> The beginning of a terror we can just barely endure,
> and we marvel at it because it so calmly scorns to
> destroy us. Every angel is terrifying.

But in Frankfurt, in Athens he was no slim teenager: he was six foot three, 165 pounds, broad chest and legs and arms taut as steel . . . what does the beautiful have to do with muscles?

There was always a box of tissues in the basement bathroom, as in the two others, thanks be Yolanda of sacred memory. Hal would not look in the mirror as he tugged three tissues out; he knew every one of his liver spots. Owl must be about the same three-quarters of a century but the Dene man looked so much better; at least the skin of his face and hands, which was all he had ever seen. Maybe never sleeping inside a White building helped. He had invited him often enough, "I've got seven, eight, rooms on two floors, plus a basement and an open, soft-carpet attic, come, sleep wherever you like." Owl smiled and looked slightly embarrassed, black eyes shifting, so Hal didn't say it any more. Once in February when he trudged home along 104th past the funeral house thermometer flashing "-26 °C" he noticed two metal shopping carts between cars behind the Blessed Redeemer Church, and then the hump of sleeping bags beside the back door. Snow drifting down, ice driven in gusts of wind and Owl sat there with his knees up and head propped against the brick wall, wrapped in double hoods and sleeping bags. An electrical cord led from the car plug-in beside the door and disappeared under his pyramid of blankets, but his face was bare, serene as Nelson Mandela in the slanting snow. The faint hum of a hairdryer? Hal stood for a long moment, watching: yes, Owl was breathing; asleep.

Owl and The Coffee Shack's blah coffee, the accidents . . . the Orange Downfill. The Edmonton City Police, he needed to contact them to see what—no no, not yet, time enough—now he needed to walk in the moist April air of melting snow, he needed coffee, he needed anything but accidents and this empty, crammed basement. And before he could think to stop, his eyes lifted: in the mirror a gaunt, grey-bearded man stared at him. He could not . . . comprehend . . . that as himself. Momentarily he had no memory of this face as personal, not even when he touched it with what he recognized instantly as his hand . . . face folds and hollows and lank white hair curling at the

Hal, really, you don't *have* to look like that. There are fifteen barbers on Whyte

Thank you *miene scheene* Yo, ever with me, my only and ever beautiful love you forever.

The telephone rang. Like a prayer always with him which he never spoke—police! No, they'd be at the door. Good to move, move! He hoisted himself up stair by stair on the banister to the kitchen phone call display. Ontario, Dennis thanks be to God work number in Toronto, he could collapse on the desk stool.

"Hey Dad."

"Hey Denn."

"How's it going?"

"Okay . . ."

But quick Dennis had caught his tone. "What, what is it?"

"The usual . . . no no, it's okay, okay . . . maybe I made a mistake . . ."

"What? What'd you do?"

"Oh I saw a . . . I . . . I looked in Gabriel's boxes, the ones in the basement."

A silence; Dennis's voice shifted from concern to his careful neutral: "Why did you do that?"

"It's the end of April, and it started snowing overnight . . . it's mostly gone already."

"That's Alberta, it snows whenever . . . sometimes September too."

Neither said anything for a long moment. They did not speak of Gabriel often, and not since Yo's funeral. They talked flat day-to-day facticity: his back and thigh aches, his right side, the birds singing along Denn's Don Valley bike route, Double Cup Ben endlessly unscrambling Mennonite family trees online and, "sweet little muffin"—as Dennis called his daughter Emma—watching a spring worm ripple itself together and withdraw into the earth. Hal realized, once again, that he had never yet dared to ask Dennis: Do you ever think . . . how you found him, when I wasn't . . .

Never there to have a memory. Now he said, "Gabe was born January 28, so . . ."

"Sorry Dad, I don't get it."

"Nine month consequences, April 1960."

"Oh, the anniversary, fifty years sort of, of you and Mom . . ."

Hal burst into an embarrassed laugh, far too loud: "There was no snow that April, not south by the Oldman River!"

After a long moment Dennis said, gently, "I could come. Easy, catch the evening flight and the weekend's in one day. We could go out to Aspen Creek, probably some snow left at the cabin, so a nice log fire—"

Hal avoided him quickly, "You know, that was years before the cabin. We were visiting Grossma and Grosspah in Taber with Miriam, she was barely a year and Yo wanted to go to the Oldman River, I'd talked so much about us in high school finding a buffalo-kill site and arrowheads and stone hammers and the weather was so warm, we left Mir with them and drove to the river, past the old church, it's long gone now, you know, and hiked all over those prairie ravines, flood plains, the huge cottonwoods, after Grossma's funeral we drove there with you too, by the Oldman, you remem . . ."

He stopped himself. What did he want to natter about? How slowly they undressed each other and lay down, the dry spring grass prickling them through their spread clothes, Yo's complete bright skin in the sunlight, the taste?

"So-o," Dennis said easily, Hal could hear his smile, "by the Old Man's playground river . . ."

"Your mom was never that sure about it."

"But it could have been."

"O yeah, I think so, yeah."

"Did you ever tell Gabe?"

"Well, I—" his stupidity, having to evade the warm possibility of talk that Dennis had offered, impossible now with what he had just done. He sagged on the phone stool. "Denn, listen, it's okay, I'm really okay, don't worry. I bent a bit, remembering, but it's okay, I've put the boxes back, closed them, I was just going out to meet Owl at The Coffee Shack on Whyte, have a coffee. Don't spend two days on this now. Come in July like we were talking, all you three together, I'm all right, when Emma's out of school okay?"

"Since when do you and Owl drink Coffee Shack coffee?"

"Never—today's unique. A Whyte Avenue adventure!"

Dennis laughed so hard Hal's ear rang; as if grabbing an excuse too. "Good, Dad! Still a bit crazy. But call the house tonight, okay, before Emma goes to bed, you can say goodnight, every day she has a different school story."

"And we'll explore the creek then, like always, she'll find more freshwater clams. The creek is too high and muddy right now . . ."

And out of nowhere his memory flipped, he should say it to his beloved listening son far away in Toronto but alive and loving him, the Orange Downfill, he would surely remember the orange—no.

"Denn, you," he said and caught himself, "you filled the gas tanks on the pickup, both tanks, I saw the receipt in Yo's file boxes. She kept every receipt forever, for everything, before Gabe got the pickup that Wednesday before . . . you had put a hundred and seventy-six litres in its two tanks."

The crinkly receipt in the box blazed in his memory; Hal got himself shut up. Why was this—the gaunt face in the mirror?

In his ear Dennis spoke as if he were reciting a court statement: "Yes, I filled the tanks. Mom sent me to Riverbend Shell, they had serviced the pickup and I filled up with a hundred and seventy-six litres at forty-six cents a litre on your credit card. But Gabe had switched off the auxiliary tank before he started the . . . only the main tank, it was empty."

"Denn, Denn! I'm sorry."

Breathing. Then, "Yeah . . . it comes back, you never know when. A carefree kid, our family seemed so fun, easy, and jacking around with Colin and Ailsa tagging along, it . . ."

Silence. So blank it seemed they were both waiting for a dial tone. And suddenly, before he thought Hal said, "Dennis, did you ever read Gabe's diaries?"

"No . . . no. I was so young then and once Mom and I talked about them, but I really didn't . . . you know . . ."

"And you and Ailsa were friends, in church, when she started high school she . . ."

"Yeah, sort of, for a little while, but she and I never really . . . and then they moved away, very soon—Dad, listen. Maybe I should come."

Hal could not speak.

Dennis said, his gentlest telephone voice: "Maybe it's long enough."

Hal repeated, agreeing, "Long enough." And then he remembered again: the police! and his stunned mind wallowed into logic, "Yes, you're right, but this is a poor time for you, and a few more weeks, they don't matter . . . save it, save it. When you all come, in summer, then we'll have time, plenty of—but thank you for your intuition."

"What?"

"Calling in your hectic day."

"Huh!" A small laugh, surely of relief. "I'm hammering at this dumb conference budget and it pops into my head, just say hi to Dad! Think something good and clear for two good minutes, oh boy."

"Sorry—I'm really sorry."

"Dad, it's okay, it is good! It's time we talked Gabe. It's long enough. Okay?"

"Yes, it is. Dennis, I love you."

"I love you, *mien leewa Pah*."

The unexpected Low German, my beloved Pa, in his nostrils the wisp of his own childhood like homestead *Tweeback*, a pan of doubled buns pulled out of the wood stove, a nudge of such warm comfort spreading from inside his mouth through his body. He swallowed and hung up. The kitchen clock: another hour before Owl.

Ailsa Craig. The great blue rock in the outer Firth of Clyde, Scotland.

Had Gabriel ever mentioned that place to anyone? Never to Hal. Another 1984 secret he left for them in a few blue words.

DAILY PLANNER 1984: *September Friday 28*

Overnight bus London / Ayr / police search at Dumfries for stolen Walkman / Ayr a.m., walk—1976 family memory of Auld Brig o' Doon, the dark kirk, Burns statue / good cider Tam O'Shanter Inn, delicious bass meal / p.m. bus to Girvan. Setting sun, and there Ailsa Craig rises out of the Irish Sea. Stunning / when you look away, you can't believe your memory. Evening in a bar with 3 "good ol' boys," very friendly

   ** Question: Why am I here? **

September Saturday 29

The boat *Glorious*, only 7 passengers / bright day, heavy rolling sea from 2-day storm—Dad would be woofing his cookies / from southeast ACraig is like the top half of a pointed head heaved out of the water, bald rock base with green hair top / tiny beach, rollers crashing, can't land, can't walk over island on this brilliant day / take rolls of heaving pics. / white lighthouse, ruined castle keep higher on rock. Nobody allowed now to live on ACraig / North Cape is blue hone—hone—for centuries the only rock cut for curling stones, west/south side gannet cliffs. ACraig there looks like a half-sunk Cree stone hammer with groove carved below north end / gannets nesting on rock spikes white with birds and manure, great gannets sailing on black-tipped wings. Ailsa my rock. Crashing smashing sea, untouchable

September Sunday 30

Sky bright again, walk to Girvan docks. They say today
sea is calm enough, they'll land, 2 hr. hike around
castle ruins and over ACraig peak   they say it's the
core plug of eroded volcano 1/2 mile wide, 3/4 mile
long, 220 acres—2/3 the size of our Aspen Creek land,
valley there 100 ft. deep with maybe 5 beaver / ACraig
1114 ft. high rock with gorse, 80,000 gannets. Curling
stones, nausea, a beautiful mountain of birdshit. Buy
ticket, walk down pier. Can not step onto boat. Fool
again. Walk back, wait for Ayr/Glasgow train. Long
Firth of Clyde, the rock on the sea forever / was/is
anything there? How/what will/can I ever know.
Does it matter   God knows

October Monday 1

In Praise of Lemmings no better than *Sex Gang Children*
yuk. Besides that spend the day in Glasgow Public Lib.
trying to research A name but get nowhere much /
librarians too small time. Train to Edinburgh, enormous
river and crowded Scotland, then discover Ailsa Craig
Hotel! Near rr station, 3 star luxury (hnnnn)

POCKET LOOSE-LEAF NOTES *(no dates)*

Ailsa Craig, by Rev. Roderick Lawson, ©1934
- granite islet of spectacular columnar
  rock rising abruptly from the sea
- the sharp shape of a huge tea-cozy . . .
  solitary in the waste of waters
- Prince of Darkness dropped it as

stepping-stone between Scotland and
Ireland
- haven for Scottish Roman Catholics,
1597, from there Hugh Barclay tried to
help Spanish fleet re-establish RCs in
Scotland. Rev. Andrew Knox discovered
plot and Barclay drowned himself in the
sea off ACraig
- strikingly beautiful name, plainly of
Celtic origin, "Island of Seafowl"?

What pray god am I doing in Scotland. Searching a
beautiful name? There is nothing here, no Prince of
Darkness passing. Get out. Get home as soon as

Obsession - that which preoccupies or vexes;
an unwanted or compulsive idea
or emotion persistently coming
to awareness; the state of being
obsessed

Obsess - to occupy the mind to an excessive
degree; preoccupy, harass, haunt

Haunt - to visit repeatedly, esp. supernaturally,
like a spirit or ghost; reappear in the
mind, or memory; to linger about,
pervade; a place often visited

DAILY PLANNER 1984: *October Tuesday 2*

Massive ACraig Hotel Edinburgh breakfast. Looked up more at National Lib. of Scotland / what is it possible to make of the name: core of eroded volcanic extrusion? curling rocks? Devil's stepping stone, church violence? Ugly list for an extraordinary solitary place. Go to movie *Comfort and Joy* filmed in Glasgow, not much but I'm happy for "small" films. Packed evening hotel wedding party / if only I could celebrate some thing. ACraig Hotel a converted 1820 Georgian townhouse, 17 rms.—free TV / free hairdryer for my lovely curly locks

Could an extraordinary, solitary person be the Devil's stepping stone?

POCKET LOOSE-LEAF NOTES *(no dates)*

Other Etymologies:

- Gaellic "Aillse Creag" modern name meaning "Fairy Rock"
- or Gaelic "Creag Ealasaid" meaning "Elizabeth's Rock"
- "Ealasaid a'Chuain": "Elizabeth of the Ocean"
- "Paddy's Milestone": traditional Irish worker route, Belfast to Glasgow; the Devil placed the rock there for easier (satanic?) travel between Ireland / Scotland
- "A'Chreag": "The Rock"
- island belongs to 7th Marquess of Ailsa, 18th Earl of Cassillis

A Lover's Discourse: Fragments, by Roland Barthes, 1979
—gestures of a lover at work—

p. 18 What the Greeks call _charis_: "the luminous radiance of the desirable being."

p. 21 I love you because I love you.

p. 67 Touching bodies: every contact, for the lover, raises the question of an answer: the skin is asked to reply.

p. 71 The Other's body—to scrutinize means to search: I am searching the Other's body, as if I wanted to see what was inside it.

p. 120 It frequently occurs to the amorous subject that he is, or is going, crazy.

p. 157 The love letter   Goethe

Why do I turn once again to writing?
Beloved, you must not ask such a question,
for the truth is, I have nothing to tell you.
All the same, your dear hands will hold this note.

Like desire, the love letter waits for an answer; it implicitly enjoins the Other to reply, for without a reply the Other's image changes, becomes simply the other.

SPIRAL NOTEBOOK (3): _October 2, 1984_
(Edinburgh) It is 3:30 in the morning back home. What does Ailsa look like when she sleeps, in what position does she lie. Are her hands under her blanket. I move through the house. How does it smell—sound— look like in the kitchen, living room—is there a record

on the stereo, what concerto was last played, what jackets are hanging in the coat rack by the front door. Is there a painting or sketch on the easel, do the parents sleep with their door open, which side of the bed do they sleep on. Has the mother looked in the mirror lately, is the wash-room messy, is the brother asleep in his room, does he dream. And then back to A's room, is her door closed yes probably what does her room look like—what was she doing last night—what face did she see in the mirror before getting into bed what does she dream how does she smell how does she breathe is her hair tangled how do her slim hands lie outside the blanket what are her first thoughts when she wakes up. Will I ever know my fairy my rock

Paris, Texas: "I wanted to see her so bad that I didn't dare imagine her. . . . I didn't want to use him to fill all my emptiness."

All I want to do is to get home, however, I know when I am there I won't want to be there either. Being near but still impossible is worse. So, I guess, really, I want to be in some place that does not exist. Where is it? Meanwhile I am always only with myself, now here in this luxurious Edinburgh, Scotland double bed room in the Ailsa Craig Hotel. I do seem to be here . . . now. Certainly alone strangely inside her name

DAILY PLANNER 1984: *October Wednesday 3*
Express bus Edinburgh–London, leave 9 a.m. arrive 6 p.m. Brief <u>terror strikes</u> but I grab my backpack, get to Hampstead Hostel room 6 bed 26. I hate arriving, yuk

October Friday 5

(Dad's Birthday) Woke up wishing A was beside me. Her smiling face, first giggling then we would get serious and kiss each other, slowly, a tongue in the ear listen   I have to cut these thoughts or I get more depressed. Check stores, get Underground pass.

FILE FOLDER / STUFF
Single page:

So you are now 49. I can't really say happy birthday; when you look inside you'll see why; but I do think of you. You are my father, even if I can't penetrate your personality most of the time, at any level leave alone with some depth. And even if in a lot of ways we are profoundly different, we are also, fundamentally, the same. And please remember I still, and hopefully always will, do love you.

Your son, Gabriel

And I do remember: you did. All your life. And more; you came and showed me your love eleven very long years later, October 4, 1995, within the time when I awoke and saw 5:16 shining on the alarm clock beyond Yo's head deep in her pillow and 7:09 when I awoke again. You were standing, your body profiled against intense, concentrated light, and I jerked upright for joy, in exploding happiness—you had been gone forever. Seeing you there I collapsed on the bed, and you lay down beside me and I wrapped your long hard body in my arms and cried, We didn't know where you were! Your strong arms held me so tight, you whispered, It's okay . . . I'm okay . . . you know that, I'm all right.

And then it was 7:10 in the morning, October 4, the day before my sixtieth birthday.

O my vanished son: did you send me a birthday card with those words in 1984? I don't think . . . I don't remember. There seems to be nothing more about me in these boxes—or I haven't found it. Yet. Did you copy these considered notebook words into a card? Were they in a card wrapped with a gift other than words? Why are there so few facts about us, you and me being together, in my memory, why do I find so little, why do I need these blue words? It seems sometimes when I have the most hope that Yolanda told me you had already wrapped a present for me in July before you flew to Amsterdam "to get away." Did you? She was to give it to me on my birthday in October—did you do that? What did the card look like? Yo would know—in your file folder pages these words seem to have been written in London—but Yo, her incredible memory . . .

What is the past? No more than what we together remember; we are what we remember, our memory? A fine word for a Gabriel wordlist; but you never wrote it out. Why not? The compact dictionary—where is the one you carried across Europe in your knapsack: on Sept 3, 1984 in Hotel Orpheus you wrote "Note: This silly dictionary I use gets me nowhere"?—"memory" in a compact would certainly list eight to ten meanings, all fumbling with "the mental faculty of retaining or recalling past experience."

So what is "past experience"? No more than whatever facticity I retain, that is the facts (from "factum": to do), the acts that haven't somewhere disconnected into nowhere from my "mental faculties," as your last, harrowing, act will never, ever, disconnect? Only whatever pictures, whatever papers you scrawled over with indecipherable words that I can still dig out of boxes? Facts: only things done—or things thought as well? Even desperately imagined? Dreamed and remembered like your confessions? Our mutual past now only everything only I have not forgotten? Is that forgotten forever? What if others—Dennis—Miriam—someone like Joan or . . . remembers? But you were alone, as I am now most often, and completely, what if no one else was there to perhaps remember and you are gone? Come, O come . . .

From what's left in these boxes—by chance? by your deliberate doing?—your visit to Ailsa Craig seems no simple, factual act. Far more than the literal travelling, the bus, the sea, the town, the great rock, the ruined fortress and white gannets, the Girvan dock, they seem to have made you lunge about, staring at whatever confronted you scrabbling in old libraries, in even older books, grasping for whatever you could clutch of language and image, lurching into words from diary to notebook to pocket loose-leaf to paper scraps to birthday notes. As if exhaustion were breaking you into pieces; but nevertheless leaving some thin string of word evidence.

Evidence. There is a long scar on my stomach; evidence: something was done there. What? When? Of course I can glance down at that unerasable memory grown and still growing in my very body, my fingers can feel the thick gnarl of it through my shirt . . . but

The fact is, your body also had a grown scar. The inside of your left arm. A scar I made on you, I remember exactly how and when and where it opened—a fact I cannot and will never forget—but could an Orange Downfill remember? These irreducible words shoved on top of each other in boxes stacked in this basement room? Words like rocks layered thinner than shale, your unique writing so sparse and repeating, such an impossible narrowness of every-thing you lived the length of each enduring day: whole days unmentioned, a bare hundred words per day at most, scratches so close to nothing of your actual lived life, no jokes, no drinking laughter with friendly "good ol' boys" in edge-of-the-earth Girvan, Scotland, overlooking the Ailsa sea she has never seen. Reading what you wrote is like trying to track the footprints you did not leave in the gorse of that rock because on the second day you found you could not step into the boat to go and climb it. Did you already sense you never would, that Ailsa rock? You travel a long night and day to get there, study it from far and near, circle its crashing surf for an entire day, a rock that sometimes appears to be a half-submerged head, sometimes a prehistoric stone hammer, but then you escape—deliberately?—to books only; to any available libraries for more re-tangled words; eventually to the films that will pass by before your eyes at their own dogged pace whether you notice/think about their existence or not. On this remaining paper your last three months of 1984 are these few repeating, so often lamenting words in a coil

Quecumque Vera notebook and a shirt-pocket UofAlberta planner.

> *Erbarme dich, mein Gott, um meiner Zaehren willen*
>> Have mercy, my God, for the sake of my tears

My tears. Gabriel: whatever your prayers, whatever your life, you were a complete gigantic rock rooted in the ocean bed of earth, a living volcano from the molten centre of life whose immense mountainsides we sometimes could not recognize for what they were when they groaned up out of the sea before our eyes. They were—they still are—massively invisible to me. But the core, your eroded core, is here thrust up out of these boxes; and even more my memory. Here it is. I grasp it.

The hard, loving embrace of two men   *erbarme dich, o mein Gott*

POCKET LOOSE-LEAF NOTES *(no dates)*
London movies seen: *The Company of Wolves* / *Jazzin' for Blue Jean* / *Sola*—*120 Days of Sodom* (grotesque, left after 15 min.) / *Psycho* / *Oedipus Rex* / *Once Upon a Time in America* (who cares? these aren't people) / *Medea* / *Paris, Texas* / *The Leopard* (what an elegant way to die. The games we play till we turn to dust. Who can live young and happy if you see the darkness all the time) / *Kaos* (humanistic film) / *The Brood* / *Shivers* / *Victim* / *1984*

DAILY PLANNER 1984: *October margin scrawls*
London: Tom Kelly—Irish   Amnon—Israeli   Peter—
Perth, Australia   Drunk—Greg? check out flights to
Amsterdam   best of all Przemyslaw—Poland whose life
is such an agility of wits, improvisation, forget yesterday
it's today, hunnnn—such an enormous laugh

October Tuesday 9
Buy books and maps. Large poster with N. Kinski   not
all—lucky I had control. Rather touch a real person than
1000 pictures   so where are you A. Meet Przemyslaw in
evening, go for a few beers, laugh laugh again

October Wednesday 10
Meet Przemyslaw and go to Canada House to find out
about possible immigration—looks tough. What can I do
to help him. And do I want to be bothered—go buy more
records, maps—Great Gabe, nice response—great human
you are, the one friend you found. Movie: *Young and
Innocent* Hitchcock, early film
Letters from parents & Mir at Can. House. Two
completed months of nothing—well—this is what it will
be may God be damned. Expect nothing when I come back

AIRMAIL LETTER, QUITO
Sun, Sept 16/84

Dear Gabe!

This is great—me writing to you at Canada House,
Trafalgar Square, London from Embajada de Canada

in Quito, Ecuador! How's the travelling going? Do you
like travelling alone? To tell you the truth I don't think
I could do it—I'd get too lonely & feel more scared of
things, ie I'm quite brave in a group but not alone.
With Sylvia it's very good, I can't believe how much
has happened to us already & we only left Canada a
week ago . . .

. . . after the 2nd bus from Lima broke down in
the mountains Syl & I and Chris a British guy we
met and a Peruvian woman and her son, also on
the bus, got a collectivo (like a taxi) and raced to the
border. We got there at 10 to 6 but they wouldn't
let us across—though we had 10 minutes to spare—
so we laid our sleeping bags on the cement floor
of the empty customs buildings & the five of us
slept there . . .

. . . Quito spread across the mountains is beautiful . . .
Syl & I found a great apartment . . . So now things are
starting to get organized here—all I have to figure out
now is "What's my thesis"!

I hope and pray everything's going good for you. If
you ever feel like coming down, there's room in our
apartment for you—in fact after Xmas when Syl leaves
for Canada I'll need another roommate! Hey?

I love you + think about you a lot, love Mir

POCKET LOOSE-LEAF NOTES

Oct. 10/84   See pictures of N. Kinski's marriage to older
man—I obviously don't know her . . . and A is just as
beautiful . . . but it is the beauty that drives me. Yet I

cannot continue to be in love with an image. I have to love a real person. Please—*bitte*—give me the chance to care for, to open up with a real feeling person. Can such a very young person bear to hear all my troubles. If I dared face them

Bitte let Edmonton not continue the same way. I thought I left to get away from A but really I wanted a total change in the situation. And in Germany suddenly for a few days, sort of like revelation, it did. A dream there, but could I face it? Not really. Can/how/will Germany continue in Edmonton after months of

Ailsa, my Fairy Rock, my Elizabeth of the Ocean: I know now I have mucked around for the last years because I'm so much in love with you. Do you have a large heart—like your mother

Please   answer me. There is/can be no other, if I look at others I feel I'm sinning in regards to you. I am still a virgin because you're the only person I can ever imagine being close to in any physical way. Please   do you still feel your Frankfurt/Mainz/Heidelberg heart, the hope

DAILY PLANNER 1984: *October Thursday 11*
Hoped today to be in Marnhull, Hardy's Marlott in Wessex where Tess lived—no, I lie in London with a fever, sore throat. Lonesome heart—rain. What to do—crud, I hate myself—I don't *do* anything! What stops me   Go see Bergman *Persona*, magnificent Liv U, then Polanski *The Tenant* again, dark Isabelle Adjani. Polanski said: When I met Nastassja Kinski she was 15,

but she was a woman. Woman and child at the same
time, the perfect Tess.

    Child and woman? If only

    Wherever I am, all I ever do is wait for . . . So okay!
Now I wait for the 17th, I'll see Emma Kirkby then
and for the 18th I've booked my flight home (Whatever
that is)

Written across March–August in "Year in Sight"

Sun. Oct.14/84   Go to corner of Hyde Park in
morning. Walk around, a sunny warm day at last.
My body is starting to go to seed because I can't take
care of it, don't feed it very well. I dislike tremendously
living in this condition. My hair continues to fall out:
I'll be totally bald by 25. My chances of winning A get
slimmer at the same time. The sun shines through the
peak of the band shell where I sit. Leaves are falling
around me

    I heard a leaf fall when I died

    Who wrote that?

    I heard that once, I think, at Aspen Creek. I'm
listening—too much ugly city noise and my mind
always stuck in the same stupid roundabout. Are
Hardy's words true, does one love/feel more at a
distance? Oh I hope not; I want to feel it close. Surely
something can happen in my life as it does in others.
Well, if anything, I can always go back to the old
routine of church, arty conversations with Joan,
and glimpses of A a short distance away   time
goes on and soon this too will pass because lives do

change   the N Kin character says "I don't know,
I haven't tried it before," meaning tried to see things
from another person's point of view. I'm so tired of
seeing with my   but then I do not excite myself, only
others can excite   oh bla bla bla   Is Hardy right,
does love end on contact. I pray and hope not   can
it   the English leaves keep falling   I can't hear
them yet   they'll be all gone at Aspen Creek

October Monday 15

Cinema bookshop, then St. James Park to read. Peter
from Perth and Amnon from Israel leave: even short
forced relation changes sadden me, though I realize
I don't really care for those two. Go to NFTheatre
but decide not to see Maria Callas in *Medea* again. Her
long, devastating face. Walk at night, Waterloo Bridge,
no rain but cool. Victoria Embankment the heart of the
great Babylon London   Paris *einsamkeit*   forests of
people laughing worse than forests of trees   two more
days   I did hear a

AIRMAIL PAPER, *both sides scrawled*

> Gabriel Wiens   London, England
>> Oct. 15, 1984

Dear Mir,

I have to write to you, even a short note, because I
know a letter from here would thrill you. I received
your letters, and it is extremely pleasant to realize that
people care enough to write.

And it's not that I don't want to write letters, it's just that I hate writing letters, and, possibly more to the point, I really have nothing to say. My mind works so slowly

crud!   this is already getting nowhere and so I'll have to start again, then again, till I finally quit and mail nothing.

Anyhow. You ask if I'm lonely travelling by myself. Well the truth of the matter here is that I expect aloneness to be my native state. I have always been lonely; however, I have not always been alone. When we were kids you and me were never alone, remember we were always together, but when one grows older we've been apart so much, college, university, you now—well—the being alone part does cause problems, especially when travelling. Both lonely and alone. Quite frankly, Mir, I don't know how you do it so well. I absolutely hate

Well, London is a nice enough place. I could enjoy living here, with a flat of my own like a few Canadians I've met, for a period of time. But London is a dump in many ways. There is nothing particularly marvellous about this or any city, not the ones I've seen.

This brings me to the point of the letter and my trip. I've found out that no place (physical place)   oh bla bla bla

what bla am I
blaing to say

Lets face it, I've been trying to find some sort of emotional relief for myself somewhere in this world. A physical place will not do it. It will either be done through mental means—i.e. through thinking things through—or with other peoples' companionship.

I hate this writing, but you're going to get this sucker anyway

I could say that I've always envied people—like you—who are so stable and always resourceful. I am driven by obsessions, very simple obsessions but they control me nonetheless. On this trip I realized they aren't justified, because what really exists? Do you think about all the stuff you fly over, bus past, what you see in Peru and Ecuador is really there? Have you actually touched/smelled, or do you just see, hear, breathe for a while and accept whatever and walk away? Are the things still there, really, after you are gone? How do you know? Even if you take a picture, as I do once in a while and a long time later develop it, it shows only what was there while I—awww—

You and me, and then Denn too, we had such fun together. I could say I would like to have spent more time with you in the past, and also in the future. But lets face it: how many of the things we would like ever turn/return into reality (whatever that is). So I won't say it; why say lies. But this does not mean that I don't want to.

I do say I'd love to come to S. Am. to you, my sweet sister, you have it so together, but I don't have any money and the prospects for getting more are dim right now. And you be careful, all those Latino machos.

Sorry, I'm so long and just send you this piece of junk   but

Love   Gabe

**note: I shouldn't send you this crap   this is terrible only the second letter   if I mail it

DAILY PLANNER 1984: *October Tuesday 16*
Old people sit in St. James Park and stare straight ahead. Could one do that for a lifetime? How long is that? A pigeon—dove?—circles me but I have nothing to offer. What can people do with each other / what have any of us to offer, really

*rent paid till night of 17th CDN$1 = 62.5p

POCKET LOOSE-LEAF NOTES *(no dates)*
Movie *Nosferatu* (Herzog) again just to see Isabelle Adjani walk through the town square. No real sound, only voices, dancing. Then *The Tenant*:

"If I cut off my head, is it 'me and my body' or 'me and my head'? What right does my head have to call itself me?"

"And anyway, what right do I have to call myself 'my self'?"

Yes, I've decided. What I want to do in Edmonton is to get myself together (physically, emotionally, financially) for my Personal Oldman River Quest (too obvious for future readers; well since there never will be one except me who gives a flying

Oldman River, south Alberta   April 25, 85–May 4, 85

Is this all I live for. I hope not, but it will be my guiding force for the next months in Canada. However I must face it. No physical space/place in this world is what I seek, but, as Nabokov writes: "not an <u>escape</u> (which is only a cleaner cell on a quieter floor of existence), but rather <u>relief</u> from the <u>itch of the mind</u>"   (I hope)

DAILY PLANNER 1984: *October Wednesday 17*

At last at last. 7:30 concert in St. John's Smith Square, 2nd row aisle seat, baroque church unbelievable as heaven. *Bach Mass in B minor*, soprano Emma Kirkby, marvellous dignity and natural elegance. She can be full of womanly compassion and also such delicate delight. She immerses herself in the music, she sings with exquisite perfection. What a divine voice, what a lovely person.

   Kyrie eleison   Christe eleison   Dona nobis pacem

   Lord have mercy   Christ have mercy   Grant us peace

October Thursday 18

(England–Netherlands–Arctic Canada) Piccadilly, platform 6 first train 5:55   Heathrow 9:00 KLM   Schiphol 13:00 CP 373 to Edmonton   60 p and 13 pds left + $120 Amer.   Ah Gabe, you're going back home—What does that mean?

   People behind me speak Spanish, where are you Mir?

   Thought: what if I were to have an accident and not wake up for 20 years. What would it be like to wake up 20 years later and feel that no time has passed but everyone else—including me—is actually that much older. Hnnnn how lovely

Lovely indeed. Dearest Gabe, a simple Rip van Winkle hesitation: twenty years en route over Arctic Canada. It is October 2004. Ailsa is thirty-three.

So: after two final weeks of again mostly waiting, waiting in London, a few beers with your Polish friend—no mention of him after the guilty (and still letter-less) embassy—"a few (unnoted) Canadians," books, maps, records, and movies meticulously noted, at least seventeen movies in fourteen days, *Tess* and *Paris, Texas* x 2, *The Tenant* x 3. And the ultimate Emma Kirkby, beautiful woman and artist, your darling classic Bach soprano, you pay to change your airline ticket home by a day to see and hear her in the sublime four-towered baroque church of St. John's Smith Square, an architectural magnificence unimaginable for a Canadian grandchild of Russian Mennonite village refugees: in over two hours of baroque Latin prayer she sings either (Soprano 1) three duets or (Soprano 2) one solo and one duet. No matter, even as she sits above you waiting to sing she is all you could desire in a woman, inarticulately all. And of course forever beyond you; untouchable. A great gulf, fixed, and you are completely satisfied. Like Tess; whose place you do not visit in Marnhull, though it is only a brief bus-ride to Dorset. You lie inert—conveniently ill?—in London, you could be lying anywhere wasting in desire, eventually you scrawl in the margin of your planner, "I'll go with a car one day in the future." And then, more eventually, you hoist yourself out of bed onto your feet, you walk across the street to a ridiculous movie shed and face 107 minutes of contrived horror to see the electronic shadow of a beautiful woman pass from the screen, again, mere seconds, and then you stay another 125 minutes for the same image of the same woman to, among other acts, seem to sleep with a death-conspiracy haunted man; again.

My haunted son. Twenty unconscious years. Could you not at least dream—act—a few present seconds into beauty? They were there; daily you recorded a foretaste of some of them; why could you not believe, and act?

To wait can be the ultimate act. And you did wait, so much and so often. But then, finally, you would not.

In the last pages of the pocket loose-leaf you took on your Scotland trip you carefully added up—perhaps in the (for you) devastating luxury of the world's only Ailsa Craig Hotel, already anticipating, dreading, the coming back to Edmonton—plodding backwards over your endured European time of "what pray god am I doing here":

<u>Days</u>   Oct: 18   Sept: 30   Aug: 31   July: 8   =   total 87 days
    —incl. London 21   Athens 25   Germany only 3 + bits of 2

Below these numbers you add:

Have I screwed up. Have I blown something that might have been. Oh please. I can't stand it

Early evening April light slanted through the barred basement window, revealing as sunrise. Somewhere a piano was playing, Yo, there were notes but no tune . . . gradually Hal recognized his own wrinkled skin: hand and arm blotched and hairy and underlaid with vein-worms. Here it was still, his seventy-five-years-of-dying body, still so relentless, feeling itself into its particular, inescapable existence, his prickly right foot, his thinning gut, his

What right do I have to call myself "my self"? If I cut off my head, am I "me and my body" or "me and my head"?

He was alone in his basement. Bent like a question mark on a worn wooden chair, the one Yo salvaged from the college throw-away heap in Winnipeg and he fixed the back of it forever—well, until now—a man-made thing so simple to fix, just glue and two screws. Sitting in the surround he had scrabbled out of Yo's carefully ordered papers, books, boxes. 4:37 p.m., if she came down the stairs and saw this mess she would be laughing at him. Until she recognized what all it was. The laughter of recognition so different from that of humour, of irony— stupidity. 4:39 p.m. He had to risk his guilt and The Coffee Shack, should have half an hour ago. Blessed be Owl.

"There were four ravens today up there," Owl said.
  "I didn't look. Up is hard for old people."

"Four," Owl said. "Real loud, right across there on top of Ten Thousand Villages, jumping on the front there and yelling at each other."

Hal said, "What'd they say?"

But Owl chuckled. "Can't say what they say to you, but you sure had to hear them without looking. They were dancing loud there, along the Ten Thousand sign."

The only good thing about The Coffee Shack was the fact they played no stupid loudspeaker music. Hal stared into his small paper cup. The sludge in it steamed; it did smell of coffee, faintly.

"What'd they say to you?"

Owl's grin grew thoughtful. He lifted his paper cup in homage across the street. "No joke, not four ravens. Maybe, 'Be careful,' maybe, 'You don't know nothing.'"

"So, what do you know?"

Owl laughed at his tone. "Police stuff, that's easy. Some say two fender-benders, not three, one rear-ender too, they had to tow it."

"People?"

"Some say bruises, some a broken arm cut, sure a few whiplash, maybe one head cut bad. All say they're looking for the old guy that run into the traffic, the guy started it."

Clearly in this coffee shop, where they never went, Hal's guilt was waiting. More than a day and he had done nothing about any of the people hurt because of his running, his—he had not even thought about them, allowed himself to—if Yo were alive the first thing she would have—

Hal raised his cup. His fingers dented it, hot, clutching so hard. He said slowly, "Have the police talked to you? Plenty have seen us together."

"They haven't found me yet."

"What should I do?"

Owl was looking out the tall narrow window; traffic on Whyte Avenue ripped by without end. He said nothing. Finally Hal took a swallow from his cup.

"Ugghh . . . horse piss."

Owl drank thoughtfully. "I don't know. Never was a horse in Fort Good Hope."

They both tried to laugh, but now there was no fun between them. Hal considered the lean face of his friend. Owl rarely asked questions, but the great lump of what Hal had not explained that morning sat in silence between them. Even more, what he had not done since.

"Orange downfill," Owl said abruptly, "that's a real old-style jacket."

"There's one in our cabin at Aspen Creek," Hal said. "It was my son's, Gabriel's."

Owl seemed to be contemplating the circle of his paper cup circled within his powerful hands. His fingers were folded together around it as if in prayer.

"That jacket," Hal had to push aside those intersection thoughts, tell a story, an easy—"that jacket, Mrs. Golding wore it the last, Mrs. William Golding later that fall in 1985 after Gabriel was gone, when William Golding came to Edmonton. After years of trying we finally got him to come to the university to give a reading in the English department, and the day after we drove them out to the cabin, show them a bit of Alberta parkland, bush, but she hadn't brought a winter coat, 'It's only early November,' she told me, 'I don't need a coat,' and then the November wind hit her whipping up from the creek and she just about . . ."

Hal got his run-on voice stopped.

"Mrs. Lord of the Flies," Owl said without looking up.

"You know it?"

"Had to read it, in school. All those boys on a nice warm island. Lots of fruit."

"Horrible boys . . . and good boys. That jacket, no one ever wore it after Gabe but it was all we had extra at the cabin. Ann Golding put it on to go to the cliff and look down at the frozen creek, she didn't know a thing about Alberta November but Golding had a good wool jacket, he walked down the valley trail with me and onto the ice behind the beaver dam, we looked at the big beaver house and their winter cache of trees frozen in the ice and Yo's brother Dave was so scared the early ice was far too thin and careless me would drown a Nobel Prize novelist; he stood on the cliff when he saw what we were doing and just prayed, please God keep them safe, please, but Ann Golding looked down at us and went back into the cabin with Yo and sat by the wood heater, she never—"

Hal stopped. Owl's obsidian eyes were contemplating him.

"Okay," Hal said. And continued slowly, "The Orange Downfill. I saw that walk past Double Cup yesterday—high collar zipped up over half the face, four seams sewn across the back, his body—that's why I ran out into the street, because that was my son Gabriel wearing it, I saw *him*."

Owl didn't blink. After a moment he said, "Yesterday."

"Yes, yesterday!" And confession raced through Hal: "On the Whyte sidewalk! Walking past the coffee shop fast, like he walked, it was him, his head and hair and he turned at the corner with the crowd to cross Whyte and I saw the other side of his head, the collar was too high I couldn't see the moustache but it was him for sure and I just exploded, I ran out to catch him but the light had changed and I was in all the traffic, the cars had to slam on . . ."

After a moment Owl said gently, "Your son Gabriel."

"Yes."

"Did he look like the age he was, or the age he'd be now?"

"What?"

"Did he look like twenty-four, or maybe forty-nine?"

"Wha . . . what does that matter?"

"What you saw, it matters."

Hal was remembering, trying to remember everything, remembering, all the human noise in The Coffee Shack spilling off the great riff of Double Cup memory rising in him like a massive rock out of the sea: the fixed-chair plastic table they were leaning over and the sidewalk in the right corner of his eye were all wrong, people just moving past in the middle of a block and no red hand "Don't Walks," but unstoppable cars endlessly whipping by with motorcycles blaring up and gone like quick, blurting beasts, and Ten Thousand Villages should not be across there between bare boulevard tree branches, nothing of that, no; he remembered exactly, beyond the full mirror wall of glass reflection where the sudden flash of ORANGE stepped out, and saw instantly the short brown hair flattened by snow on the skull and curling up at the collar, the high forehead and straight nose half-hidden in the zipped up collar and the long body walking, jeans, faded blue jeans and absolutely the body, yes! long bare fingers and the shift of blue legs so fast and lean: that was fixed, immoveable as Ailsa Craig.

"It *was* him, walking, I'll never forget that walk, his nose inside the stand-up collar and his forehead, I can never forget how he walked. It was him."

Owl was studying Hal's knobbly hands locked into each other on the table. "Sometimes," he said, "when somebody dies too soon, a baby is born somewhere."

"What?"

"Yeah. People . . . they say that."

"He wasn't born one of your people."

"Sure. But, sometimes, something happens anyways. No matter who we're born."

"What do you mean, 'a baby is born'?"

"I never listened much, not enough, those Old People stories . . ."

"You don't know?"

"Hard to say . . . what do I know."

"And what you know you won't tell me."

Owl faced Hal across the tight table eye to eye. "I can't tell you," he said. "Not that I shouldn't tell you, not that it's forbidden, I can't because I don't know. I was young, I was stupid, I never listened enough."

They considered each other; their hopelessly different worlds: Hare Dene gnarled by Christianity, Mennonite Christianity twisted out of Anabaptism and Catholicism and Pietism. Sitting face to face in a raucous twenty-first-century city of coffee and doughnuts and surveillance cameras staring at them every second. More and more brilliant technology and the same old dead.

"People mourn," Owl continued. "That's the way it is, but they remember too, and sometimes a baby is born, later, and laughs or walks or yells and then somebody will remember, something."

And then they will do something, too?

Suddenly Owl smiled and Hal realized, as he had so often, that he had never met this warm, beautiful man before they found themselves sitting side by side at Double Cup on Whyte. And they both looked up, and their gazes met. *Deo gratias.*

"You poured his ashes into running water, Aspen Creek?"

"Yes."

"Could be that orange downfill is in the river valley."

"The river valley?"

"Your creek runs into the river."

"Yeah . . ."

"And that jacket's real old style, but good shape. Something warm you could find in a thrift store."

The Edmonton North Saskatchewan River valley. Mostly long narrow parks and small clusters of houses, but also age and winter-broken trees, tangled brush, deadfall, homeless, down-and-out, vagabond, bum, loner, handicapped, drifter, pan-handler, free spirit, alcoholic, misfit, disabled, mentally challenged, drug addict, mental defective, crazy, outsider, nut, outcast, beggar, deranged, insane, screw loose, unemployable, brain-damaged, cracked, addicted, homeless, free . . . insane . . . loner . . .

"That's impossible."

Owl had twisted his head and was looking out the narrow window over his shoulder; backwards, as if he saw coming on the street what Hal was thinking.

"Maybe a start," he said, and faced Hal again. "If we want to hunt. Whyte's no good, too many police."

"*Acch* . . . police. Those rear-enders were my fault, I should . . ."

"You want them police to help you look?"

"No! They're looking for me, sure they . . ."

"Okay. So when they find you, you tell them why you run into the street?"

"Maybe . . . yeah, maybe I should do that . . . just go tell them."

"Tell what? He hasn't done anything, why would they help you look for him?"

"I saw him!"

"And you run after him into the street."

"And some people got hurt."

"Yeah, they say some."

"But if I told them I was overwhelmed, my son after twenty-five years, cops would understand, they have to, every day they know people do crazy things because they're overwhelmed."

"Yeah, cops can understand, sometimes."

"I mean, twenty-five years."

"For sure. But first I thought you wanted to hunt, first."

"I do. But if we could, maybe . . ."

Owl laughed his quiet Dene laugh. "Okay, maybe. The cops we have always with us. We can always find them, they'll always find us. They're hunters too, so leave them for now, first we hunt what we want to find."

The North Saskatchewan twisting its shifty channels down from Rocky Mountain glaciers through mountains and foothills and forests and farmland toward Edmonton glowering high on its banks, and on, rapids and lakes and forests and dams and cities and swamps and countless creeks and rivers to Hudson Bay, to the polar ocean. But not the streets and parks manicured into the deep bends and flood plains of the river in Edmonton, not the trails groomed smooth for joggers and skateboards and dog walkers and bikes. Police cruisers. No; the natural bush chaos of the valley cliffs; of forgotten, avoided, loners.

"Better not before noon," Owl said. "After they go to Recycles and get their money and buy stuff. And maybe wear boots, lots of wet snow down in there."

Hal edged himself out of the bolted chair. With Owl talking he was tremendously awake, suddenly rushing energy. Almost an explosion like joy—tomorrow, yes. The river valley he had known all his adult life.

RIVER: always ambivalent; it corresponds to the creative power both of nature and of time. On the one hand it signifies fertility and life, the progressive irrigation of the soil; and on the other hand it stands for the irreversible passage of time and, in consequence, for a sense of gathering loss . . .

North Saskatchewan, Oldman—no boots yet; it was still today, settling into the long northern spring evening. And all that Gabriel wrote after he came home, October 18, 1984, was still waiting.

DAILY PLANNER 1984: *October Saturday 20*

2nd day back. As always I drive pickup, help Dad, Uncle Dave, Big Ed move heavy kitchen stove from Edmonton to Aspen Creek cabin. I feel like dying. Everything is exactly like before, including me on my basement bed, gobbling Mom's great food, staring at the same ceiling. What did I expect. Why did I return. I hate myself

Sunday October 21

With parents/Denn to church, and first thing saw A (not since July 30) from the top of the stairs, standing in the doorway of the youth room below. So perfectly there, I could be dreaming. She saw me too, then quickly walked out of sight, but as I walked down the stairs she came back, for a moment looked up at me again. Those beautiful green eyes, sad, what—Hi. We were face to face, and I—I turned left as if I needed the washroom. After that I never saw her, she disappeared. She wasn't in their car going home / talked with parents, told them I'll move out, as soon as I find a job

Monday October 22

Made an even bigger fool of myself. Borrowed pickup, at noon I parked near Rowand School and waited—but A didn't go home for lunch. I stayed the whole noon hour, then parked in a different spot and saw her in the schoolyard, just watched her stand around, talk with other kids. After school drove to Rowand again. She came out and I followed until she was walking alone. I drove up beside and offered her a ride home. She took off her glove and glanced at me once, but she says, "It's okay, I'll walk." I drive away in a daze

Written across Tuesday 23–Friday 26

Feel like suicide the next few days. She doesn't care one bit   letter huh! / drove blue pickup out to Aspen Creek / alone, empty cabin, bare trees at night groaning in the wind. Good music for me. Ripped open the 2 metre beaver dam below their lodge, twice, but they just patched it together every night / why am I anywhere

October Saturday 27

Our family at Grant and Joan's for supper. Ailsa with Denn and Colin in family room downstairs but of course I have to stay, talk with adults. Then A comes upstairs face painted and dressed like a clown! Hallowe'en child

> Like the buffoon, the clown is the mythic
> inversion of the king, of the person with
> enormous power seemingly reversed

All of a sudden I'm shaking. A dances around the living room close between us, doesn't look at me, the boys come and yell and chase her back downstairs. The red ball hides her perfect nose. Okay God, your joke   good for you

November Wednesday 7

I have not—no, I said a couple of sentences to her in church—she said Hi in a crowd but otherwise she ignores me—runs away in fact. I see no future. Just end it. I can't Three day job, Edm. National Film Theatre, attendance survey.

SPIRAL NOTEBOOK (3): *November 7, 1984*

I can't forget that distorted clown. Things are worse than before I left. Such a waste— what am I doing? Is there a pattern I could figure out—

God (reason behind/beyond existence)
NKinski (innocence) / ideal / EKirkby (maturity)
Ailsa / closer to reality / Joan

So maybe if I talked to Joan more I . . . but obviously A and her mom are still not reality to me, I don't really . . . what are they really like, what they think, what   in *Paris, Texas* the NK character says she hasn't tried to see into another person's mind, from their point of view—I do not even want to see into my own mind, but then I do not excite myself—only some others excite—o bla bla bla   I miss Miriam, researching her anthro MA in the old quarter of Quito, Ecuador—and her letters, not since September in London—"travelling alone . . . I'd get too lonely and feel more scared of things i.e. I'm quite brave in a group but not alone." Ahh Mir, the heavy, heavy difference of "lonely" and "alone" / I've never even talked to sweet Mir about A   never to a single soul   but she's always been so considerate and gentle, every minute since I was born, my beautiful sister full of fun and forever friend, I can't remember one quarrel or long yell leave alone fight, it sounds brother-and-sister impossible but its true because of her / maybe talk to her I should I should "I love you and think about you a lot"   yes, I do both too my sweet and only sister, and do you have an inkling of what I feel? I should visit you in S.A., bury myself in Spanish, learn to be a different person—   But now Leo says he's quit his job at Edmonton Transit as of November 30 and will fly to Miriam in Quito for Christmas. And what will happen between them—o Mir, the dangers of studying Spanish—maybe if I'd been born like him, in Argentina and tortured half to death by politics and been forced to flee (not try to escape) my own country, maybe then I'd know what I wanted when I wanted it and do something. Not just sit at cafes below the Acropolis—in the bedroom where I grew older.

Okay folks, why'd you give me such a great Canadian childhood?

Hopeless

The problem is you can't have anyone else, you only— maybe can't even—have yourself. So why do I worry. I can't help it if my emotions take control of me   can I

DAILY PLANNER 1984: *November Sunday 11*

I hardly dare say a word to Joan who's as lovely as her daughter, just to be in their presence is . . . I play my silly thought games—A will save me—fool, no one saves you, only yourself. I do have a few things to say, I just can't do

anything. Not even shovel snow off the walks unless
Mom asks me. If only my being would cease

November Wednesday 14 and across Saturday 17, Sunday 18
Life mucks on, always, somehow. I still exist at church, to
be ignored with a "Hi." If only Germany and Duino—
ugggh—this mind bullshit   why A why did you go after
me in Mainz only to ignore—yuk—all I do is ping-pong
back and forth about that stupid letter, never yet mentioned but there in every glance we
     Edm. National Film Theatre, "a non-profit organiza-
tion devoted to the study and appreciation of cinema."
May hire another assistant if gov't. funding comes
through/January. Fat chance.

November Friday 23
Lucked out: hired by NFT, assistant administrator, $150/
week, start Monday 26, yes! And I can get out.

November Sunday 25
Stay at church for open lunch. A has cut her hair short,
comes in and talks to BR, must be dating him. I can't
stand it, go down to washroom.

SPIRAL NOTEBOOK (3): *Nov. 25, 1984*
The problem is, if I could distance myself from this entity
called "Gabe" I would laugh loud and sing: but since I am
I it seems I can only weep.
     I seem to hear chuckling, somewhere. Laughter in the
dark. I hope I'm providing these beings with a good time,

because I certainly hate it. Why create feelings only to laugh at them. I say, who wants to exist only to be tortured

Hey! What am I doing? I'm free.   But I have nothing to say.   Or I do have a few things but I just can't / in this basement room I can't / things leak out of my head, that's what eyes are for, to leak tears—or get mad at—poor Mom

Naturally I'm too feeble to go through with anything because the right time, right place would be the Oldman River the last week of April c. 21–30/85—but that is a long way away. Too bad I don't get run over in the street / like Dad says of poor stories his students write all the time: things get too complicated to handle so here comes the Big Truck, Smash! All problems solved, end of story. Just step out

Just "lucked out" with a possible dream job, and you talk The Big Truck Ending. In your life, Gabriel, there was a truck, but it was no easy gimmick ending.

The Oldman River—Hal suddenly remembered, startled: was one thread of that longing a subliminal Paul Robeson bass with which he cradled his tiny son around the room when he would not sleep, arms tight but hopefully comforting

> ". . . tired of livin' an' scared of dyin',
> but Old Man River he just keeps rollin' . . ."

Not "Old Man" Mississippi; Gabe named it right: Oldman, that mythic Blackfoot glacier water winding across Alberta

500 kilometres south of Edmonton, past the town where Hal lived his teens and they sometimes visited Grandma and Grandpa fast on a weekend, driving down most of Saturday and leaving again Sunday just before they had to go to that prehistoric Mennonite service Hal did not want his children to suffer, the church where Gabe and his cousins were teen pallbearers for both grandparents. Dearest Gabe, always so precise: on the last page of Daily Planner 1984, on the complete 1985 calendar, April 21– May 4, was underlined. And in both years April 28 was circled in heavy ink.

How could that—in what kind of thinking could that be "the right time, right place"?

The story of that river place Hal blurted out after he accidentally cut Gabriel's arm, the yellow chainsaw he later hurled into the county dump. He was talking and talking, anything to keep Gabe awake with that curly head in his lap in the back seat of the station wagon with Dave driving gravel roads like a fiend to get to the Breton Hospital, holding the twisted tourniquet above Gabe's left elbow not too tight and his cut arm wrapped—where was Yolanda! Not in the front seat—missing? impossible—talking to keep those brown eyes staring, conscious and open as the stones sprayed in the wheel-wells, the car swerved and leaped, nattering anything that slammed through his head and Gabe breathing, held . . .

Is it "Me and my body" or "Me and my head"?

You in my lap, in my arms.

DAILY PLANNER 1984: *December Wednesday 12– Saturday 15*

Got pictures developed:

<u>Solitude</u>: Sanctuary of the Sensitive Soul (Duino Castle in mist)

<u>Ardor</u>: A Demiurgic Quest (A walking away, forest)

Neither pic really much of anything?   hnnnn

Finished Nabokov's *Glory*. In the end Martin finally ACTS. Sadness soaks me. ". . . to create such a protagonist but not include talent with his keen sensitivity . . . how cruel to prevent him from finding in art—not an 'escape' (which is only a cleaner cell on a quieter floor), but relief from <u>the itch of being</u>!"

So much feeling with no talent; uggggh

<u>Demiurge</u>:

> Plato - deity who fashions the sensible
> world out of eternal Ideas
> Gnostic - creator of the material world

an autonomous creative force, uncontrollable   yes indeed

December Sunday 16

Church concert p.m. A there with J, Grant sang tenor. After A came straight to me, said she was so glad she was old enough not to sing in the children's Christmas program. She looked me in the eye unblinking, surely she was hinting at my only letter? She definitely does not hate me but—how can you talk in a packed church lobby chattering Christmas

December Friday 21

Finished Nab's *Laughter in the Dark* hmm a cruel
novel, to be in such clutches. Denn went to Youth Group
swimming party. Much too young for me, but I imagine
Ailsa in a swimsuit—God you do create beauty, it exists
in this world. Thank you for letting me see her, only
please, now let me get to understand and see the mind
behind those stunning green eyes.

December Sunday 23

Didn't go to church—not up to seeing but impossible to
be close situation. Suddenly remembered a song we
learned in college, singing in my head:

I sing of a maiden that is makeless . . .
he came all so stylle where his mother was,
as dew in Aprylle
that falleth on the grass

Happy memories of Xmas singing . . . why didn't I sing in
that choir after the first term? So many questions

December Tuesday 25

A and J, Grant, Colin come over in evening after Mom's
Christmas turkey dinner. We all play games on family room
floor. Fireplace fire. Always nothing but family, very good
for what it is, laugh and snack and joke and chatter and
everything warm / the back of her head, her slender hand
reaching / she plays every game so intently, completely /
friends, family happiness / lying in me like a burning log

December Thursday 26

With parents, Denn to Aspen Creek, cabin in deep snow.
Plowed a track in. Tree trunks a grey wall splintering,
crashing with cold. Chain-sawed firewood, shovelled.
Then Fred arrived from his home in Winnipeg, great,
played ping-pong, pool, lots of crazy laughs remembering
Italy and Greece. Karen O now at Ohio State / Fred
phones her a lot. He wants to study law at UofA starting
January. Great I have a job / find apartment together?

December Saturday 29

Fred and everyone left p.m., no church for me. I scrape a
few inside logs, sand smooth knots again. I love the long
bulges of warm walls. The moon over the creek. Moving
around in this empty house silence.

> Alone. With my futile dreams.
> Why am I?
> The universe even if beautiful should not
> exist. A bad dream in God's sleep . . .
> Laughter—somewhere there is laughing—
> Do I make you happy?

Silence. Sometimes a log in the wall cracks, not loud like
when we first built it, more like an afterthought—hey,
don't forget me. Logs fit together thick, round, each
trimmed and layered in its exact place and shape, holding
its weight. Good to be a log.

December Monday 31

Usual four families back at cabin for New Year's—including J, Grant and Colin but no A. Usual celebration, enormous bonfire in deep snow, Dad pounds it with logs, showers of flames shoot above trees / take photos, eat, sing, talk, listen to music till 3:30 a.m. with J the last to go. She's so exquisitely gentle. She nor I say a word about A. She stayed in the city—with friends overnight it seems.

DAILY PLANNER 1984: *Telephone Page*

1985 Options

- continue as I am
- continue: leave next summer for good   (where)
- end it
- just spill my guts to someone   (who)
- talk to Fred, we go to Australia
- if only I had more imagination   (less)

DAILY PLANNER 1985: *January Tuesday 1*

Make vow at cabin not to enter Mennonite Church Edmonton in 1985. Joan, Mom, Grant hear it / the people, the place has never helped me live. And I've had enough of seeing a distant A (didn't say this out loud) no A, every Sunday—enough already.

Make series of photos, snow patterns, little Sara N (6) dancing in snow, beautiful profile, always turning her laughing face away just before I snap and breathing clouds.

January Thursday 10

Have not seen Ailsa since Christmas Day in family room.

James Joyce / "Araby": "Gazing up into the darkness I saw myself as a creature driven and derided by vanity; and my eyes burned with anguish and shame."

I realize I have really nothing to offer people / the sadness of it all, lost due to my extreme nervousness of character. And always, foolishly, thinking ahead.

January Monday 28–Tuesday 29

At last! Away across the river! 2 bdrm apt. with Fred in Westview Tower, 108 St. #305, split rent $485 a month, phone, cable, everything except parking (who needs it). Good walk to NFT across town   the winter city white and cold.

Socrates on being after death: "I have to see. If I survive there can be no fear about it. If I don't survive, how can there be fear? If I don't survive, I don't survive. Then where is fear? There is nobody there, so fear cannot exist. If I survive, I survive. There is no point in getting afraid about it, no reason. But I don't know what is going to happen. That's why I am so full of wonder and ready to go into it. I don't know."

(Doesn't sound much like Jesus)

February Wednesday 13

Spent today: food - 20   drink - 50   sweater - 20   dishrack/ tray (brown) - 11.26

5:30: Joan's Master's degree exhibit, UofA Art Gallery. Beautiful surround of washed watercolours, much blue. A present of course, walking, looking so intensely young,

beautiful. I nod and say nothing to her, mind numb.
Crowd of university, church people, I can't even say
"Chagall"—what a complete WUSS I—o give it up

> In the vague mist of old sounds a shimmery
> light appears: the speech of the soul is about
> to be heard. Youth has an end: the end is
> here. Framed like a blurring picture. It will
> never be, you know that perfectly well.
> What then?
> Wait

What is reality? Did I see it looking over that gulf at
Duino Castle fading into deep distance like a cloud in rain
over the great cliff and thinking only of A? Did I see it
then, and did not know? The impossible letter

February Friday 15–Sunday 17
National Film Theatre Marathon: Stayed up for a total of
61 hours 27 minutes 9 seconds without any sleep, not one
wink. Get to apt. and in bed by 7:27:09 pm Sunday

February Monday 18
Day spent sleeping   listening to music   decide not to
go see *Night of the Shooting Stars* by 7:20 / going insane,
o Ailsa Craig, where is the Fairy Rock of Comfort

Going insane. The impossible letter. WUSS: both "wimp"
and "pussy"? Drink: 50 . . .

The light beyond Hal's barred basement window was almost gone. Much too late for him to make the call to little Emma in Toronto; her school-day story would not be heard today. He could be there, walk hand in hand with her across the street and into the park, watch her climb, slide, push her higher and higher on the swing, her curved little body yearning upwards. Was the gorgeous catalpa tree now in blossom there in deepest Ontario?

Never yet without Yo.

The buried pasts: diaries, notebook pages, loose and random scribbles surround him wherever his glance falls. The body language of a blue ballpoint groping across paper: like a residual cancer, a spiritual gangrene gnawing its repetitions out through Gabriel's fingertips. An entire page labelled "March 17/85" lies open as a column, and on every line

Ailsa Helen
Ailsa

repeated top to bottom, twenty-two times, ending with

I sit here alone and where are you, what are you feeling / please

Paper suddenly so toxic it burns Hal's hand; he drops it. For the love of God, Gabe, DO SOMETHING WITH YOURSELF!

And recognition slams him: Gabriel's "dream job" at the National Film Theatre, "the study and appreciation of cinema," was the worst work he could have found in 1985. Far worse than tiring body labour, worse than a course which would have had some instructor direction: here he was paid (minimally but enough) to evaluate and advise on movies to be shown in repertory theatre—his job was simply to sit and watch any and all movies. And he did: twenty-two theatre movies listed in January, twenty-one theatre movies in brief February, PLUS TWENTY-NINE MORE at a <u>Fifty-Hour Movie Marathon</u>. Gabe organized it; it ran without a break from Friday evening to Sunday night, living hell! Hal unfolds the NFT poster like a trap:

> The idea is really very simple: we want 50 celluloid junkies to attempt to sit through 50 continuous hours of movies. And we want each participant to find sponsors willing to pledge money for each hour of film watched. This is an ideal opportunity to catch up on 30-odd features in one short weekend, Feb. 15–17!

Hal cannot remember how much he sponsored Gabe—he must have, a lot—hour after relentless hour to stare at a screen; he does not want to think of it, he shudders to remember. That lean 6-foot-3-inch body, 165 pounds doubled for fifty hours in a chair—no matter how "amazingly comfortable!" the brochure bragged it would be—fifty hours after having already been up for twelve hours, since six Friday morning, moving "a comfortable lounge full of comfortable armchairs" into place with "large-screen video projectors." And such superb, psychologically shredding films lurking everywhere throughout the program: *Psycho—Cat People—Dr. Strangelove*, and especially *La femme de l'hôtel*:

> Three women: a film director, a mysterious suicidal woman she encounters in her Montreal hotel, and an actress who acts out both their traumas.

And, O blasted thought, John Huston's new *Under the Volcano* at 10 a.m. on Sunday morning, Malcolm Lowry's drunken meditation on the Sermon on the Mount—what a Sunday worship—that drove Gabriel to his only marathon comment:

> Finney great as the alcoholic who's given up on everything—sounds familiar

With scribbled sidebar:

> Yes okay. and what did you have for breakfast.

Gabriel, no wonder you scrawled "going insane" over and over again. No wonder two days later—day after day you kept on punishing yourself with these pitiless movies, bending your long body inert while virtual violent worlds reeled through your total attention, you need do or decide nothing, you were totally controlled by a fiendishly skilled camera—two days after the marathon you submit yourself to what you name "the brutish lyricism" of Sam Peckinpah, twice in a row! and confess:

Extremely depressed. Started that night before *The
Wild Bunch*, then depr. renewed after seeing . . . *Bunch*
again. Alone in apartment in Edmonton. I am obviously
living in some dream world if I think anything at all exists
any more. I smoke   I drink   the wind howls   time
twitches on

> And suddenly in this <u>Tedious Nowhere</u>, suddenly
> the ineffable place where pure dearth
> is inconceivably transmuted—changes
> into this empty surfeit . . .
> Angel, if there were a place, some ineffable carpet
> where this column of total zero . . .
>
>   (Rilke)

Gabe! Where was your work community? The convivial,
witty, artistic, stubbornly opinionated people with whom
you ate lunch, had drinks—too many?—talked Oilers,
ideas, winter weather, politics . . . were you locked into
shame at what you felt? With them especially?

All the Marathon Program could note was: "Special
thanks to Gabriel and Ross for putting together . . . manag-
ing . . ." Ugh.

And Fred? By then he must have had, however unaware,
more than a Europe Karen whiff of your "obsession." Did
you simply, wordlessly, shift past each other in the narrow
aisle kitchen of your apartment?

Did you ever talk *with* anyone?

DAILY PLANNER 1985: *March Wednesday 13*

Okay read—I know you're reading this, some day, these repetitious scribbles of a trite, obsessive mind / reflection is needed. However, with the phenomenon of Gabriel Wiens something more is necessary. Remember dignity. Remember how to forget?

To b&w *Cul-de-sac*   7 minute beach scene.

After out with Beth to Ninth Avenue

Beth. Beth, in the Vancouver Airport, that Beth. Hal remembered her like a splash of frozen memory: cropped hair, tall, dark blond, it must have been the mid-nineties, 1994, '95 and he bought her a latte . . . she was a volunteer driver at the Vancouver Writers Festival. She had picked him up at the hotel in lots of time to catch his flight back to Edmonton and said she had time for coffee, Joy Kogawa's plane from Toronto wouldn't be in for an hour.

Hal told her, "Joy was in Grade Seven with me, my school."

"Really!"

"Taber, Alberta, and kids and sugar beets, that irrigation slogging, her first novel, *Obasan*, it's superb at describing that mind-breaking labour."

"Did you do it too, hoe beets?"

"All Japanese and Mennonite kids did, that was South Alberta after the war."

"Why didn't they ask you to have a conversation with her too, here at the festival? Not just Clark Blaise?"

"Hey, that's a great idea—World War Two: the Vancouver expropriation and prairie exile of Japanese

Canadians—let's pick up Joy and go back and tell them!"

But then, abruptly, she stopped laughing with him. He looked up; she was staring beyond him, her grey eyes fixed as if something was there, coming. She said, deliberately,

"I used to live in Edmonton. I knew your son."

She had picked him up at the airport two days before, and he had noticed her in the festival hotel, checking tickets at the door for some events. Then she was in the audience, front row, for his "A Conversation with Clark Blaise" and in the van returning to the airport she had talked about nothing but that: "I liked the way you pushed him about 'beginnings,' that was so strong, his 'beginnings' comments."

"You really feel I pushed him?"

"You were very good, evocative, when he said, 'To begin, to begin, the first paragraph of a story is an act of faith,' and you pushed him and he's so quick: 'It's in the nature of story, story seeks its beginning like the drop of the baton seeks the first chord in the symphony—'"

"You knew him, Gabriel?"

"Yes."

"When?"

"Working at National Film Theatre."

"You weren't at the funeral."

"No . . ."

"Half a dozen NFTers came, they signed the . . ."

"I couldn't come."

"You just got drunk."

"How do you know that?"

"Guess . . . easy oblivion."

"Yes. Gabriel never was—he drank but he was never really drunk."

"You sure?"

"Not that I saw, not the eight months I knew him, not . . ."

What could Hal remember? Surrounded in his basement by notebooks and paper, holding in his hands the 1985 diary with those suddenly pale blue words rolled across the last line of March Wednesday 13:

To b&w *Cul-de-sac*   After out with Beth to Ninth
Avenue

A class restaurant, a neurotic Polanski film. Hal clutched his head: my memory, my memory's so overloaded it's . . . that latte, those airport lattes . . . I drank them then, all the time, but this . . . the old Vancouver Airport . . . my memory is inventing . . .

Gabriel wrote all his '85 diary in black, why this single line return to blue? Hal tried to calm himself, to organize his thinking into discrete areas, complete one single thought, follow it through—how often does Gabe name Beth? In the diary, he must look through all the NFT days again, and also after he was laid off, was there any Beth after, when was it, May, when he turned in—Yes! May Friday 17:

Phone NFT office, bring them the keys
out with Beth, Ross, Jack

In blue pen. But also two guys. Was it inside Vancouver Airport she confessed she knew Gabriel? At a coffee table, where surely they sat face to face? Didn't she say it driving, where the traffic would allow him no more than her profile? Her handsome face—not beautiful but character handsome, certainly older than Gabe, early forties by '94, such a face chiseled from marble—and the same stab of sudden rage, he knew that! hit him: why didn't she seduce Gabe? Her body, her powerful character could surely have overrun that fixation on an avoiding child, soak him in pleasure, let your body roll and stop torturing yourself, stop fumbling around that confused kid you never see anyway except in some crowd, embrace this, now, and whenever that girl grows mature enough to respond—accept or reject or play, whatever—well then that will be—Beth, why didn't you!

Hal was hunched around himself. Oddly down on the floor.

And still his stupid instinctive male thinking: the first, the simplest cure for all men and women: sex. After all his decades of growing old. *Ach Gott.*

Love, let it be love.

He must find what he had known, then. He rolled to his knees, hoisted himself onto his feet, crunched through papers, began to climb the two stairs up through his house. His legs were heavy as logs but his head light as a single thought; the space of the house seemed to be turning round and round around him but the weight of his legs balanced him upright, as long as he was upright the turning cannot waive his lightness. Inside his office finally, he leaned down against a filing cabinet and reached for the bottom drawer handle. Still he did not fall, not quite, and

there were the heaps of his diaries: on his knees, searching,
October 1993 . . . 1987 . . . 1994 . . . only October it could
only . . . yes . . .

> Sunday October 23: Van. Fest.
> Author Brunch   Edm. return
> Beth G drove me to airport / friend of
> Gabe at NFT 1985! told me in van on way
> in Montreal (film scout) week before his
> death / so not at funeral / very hard alone
> almost ghostly experience / still dreams
> of him / thinks of him / he comes in
> dreams but never speaks

So. His thick, pocket-size 1994. Hal stared at the flat
words. And inside the "Name and Address" back cover:
Beth Garneau (knew G) 604 654 3219.

He could call her. She offered him her number, he has
never called her. Fifteen and a half years. Late fifties now,
almost catching up. He sat in his armchair and lifted the
phone. What will he say? The Orange Downfill passing,
did you ever see—the mechanical voice comes: "There is
no one available to take your call right now, but if you"
hung up.

And sat staring at the ends of files lining his wide desk.
He has tried off and on to arrange what he did with his
lifetime. His sieve of memory. They drank airport lattes,
he was suddenly absolutely certain, yes, so why didn't he
write down what they said—words wasted on driving—
they had, they must have said it.

He: "Did you love him?"

She: "I would have, if he had let me."

The closed computer on the desk beside Hal's arm. Flat, coiled, waiting with mind-boggling Google, uncountable Wiens sites and images—his e-mails, uggh. Hal fled back to the basement, to the specific, limited paper Yo stored for them alone in such restricted order. What a thin life to find in this scrambled chronology of scraps jotted down. Thinner than skin, but enough.

SPIRAL NOTEBOOK (3): *March 18, 1985*

I phoned your house, asked for your mother—and it was you! I didn't even know it, your voice was so different I hung up. Then I caught on and phoned right back and talked nervously to you, about Joan. But I couldn't talk and foolishly hung up again without giving the phone number, which you even asked for, your voice breaking in a cough. I can't talk to you, not even when I don't have to face you.

Ailsa, how have you been? Your cough, are you ill? Do you still think about me? How did you feel just now talking to me. Do you want to hold my hand again. I see you sitting on your hotel bed in Frankfurt (that early morning, we were driving to Chagall in Mainz, your dad and brother were already gone to Marburg with mine) looking so sad, why? Oh all I want to do is hold you. Are you lying in your narrow bed, are you really sick, can I comfort you   get you some water, pills, put on a record, wipe your forehead. Or just sit silently beside—or perhaps you want me to leave. Ailsa, your voice was so harshly deep . . .

Gabe you're a useless human being
Run away   run away
    Existence is an ugly pain.
Please tell me why I exist,
in a neat English paragraph
    I can understand. No thank you
Mindless dribbly stuff   looks more like the rantings of a
    fool than
  I sit here alone and write your name   down the whole
    page again
        Ailsa Helen
            Helen fatal beauty
          go abstract
    line   curve   colour   gesture
            left foot   right foot
                    eat, eat
            stand talk
                    talk of   eat
        tea / coffee   sit   tell stories
            soak feet lovely feet
        heart pounds long thin limbs   thighs
              move
                    move
        eye movement   voice   fingers
            like pen on paper
                        trivial
            I don't remember what   what
  I remember remembering but have forgotten   go back
  Re-membering, putting together lost parts of the
      dearest lost body

where are they
Ailsa Helen I'm sorry to think of you
as a saviour
you're just a lovely
young girl—nothing more—nothing less either
Please—I know not what I do

DAILY PLANNER 1985: *March Thursday 28–Friday 29*
Ailsa—I look at your picture and I weep. You are so
beautiful, what have I done. I drink and smoke. Where
are you, where in the empty world? Please God give me
the courage to talk, please, it's not much to ask—

Great! Gabe you sound like a most mature person

I think I've been sick since childhood, I realize I should
not project my desires onto one person but my life drags
on—I repeat the same babble—why can't I escape, to
where, I am nothing but a creature of continuous hope
for the nothing I seek which I know is not in existence.
The mind keeps bumbling, to kill the mind, to kill
nothing. Take my life—please I would

Gabe. Shut up

March Sunday 31
Palm Sunday. Church choir very good   "If these voices
are silent, the very rocks will cry out." Where are you,
rocks? Cry!

In hallway I look for A, she's there and once looks
directly at me. Then what? Not a flicker in my brain,
what   in that church building where I've gone for 18
years, surrounded by people warm-hearted and laughing,

elders good as any grandparent— and smiling me a
gutless jelly

What am I blathering! Face it: I need a lover and A is a
child. Once upon a time we held hands, she was barely 13

April Monday 1–Tuesday 2

Fool's day. The world is alive with beautiful women and I
am a fool.

I need to cut this desire to write because I never edit
this dribble, as trite as

Lunch with Oleg at U, he's still studying philosophy
and a teaching sessional. To have a mind to think like
that, clear, logical, straight ahead, and act. Like Socrates

Don't go near Dad's office in English   he'll be there,
offer Java coffee

April Saturday 6

Easter Saturday, Auditorium, Bach *St. Matthew Passion*. To
the second performance, alone, parents with Grant and
Joan went to first. Oh the beautiful contralto, she sings
"Erbarme dich":

Have mercy (no—pity, pity) on me, my God:
for my tears' sake, look at me.
My heart and eyes weep bitterly before you.
Have pity.

Under the singing violin, the beat plucked by the violon-
cello, gently steady, relentless and harrowing. A beat steal-
ing your heart

Scrawl at right angles to full page

I weep. What have I done. Please, I

—why do you read this whoever you are—

I realize this (madness) must end. It's not the greatest choice a person can make, but really, what choices does one have. Being human does not give you profound choices, because one has to make these choices within the given moments and within the given personality one has that creates the existence we call "being human." To void is simpler. Do I make myself clear?

April Monday 8–Saturday 13

Best Boy for 6 days. National Film Board *Where Is Lily?* shoot in Jasper National Park. Mountains and grey braided rivers. Pick up van at 8:30, drive

And that's blank. Not one word about that Best Boy week of work. Nothing of film people met, of technical skills observed, of creative connections. And the mountains— as a boy you "played mountains" in our backyard sandbox, lines and ridges of stones relining the Machu Picchu we visited when you were five, that picture of you and Mir beside the Great Sundial against mountains and Inca bright sky with your jackets tied around your waists and laughing, the Urubamba River far below—didn't Folding Mountain and the milky Athabasca River jog a single slip of re-membered happiness?

Not one intriguing person in the *Lily* crew? Not a word.

April Friday 26

    Paris, Texas opening at Varscona, maybe for a month /
let's hope / stay and see second showing till end of
Super 8 part. License Plate: 78734J

        Shave off moustache a.m.   Start reading Nabokov's
Ada

April Sunday 28

    Start growing new moustache immediately

Gabriel, what happened? Your Oldman River Quest
was marked so emphatically in your calendar. Was it
the ambivalent doubleness—duplicity?—of river: both
the life of the soil and the oblivion of irreversible time?
One moustache shave was enough, and Nabokov's
indulgent novel?

    Hal recognized he was in his basement. The ceiling
light was on, his hand gripped the edge of the box, a
red file folder lay in it. Neatly labelled in that familiar
hand:

    Oldman River/25 Years Later

He opened it. A sheaf of blank writing paper; the brooding
grey image of "Duino, Castello: dev. Jan 12/85," then fifteen, sixteen pages more, blank or dated erratically: "Feb
2/85 . . . Feb 4/85" . . . no date after "Mar 5/85." Line quotes
from Rilke:

... we don't love like the flowers for a single season ...
... the fathers who lie at rest in our depths
like ruined mountains
and the dry riverbeds
of earlier mothers ...

And then again page-long lists of definitions: "tedious ...
felicity ... dinge ... bore ... perversion ... obsess ... smug
... things—bah not getting anywhere!!"

But between the last pages in the folder, a small, heavy
Ziploc bag; half a page doubled inside, covered with Yo's
writing and folded around:

Ceramic Pottery, Oldman River Dueck Site
Taber, Alberta, July 6, 1971
Rim Shard: roughly triangular, slightly convex. Blocky,
    well-rounded rim
Colour: interior tan grey, exterior grey black. Compact
    textured clay
Size: roughly 8 cm x 4 cm x 6 cm   Thickness: 3–11 mm
Period: AD 150–250

The tan and grey and black fragment lying in his hand: a
prehistoric piece of prairie Aboriginal pottery. The memory of that day unfolded like an opening flower.

The '71 summer holiday trip home to Taber when
Gabe was ten, and Hal's old school friend Jake drove
them in his jeep to his ranch along the river, wound
down ravines and through coulees between his red cattle
and showed them the eroded bends of the Oldman

banks, the black blotch of ash in the face of one sheer cliff.

"See, it's a very old campfire site," Jake said. "Prairie Indians always camped in a valley in winter, where there's lots of trees for firewood, and shelter from snowstorms."

Gabriel said, "But it's deep in the ground."

"Right!" Jake said. "Because long ago the river flooded and hid it under mud, but now after hundreds of years the river has washed it away again—see, so we can find it."

The two were ten feet below Hal in the eroded edges of the bank. Hal was peering down anxiously—ever Daredevil Jake!—he could see Jake's left arm braced against the steep cliff and his right holding Gabe very tightly. The boy's hands were scratching, poking at the cliff, black ash falling on the spikes of crumpled clay all around them and down to the swirling brown water.

"Hold it," said Jake, "careful . . . there's some big piece . . . wood . . . hold it . . ."

Not wood. Gabriel had exposed a shard, the broken rim of a clay pot almost as long as his small hand. He was so happy, they were all laughing and talking that evening, a future archeologist for sure! Jake said he would send the find to Calgary for analysis, but Gabe would get it back, there already were plenty of artifacts in the Dueck Aboriginal Site collection. A beautiful day at Grandma and Grandpa's, two-year-old Denny was dancing with Miriam and—

This jagged clay shard. In his basement Hal was holding it. And suddenly he understood that this too would have been part of Gabriel's Oldman River Quest: this childhood, discovery, happiness, family, laughter; this being held safe.

There was one more page in the red file folder. On it two lines written in blue:

Abandonment: to feel abandoned is essentially to feel forsaken
by the god within us—to lose sight of the eternal light

The piano was playing. On the blankness of Gabriel's page Hal heard the syncopated words Yo loved, loved so completely the first time the church choir sang them. She borrowed a copy and played and played and played it until she played it by heart:

We are not alone we
are not alone we
are never alone God is with us we

DAILY PLANNER 1985: *May Wednesday 1*
We don't know a thing. Walking streets   footsteps
sometimes a breeze touches you and you feel you are
spirited away . . . Athens? Poor crippled beggars, crippled
me. I run and run. Athens is such a waiting hole—why do
I long for it here—my life is a Tedious Nowhere. But May
in Alberta is shining spring

May Saturday 4
We planted blue spruce, Dad and I, dozens long as my
hand along the bush road leading in to Aspen Creek
cabin. Lovely. Also potatoes in the lower garden clearing

seed it and the earth makes food   every human is made
of earth? That's Genesis

   party with whole NFT gang, at Beth's, 115 St.

May Monday 13

Mom leaves for Miriam in Quito, Ecuador / till June 16.
Dad, Denn, me with her to the everlasting airport. Then:
room with a view! Move up, #1004 in Westview Towers /
rent $495 and huge bend of North Saskatchewan River
valley.

   Last NFT day Friday 17/85, turn in keys, their grant
finished. Fred completed semester studying business,
rent's up $10, and I have no job. Savings for 3 months rent,
no food.

   Out with Beth, Ross, John

May Thursday 16 down Friday 17

Finished *Ada*. To have such a mutual love, so
responding

   Paris, Texas again, invited Joan. After talked two hours
over coffee. I said I get obsessive about things. She said,
"Yes, I know." What did she mean?

   If it's not tedious nowhere, it's the distant unobtain-
able. Doesn't end even with endless spring light

   <u>Obsessive</u> - a persistent, disturbing preoccupation
               with an idea or feeling; intensely or
               abnormally   (me all right)

<u>Narcissus</u> - no mature independence, but a
dependence both greedy and desperate.
He is always liable to identify himself
with his object rather than differentiate
the object from himself . . . The
narcissist is not the self-lover, he is
the self-hater.

CRAP! The birthday, I should have put together a print
collage of my pictures of Ailsa Craig, Scotland—with a
list of meanings of the name and the strange stories
about/shapes of that startling rock in the sea: give her a
gift—Sunday she'll be 14. This would have been something to <u>do</u>, not just feel and hide . . . constructive—even
imaginative?
　　TOO LATE IDIATE
　　Out with NFT gang Peter, Beth, Ross, Jim　a laugh
evening carried on blues

May Sunday 19
Ailsa Helen's Birthday. Fourteen years ago. What
was there I could dare give, after nine months of no
answer　　hi
　　(Note written to myself Sept 14/84, last day of
waiting in Athens: Where will I be on this sacred day?
The day Joan brought lovely Ailsa into the world; and
I cry because it will probably never be spent with the
one I love—how prophetic of me)
　　Don't dare church. *The Bostonians*　　*Paris, Texas* x 2
again

May Monday 20

Pickup to Aspen Creek   eat   tan on deck   water every
tiny spruce and walk in endless poplars, new leaves bright
green turn over pale singing in the wind   did Cree call
poplar leaves lady fingers? Sap perfect, make whistles,
blow 3 at once—almost make harmony alone

May Wednesday 22

Fly away. <u>Vancouver</u>, Uncle Joe lives near Jericho Beach.
Sleep on his couch

May Monday 27

Visit Surrey cousin Elaine and husband / my age and
already two little screamers.

May Friday 31

On the beach as daily   walked around False Creek
where are you A   I feel your fingers—stop it. Huge
rusty ships anchored on the horizon   the world
waits, poised to act.   Uncle Joe so good, talks but
never pushes

June Thursday 6

Flight Van–Edm   Dad says Mom called from Ecuador
Miriam and Leo want WEDDING this fall   so that's it
then

   NFT for *The War Game*   after with Jim, Ross, Beth to
9th St. bar   money going fast

June Friday 7

Edm. same old same old. The one life one is given—ahhh
Velcro trash, tear it open

June Saturday 8

Wrong Move: Nastas. Kinski film debut at 13! Lucky dogs
Wenders, dad Klaus

June Sunday 9

After church go home with Dad and Denn for lunch,
catch up with A's parents' car, see her shadow through
tinted glass   shadows only   looking for work

June Thursday 13

Paris, Texas ends at Varscona   49 days/7 weeks   talk to
Jim/nothing. Visit Joan in her studio at UofA. Magn.
colour everywhere, esp. blue   talk, such a thoughtful,
attractive woman. If only A had her heart   perhaps she
does, how would I know

June Saturday 15

Joan invites just Denn and me for supper, then we'll go
see *A View to A Kill*, James Bond (R Moore) chasing a
microchip

SPIRAL NOTEBOOK (3): *June 15, 1985*

Joan's for supper. Very lovely meal, eat, laugh, eat. Then
talk openly with Ailsa while we two do dishes, alone
together in the kitchen. She'll go to Merryville High in
September, basic courses, she's poor in science, likes art,

take one year of gym and that's it, doesn't like swimming—bad lessons, when she had long hair the instructor pulled her out of the pool by her ponytail, yuk! Films she likes: *Ghostbusters* (seen 6 times), *Breakfast Club*, she listens to Christian rock on tape, likes Fears for Tears—huh, their first song came from a Jesus story, "suffer little children"—loves clothes, has lots (her breasts have grown slightly, she walks with very straight back). In back seat of the car driving to movie déjà vu of Mainz, but Grant driving and Denn, Colin, A and Gabe are so tight all arms are crossed. No exploring hands. Thighs did touch several times but back off quickly. She does look me straight in the eyes, fearlessly. Skinny Joanne still her #1 friend. After film we drive back and sit in their living room, Grant in single chair, me on couch near window and Joan and Ailsa on couch opposite. Grant puts on quiet strings music, A lifts Joan's hand and kisses it loudly, smiling. Full lips. She listens to our film talk but Gabe, of course, has to act superior, cut down spy-formula film—A loved it. She goes to the kitchen and brings us coffee, and then disappears to her room, to sleep? Denn and Colin play games in the basement.

On the whole a very pleasant evening, the parents obviously like me, try to be diplomatic. Ailsa comes across as an extremely typical very young teenager with childish traits. She is lovely, more rounded breasts and buttocks, her bare feet perfect and her lower lip so full. She has no driving loves except clothes and having fun—how can I get to know her mind. Please God, I don't ask to hold her and kiss her—just let us meet again, open

up more, I continuously say the wrong things—she seems
a bit like me, we don't know how to start saying things
and keep them going. Please let me be more positive,
find good points in bad art, so to be able to talk about
something, anything.

JUST REMEMBER Gabe—don't push it. She's barely a
month over 14 / what were you like then—innocent,
mind unshaped—you have lots of time so don't push and
act stupid—as in past. Have to learn to look at her in
company   she is so lovely

June 16, 1985

Mom home from Quito. In evening already feeling
lonely—when will I see A again. I suppose it was smart to
take J to *Paris, Texas*—she caught on right away the film's
about loss of communication. Perhaps that was why I
was invited over for supper, placed right beside A, was
alone to wash dishes with her—And no guts! Not one
word about Germany—too scared to spoil   arrgggh

Lots of Miriam stories, and Leo. Wedding middle of
September at Aspen Creek? Mom & Mir travelled jungle
rivers, mountain passes by bus, saw volcanoes and
equator / they like meeting the world together, and so
curious everything becomes fun for them, even jungle
diarrhea. What happened to one-track me?

Talk, good talk—but actually, already lonely right there
with her in the kitchen! How dumb is—look her in the
eyes boy, now! Red-striped dishcloth. God have mercy—
please—let me get that job with the Provincial Film
Censor, it would be perfect—I'd see every new film and

have something to talk about. Please let J ask me to house-sit when they go on holidays in July   it would be the perfect chance to dream walk through A's house

Hnnnnn. What would be, for me, the perfect way to live?

June 17, 1985

Well. I look at (in my mind's eye) A's family and they are nothing special. Middle-class ordinary. And let's face it, what I've observed is that A is physically beautiful but otherwise nothing at all special either—I'm being very cruel—lousy school marks, Christian (?) rock, clothes clothes—why have I created her (with those incredible green eyes) into this legend? All of us, me in particular, are nothing special / I love her, I love everything about her, the things she likes, does, wears, I love every part of her body I have ever seen

What does one do with love, emotions, tenderness what stops me

As the old joke goes: I refuse to worship a God who creates a pathetic lump like me. No way.

To Oleg's for supper, 6:30

DAILY PLANNER 1985: *June Thursday 20*

No Prov. Film Censor Board job—should be 42 not 24. Apply for unempl. insur.

Out with Beth, Ross, Kathy   can't handle wine any more

June Saturday 22

A, I dream of you beside me in my narrow bed. We are naked. We are both very tender, your arms bring me in, enclose me. Then we lie together, going to sleep. Oh Reality, Reality, where for art thou??

P.M.: At parents with job painting garage door when Grant phones, will I take care of their house while they're on vacation July 4–10. In background A interjects comments several times—to let me know she's there? Good— she cares enough to play the same games I do. And I have her parent's approval to stay in their house, yes! Fun.

Was it? During that last summer, what could Gabriel experience as "fun"? Hal knew he would never know. Personally he remembered nothing—though he sometimes tried—of that July. Was that the hot month he dragged out building the stone retaining walls overlooking the cliff at the cabin? The rocks in his hands such concentrated, heavy, absolute exactly-what-they-are and nothing less. Fitting them together, round granite, flat and breaking sandstone he hauled up from the creek in the pickup or from farm rock piles along the road allowances, selected and fit so carefully leaning against the sheered clay wall of the patio deck ending on the cliff high above the trees and twisted creek water shining between flickering aspen. Lift the rocks with your two hands, place them and they lay, a declaration of solid, unchangeable earth; like Canadian Shield bedrock billions of years . . . and Gabriel wrote not a word in his diary about that week of "taking care of their house," July 4–10 1985.

Indeed, not one diary or journal mention of Ailsa from June 22 to August 12: seven weeks and a day.

Though he named twenty-eight different movies.

And there were three loose pages; torn out of something. No dates.

Page 1: lists birth information, including "6 lbs 10 oz May 19, 1971" and the names, addresses of "Jordon from Brooks, Lee from Bow Island, met at the Roy Salmon Praise and Worship May '85 weekend. Favourite saying: Right on!"

Page 2: an outline sketch of the bedroom with full page list of items and rectangles of drawers labelled with contents: "make-up," "letters Lee, Jordon," "underwear," "socks," "in bank: $76.00 babysitting," "sweaters," "bed-clothes," "skirts/shirts" . . .

No "letter Gabriel"?

Page 3:

> Petals, petals falling
> It's just a flower
> She's barely a teenager
> The flower doesn't even have the sense to
> completely denude itself

Oh, I feel soooooooo bad!!   (I'm writing like a little kid)

She is so common as to be banal. Her dreams—huge Michael Jackson poster, *Ghostbusters*, Fears for Tears, handwritten recipe for lemon sherbet—nothing more, nothing less. A Bible—ever opened? not noticeably. But, then, after the day or two of hate, after thinking that

the rose is finally, absolutely, dead, you realize suddenly
(like a breeze washing over you) that you still love
her. After you noticed that she is not quite as beautiful
as you thought, you find you still love those full lips,
those eyes, yes more than ever. The feelings are human.
The family album pictures, the ones that captured her
off guard, looking right, staring over her shoulder, at
what? I listen to her tapes, tapes she has gone to the
trouble of making, she has held how often in her
slim hands

> It's a sad affair
> When there's no one there
> He calls out in the night
> And its so . . .
> Suffer   suffer the children

And beyond the three written pages there are pictures.

Seven prints. Hal could not believe it possible these were
all Gabriel with his unending demand of camera took the
long week he stayed in that house—if he did stay. More
likely he could not endure even one complete day in a
place so haunted, especially at night—in what bed could
he dare sleep?—especially the kitchen sink over which
they once talked, side-by-side, handing each other dishes
(though surely Joan heard them, and Grant, from wherever they were in the spacy bungalow with all those wide
archways opening to kitchen, dining room, living room,
hallway to three bedrooms). He could not have endured
that smallest bedroom nearest the hall telephone—five of

the seven pictures he kept were of Ailsa's bedroom. The tightening order of black and white obsession; no colour, nothing touched:

Picture 1. The unfocussed backyard seen through the curtains above the kitchen sink: one of the curtain folds could be a pale slender thigh with knee bent, leg and ankle slanted forward as if running;

Picture 2. The pale telephone: hung up beside the closed hallway cupboard; the cord dangled in coils to the baseboard;

Picture 3. The bedroom, clothes closet: twenty-nine black wire hangers, thirteen with clothes hanging unrecognizably together; long dresses, perhaps a robe, jackets, shirts, skirts or slacks;

Picture 4. The bedroom, bed: brilliant light on the shadowed bedspread like a massive, winged creature; between its jagged upper leg and wing lay one small pillow, and on it the embroidered word "HOME";

Picture 5. The bedroom, vanity and corner of large mirror: a reflection of the bed with ribbed throw and cushions, sunlight shone through lace window curtains, end table with radio, writing desk with lamp; the edge of the mirror lined with head-shots of teenage girls;

Picture 6. The bedroom, full mirror: "star" pictures pinned over each other on poster above bed; mirror outlined with portraits, the left side all Ailsa school photos from kindergarten to grade 8. But also: above the portraits along the bottom edge of the mirror a faint shadow of Gabriel's head. Very small and in profile, looking right.

- 182 -

Picture 7. The bedroom, full mirror: the blurred double-image of the back of a man from the waist up, naked, pointing the pistol of his left (right) hand into his ear.

Not a word written about the pictures. Nowhere.

The '85 diary from June 25 to August 3 named only movies and minimal acts; but then, suddenly, two intense personal statements.

DAILY PLANNER 1985: *July Monday 1*
    I owe Ross a beer   tennis with Denn

July Wednesday 10
    Fender-bender with parents' pickup—changing lanes, my fault

July Thursday 11
    V. Nabokov, "To Russia: Will you leave me alone? I implore you!"

July Wednesday 16
    Reading Robert Kroetsch, *What the Crow Said*
      People, years later, blamed everything on the bees

July Tuesday 23
    Tennis with Denn

July Friday 26
    Four days cabin work   9 hrs 6 hrs 10 hrs 6 hrs

July Wednesday 31

Unemployment Insurance application accepted.

Miriam returns from Quito with Leo   I cry for what's to come

Thursday August 1

Trampoline with Denn. Out with Ross, Judy, Beth

August Saturday 3 across Sunday 4 and Monday 5

Writers weekend, about ten talking with Dad at Aspen Creek, they read their (often pretentious) work. Isabelle o you are such a flake. Sure you have brilliant eyes, but real intelligence? To argue that females should get male roles is ridiculous! Why on earth or heaven would anyone want a male role, always lonely, shy, timid, yet always expected to be endlessly competent, to forever compete! We're so loaded down with old shit, females should want to invent totally new roles for themselves.

Image, the evening campfire (Isabelle sat there, she saw it too): A moth flying out of the darkness, beautiful swoops, flutter, dive, a faint hiss, a wobble, it falls to the ground beside me. The end.

Memory Image: when I returned from Europe, first time back in her house, A came up from the basement dressed like a clown, face and all, October 27 1984. She was playing the buffoon, the comic inversion for what is all-powerful and controlling—she wouldn't know it, but I know now, for sure.

So okay God, you create a world, a world we have to exist in. Why?

I never asked to be me   I can refuse

August Monday 12 over Tuesday 13

If I do have love, complete love, I should be able to live forever, no matter what the outcome. If all I have to offer is death, obviously meaning, literally, the ceasing of this love, then it can be construed as not being a completely obsessive love. But non-existence can also be seen as an easy cop-out, a pathetic choice of evasion: even if the world is full of useless, trite things, including myself, I should fight against exactly <u>that</u>. However, to end now will be to undo the triteness A is, that I am. And I'll be forgotten within months by the few who still remember, I'll be missed by less in even less time.

It's not that I don't want to live, it's that somehow I've lost a means by which to function. I'm as hollow as a pail filled with only one thing. Has there ever been a more nervous and shy . . . if only I were a beautiful female some Big Strong Manly MAN would save me. <u>Laugh</u>. What can I say if you don't know and understand already—when you're empty, what is there to miss? I'm sorry, I don't mean to hurt anyone—I did not ask to come, with my personality, into a place in time and space to hurt anyone. Okay, refusal to be is an act against the God in us. I refuse to make choices, oh, obviously death is a choice—an extremely clumsy and awkward one at that. Can you imagine the discovery, poor person

Yah sure Gabe, your empty life is a continuous ravenous process, always a wanting more, always a somehow feed yourself   hnnnn   feed   feed

Feed yourself. Hal remembered a morning in January, when Owl was leafing through Double Cup newspapers as Hal watched a pigeon on the sidewalk outside. It was bird busy, eating. Fluffed fat in the cold, it ran and fluttered between passing feet while pecking at what seemed to be the brown crumbs of a cookie. The crumbs were scattered everywhere, crushed into the cracks between sidewalk bricks, but the pigeon was finding them, pecking them out quick as fingers tapping when Owl spoke suddenly:

"Feeding them is the least of it."

Hal glanced up at him. "What?"

"This news again, East Africa."

"Oh, yeah. Starvation."

"Getting worse, every week . . ."

Hal said, "I can't remember that, ever starving."

"For what?"

"For . . . ?"

Owl was staring out the window. Momentarily no one walked there in the brilliant cold; only the pigeon huddled into a fluffy ball now, and on the street motionless cars in shrouds of winter exhaust.

Hal said, "Starving, for food."

"Yeah. That's what I meant," Owl said. "And I've needed food, not now, never in Edmonton, really, but where I was a kid."

"Actually, my parents starved too," Hal said. "Plenty, in Russia with the Communists, '*Hungaschnoot*' they called it, hunger-need, agony. But I was born in Canada."

"Me too," Owl said. "But north, way too far north. In winter on the Deh-Cho Mackenzie River you need more. For a few days it's not much, not so bad, a ache you feel up there lots of times, but sometimes it gets real bad and you all know Hunger Animal has come. Hunger Animal is different from 'being hungry,' we have a different word for her in our language, nobody ever says that name out loud, but we all know it, in English it would be sort of like 'Hunger Animal.' She's like a black beaver, huge mouth full of teeth curved for gnawing, she starts small and eats herself bigger in your gut, you feel her chewing out your gut, the hole gets bigger and bigger and pretty soon it's so big she's gnawing in your chest, your throat, Hunger Animal's in your mouth and eye, everything you see is something you have to eat. There's never enough then, you see a bit of caribou fur, a piece of dog shit, whatever you find you take and put it in your mouth, it doesn't fill the hole inside you but you chew it, you swallow, you see fire and a pot of water and your sister's toes are a row of little sausages, they're soup . . ."

Hal stared at his craggy friend. Owl, cold coffee forgotten, continued in what had now soaked into monotone:

"It's way past having to eat, wanting food. Or being together . . . together is just something watching you eat. Nobody else is there anymore when Hunger Animal eats you empty, just you alone with her, there's nothing left, just her. Eating."

Beyond the glass wall, the pigeon was gone; only people, cars crept by, so slowly in the groaning, rutted snow it seemed they were hunched forward in weeping.

Finally Hal murmured, "You said, 'For what?'"

"Oh yeah . . . food. Just having no food is pretty easy, even one rabbit or ptarmigan can start chasing her away, then, but she can come different too, you sometimes don't know what she is but you know she's there and she wants something. It's not food—stick it in your mouth and chew and swallow—no, if Hunger Animal finds you she always wants some big thing you haven't got . . . or can't have—she's inside you, gnawing deeper. When you can't think or feel nothing else, that's her."

Abruptly it seemed to Hal that Owl no longer spoke English; he was somehow talking a Dene translation so thin it was diaphanous as vapour. And more so when he continued:

"When I was a boy, our medicine man who had four songs, while he was chopping down trees for that highway the Americans made to Alaska during the war, he told me he had once seen Hunger Animal. Huge, black, coming through the trees, you could tell it was her by the light following her. Big like a spruce all on fire, but coming and no other trees burning. He warned me, I was just young, he said if you ever see that, just run like hell."

The warm surround of the coffee shop held them motionless in their soft chairs. After a time Hal lifted his Monday cup; took a swallow of cold coffee.

"Did you ever see that, in the trees?"

"No."

"You believe what he said?"

"It's not just food," Owl said. "When she's in you, he said, she wants what you haven't got. And you have to have it to stay alive, you need it more and more because there's only less and less of you to want it."

Music was playing from the ceiling, a familiar Beatles song but Hal could not think about that. He was concentrating on Owl, and asked him again,

"Do you believe what he said?"

"No," Owl said. "No. But one bad winter, in the snow I saw the tracks."

"Tracks?"

"Yeah. And you run like hell, but you can't forget."

DAILY PLANNER 1985: *August Wednesday 14*
　　Hi.

Loving son: we will never know how much you thought, and wrote, and then destroyed. But you deliberately left us these spare diaries: they were to be, they are your message to us after you are gone. And on an otherwise empty day during your last August you offer us greeting:

Hi.

And suddenly Hal could not endure what was approaching through the shredded trees of his life; what had come, what was forever already there since that tiny word was written.

Like the final exhalation of a breath.

Oh Jesus Christ, Son of the Living God, have pity on me a sinner. Up the basement stairs thump by thump and across to the back door, unlock, walk out on the deck. Face the last April sun blazing down through snow-spotted trees tipped with green buds.

The houses and condo blocks of the city loomed there as ever, piled blankly dark around him. A helicopter—the city police?—beat somewhere, fading east. Why didn't they come and get his official guilt registered, take him and throw away the key, oh sure it was that old guy, he's in here every day, name's Hal, he comes and goes on 104th Street towards Saskatchewan Drive, he's sometimes with that Dene guy, Owl, yeah, usually straggle beard, he run out yelling a name like crazy—why didn't he go, what was the matter with him, why—

He heard a sound he has known since before memory: he stared at the sky, high and west, where the last blue light played in burning clouds and he saw the bent line of Canada geese, he heard their honking even more distantly clear when he found their ragged, undulating V, their giant wings stretching their long necks, their bodies yearning relentlessly north. His heart leaped as he watched, their sound, one arm of their V shifting steadily forward, shaping them into an N and then gradually out of it as they cried into a wobbly W and then bent slowly out into a larger variation of V; they were calling north high over the bright city and the dark river valley and the luminous sprawl of streets beyond, and it seemed to him they were writing their shape-shifting story letter by letter on the sky, he read it bright as memory:

Thom, his *Groota Brooda* / Big Brother Thomas, Thom, forever nineteen. And he was little Hal, almost nine then, he was looking up at Thom so huge beside him in the wagon box bumping towards the Wapiti Post Office and Thom's big right hand lifted from the reins, pointed up. It was not spring, it was autumn and the V of the great geese were crying south. That last autumn before the winter

Thom enlisted in the Canadian Armed Forces though no one drafted him. Two years earlier he had declared himself before an official government Registrar as a Mennonite Conscientious Objector and had been judged and lectured and granted exemption as an essential farm worker—with Mam he ran their Wapiti farm far better than their father was capable of—but the day after Christmas 1944 he travelled eighty-two miles to North Battleford, Saskatchewan, and enlisted in the Air Force and on Sunday January 28, 1945 he was dead. The telegram said he had been running a Basic Training obstacle course in Ontario when he lost his grip on a high bar, and fell. His neck broke.

Sixteen years to the day before Gabriel Thomas was born.

Their Wapiti Mennonite Church deacon Peter Block holds the telegram low in his left hand. Backed against their closed kitchen door in his black buffalo fur coat, but they are all staring at the dirt-yellow English paper he has translated. "A horrible accident," he says in Low German. And again quietly: "Accident."

On his Edmonton house deck, the distant Canada geese gone in the darkening spring sky, for Hal that word was like a bell tolling: "*Onn-jletj . . . Onn-jletj.*" And he thought again, "*Jletj*" means "luck," the word literally meant "un-luck," and his father's Low German words ignoring completely their mother's piercing shriek, words so fierce little Hal had never heard his mostly silent father speak to anyone like that, leave alone to the all-powerful deacon who spoke English as well as any school teacher:

"You always say there is NO UN-LUCK! There is only GOD'S WILL!"

And the Deacon gestured helplessly with one empty hand at their wailing mother and sister Margret, and then at Hal as well: who had read and understood the telegram words perfectly without translation, he had been at enough Wapiti funerals to know about dead.

Accident. Un-luck. Noun or verb—at best, stunning evasions.

Whatever it was, you could do nothing. These were the facts, you had to accept. Accept your big brother Thomas would walk those winter miles alone to the highway and flag down the Meadow Lake–North Battleford bus and after five weeks come grinding home through snow in a box on the back of a truck and in the corner churchyard beyond the barn four Royal Canadian Air Force soldiers would surround that box like posts and hoist their bayonet rifles up at the sky, Yes! you thought then, stab him, shoot him, God!

And when your oldest son so carefully backs up your truck, parks among small birches.

Facts.

The geese over the city were gone, and the sun. A last brightness flamed against clouds above the patches of roofs, beyond the six high-rises clear through a spray of bare trees: how long since he had remembered his beloved brother's rigid face in that coffin, that dreadful uniform . . . he will not remember. No. Owl and tomorrow would come as certainly as the moon rising and now the sun was gone and it was time, yes, time for the detailed and programmed evening rituals that led him steadfastly through his life wilderness of utter avoidance into the blessed, daily blank nirvana of unconsciousness. Go, not down into the basement, go upstairs, go up. Abandon this.

Gabe's word: abandonment. No, impossible now. Down again.

DAILY PLANNER 1985: *August Tuesday 20 and across Wednesday 21*

Yes—I'm sorry—I'm sorry—I'm incredibly sorry

Listen to pop music on the radio trying to hear a certain song. Go to Music Centre to look, their PA is playing like vibrating thunder ". . . and she knew that she would never drive through Paris in a . . ." I slam the door on it.

Where is there a saviour when you need one. It's too much a romantic dream.

The effort needed to write down words thought in the mind is never good enough—words put down, even sung, are never, ever—o banal—somehow this Gabriel Thomas Wiens does not have the stuff to write down . . . too full, too empty

Arrange something beautiful, an image . . . I don't know if I can do this, even for my darling Mir, this white and red rose picture wedding present, rolls of shots, they develop so trite. Vases all around, vases bought or hand-shaped—and I don't know what exists inside a female—hence they are all <u>empty</u>, not even two transitory flowers—the colours alone don't do it.

In evening meet Shirley, Susan, Donna, Mary, Simone and friend / feel like expired high school—feel like a <u>twit</u>

I need to start everything all over again; life is good, lovely—but how can I do this living? Oh skip it

August Monday 26 and scrawled across two full pages to Saturday 31

Gabe: you must remember that the ramifications of this act before the 21st of September (M&L wed.) are going to put great distress on that whole happy situation. If you were a strong man you would wait at least till after. But Mir getting

(Saw A and skinny Joanne through the girders walking across High Level Bridge on opposite side as I walked to play tennis with Denn. A on railing side, her hair permed in gold streaks since I last saw her. When? Did she see me? I'll never know)

Quit reading this, trying to find clues to who I am. Shut the case and go on with your lives. Cause here I sit and I know that I would preferably do no different— I'm no better than you. (I know / I do seek romantic crap)   (NFT Board meeting 6:30 Citadel)

It's going to be so messy. How long will it take   a week   imagine the poor person

Sorry Mir, I have no gift to give you—I have none for anybody. Even God—he just   I would rather burn in hell than go to a "Father" who just creates and then leaves you on your own / I don't want to go on living this given life: I <u>refuse</u> to accept being my self any longer. Therefore, I guess, proving I have faith in, I value my self.

Oh well, I can certainly babble contradictions

(*The Trial*—lovely music)

These photos I took to make Mir a present. I should
have put the camera right up to the white and red roses in
Clara's stacked-clay vase, with a wide open aperture, that
way the background would be blurry and foreground in
beautiful focus. But I kept the camera back about 3 feet:
crap, should do it over again // but I don't have the
money, and to make the effort, and time . . .   Not
drunk yet—suck some more.   That's better—the first
waves of warmth pervade my being—and at the same
moment I feel that I shall continue. hunnnnn needs to
be seen   All this stuff written Aug. 25/85
     The long walk, bridge, university, valley, dining at
home, Mom always so good to me I sometimes can't
stand it, yell, yell and walk out. Feel worse with every step

Top border of page, tiny, written at right angles
     I cry for what is lost, and conversely for what will be lost,
losing lost, losing lost, a nice skipping rhyme for a little
kid but I'm too old. I look to the future at some date; I
will be forgotten, the past over. I wish I could cry for and
cry with all who cry, everyone crying inside their laughter, but I am selfish, I can barely cry for a few. I laugh but
I cry. The white rose wilts, the red petals fall—why create
at all if all your life is losing lost Aug 31/85 Does this help
you   I don't know

September Sunday 1
     Dinner at Mir and Leo's, whole family. Travel and wed-
ding talk and laughing. I egg Denn on too loud, Dad as
usual not amused

Wide waterfall on High Level Bridge lit for Labour
Day / bridge steel burns a sheet of light far down into the
river   it just keeps rollin' along

September Monday 2

Cross the High Level, play tennis with Denn, all UofA
courts full and more people come, they watch as they
wait; naturally; but, my game totally falls apart, I can't
play with people watching me, I want to run away, I
continue to hit the net. The joke is that they're not even
paying attention to me, why would they give a hoot how
I play a game? And yet I fall apart

September Tuesday 3

How can that be my last entry? It at least indicates a
character trait of mine, the shy nervousness when people
watch me / maybe more than that—these are the kind of
things that are so useless in the late discoveries of one's
existence   And also my accidental, my accurate
double-meaning choice of words

September Tuesday 3 across August Thursday 15 to Sunday 18

Please, if you must insist on a funeral, do not have it in
Mennonite Church Edmonton, I hate the place: it never
taught me how to live. Oh stupid again, blaming others,
actually good people, making requests: did I want to
learn? Do whatever you want—you made the effort
to bring me into the world (what? a moment of joy?)
you (and the world) can make the effort to clean up
what remains

(Note: if you don't have it, you just don't have it. I can talk all I want about that and what would that explain? Extreme double meaning here, and do you know what I'm talking about? No? Can I talk more clearly? No.)

As for the people I love—forgive me, I am obviously not worthy of you. But I have, and I do, love you.

If I could write out the words of a song for you (in your style), I would do so, but for all the songs I know, I don't know any that would do justice—I weep—I cry   Oh Lord, why can I not show love—I can't do anything without you: and obviously can't do anything with you. Have pity

Grrrrreat

September Wednesday 4
I'm sorry (
Well enough of this

Well enough of this

The only words in the journal written in pencil. Hal had just enough control to check: the last words in Spiral Notebook (3) were dated June 22. He already knew every remaining page of the black Daily Planner 1985 was blank after Wednesday, September 4. He knew he would never find another Gabriel word, however often he might look; not an ink or pencil mark on thirty-four dated week pages. Except one:

September Saturday 21
   Wedding, Mir, Aspen Creek / white rose, red rose

O Gabriel my son, O my son, my son Gabriel

The leaves did nothing
neither did the trees, nor the birds rehearsing
their long fall journeys to their homing
south, they all saw him back the pickup slowly
between the pale black-knotted trunks of aspen
along the track bent away from the cliff cabin
very carefully so the wide tires crushed no
small birches, the youngest already thinking winter
and bowing down to let him pass over and straightening
again so that two days later it would seem the pale
blue steel and glass and white fibreglass
had simply grown, been sifted over
by autumn snow, a strange extrusion suddenly there
on the insistence of some green and barely yellow
lightning and the moist soil where peeling aspen
stood dead grey, enjoyed for too many summers
by armies of insatiable worms, a month
after we two were together exactly there
cutting a narrow path through grass, brush
together, sparing those very birches
to contain this indifferent hiding. But now
you are alone. There is no need to work quickly
because of course you know you have all the time

there is and not even the thickening night
need hurry you in this boreal stillness
　　　where am I
why am I not here as you make your bed
so neatly, your cabin pillowcase and sheet, sheathing
the foam mattress in a blue matching the ribbed
metal you lay it on, as you miter the brighter
blue corners of the blanket as your mother
taught you, as you raise your head
stare into the deepening perspective of trees
hear a pest of robins harry a great horned owl
before you steadily continue—why don't I stretch
out my hand to your shoulder as you drop
to your knees, bow to the chortling exhaust, as ever
do such neat work, not a fold or wrinkle in the winding
tape, when you climb in again and clamp
the tailgate up tight and pull the canopy door
down firmly over the white hose, as you remove
your shoes, fold your favourite tan jacket beside you
to the acrid mutter of motor
all this relentless, steady work
　　and when you lay your long body
down on your back and pull the blue blanket
up against your throat and breathe
　　　smell
why am I not there, my arms around you
saying Gabriel
　　Gabriel

Machine: - from the Greek *mechane* / machos, contrivance

       - from the West Teutonic *magan*, to be able

       - any instrument able to, employed to transmit, force

Humans rely on countless machines without thinking

Because that is why they have contrived them: to apply

Mechanical force through their various connected parts

In order to change our environment, to control and alter

Our surroundings or ourselves for our convenience, our

    comfort

They are built by imaginative logic, they operate by logic

And logic tells us that at some point they will invariably

Break down and then there will be a discoverable

Logical reason for how they must be fixed in order

That they will function again   this is unlike human beings

If you hold that humans function like machines

A Chevrolet three-quarter-ton truck, in Alberta mostly called

A pickup, is a contrivance for moving things, for 96,773.8 miles

This blue pickup has moved things, from a family camper

To lumber or a kitchen stove or garbage or comfortably carried

People from one place to another, whatever it is loaded

With and wherever it is steered, besides all the hours

It has been forced to stand and idle in searing cold

       Why is it so reliable?

A machine this used, this complex, has infinite reasons

To stop functioning, to sputter, to hiccough, to rattle

To a stop. So why, here among these small birches, to the last

Whiff of gas vapour in its tank, why is this particular machine
Of such staggering reliability, how is it possible that such
A ludicrously finite contrivance for moving things
For standing inert
Is able to transmit such unending
Force

The black grid of the high city bridge
was long my fear, the quick valley
with rocks and trees and gravel-bars
and water motionless as sky, the deep
welcoming air
            I should have known you better

That night the animals came
First the twitchy squirrels, perhaps they heard
the engine sputter as they leaped from spruce
to poplar, heard the click click click of the machine
cooling, having done everything it could do, so completely
reliable, and then the flutter of bats and the invisible insects
they hear, the porcupine climbing down ponderously
from the tree notch where she slept sunning herself
all day, humpling through fallen leaves, the nosy badger
a scurry of mice, two beavers heaving themselves
up the cliff from the creek and snipping, peeling
an evening breakfast of aspen before settling to their night's

work of cutting. Four white-tailed deer wandered by,
nostrils wide, a spruce grouse treading so lightly
two hesitant rabbits, perhaps the black she-bear the Cree
trapper said lives in the valley though neither he nor anyone
has ever seen her track, not yet, his medicine more certain
than tracks in that shadow, there, beyond the edge of your
left eye, the hunched darkness that isn't there when you
twitch to stare at it, but if you walk quietly
enough you may smell a faint musk, like a memory
of black not quite touchable. Three stepping deer
muleys this time, and then evening coyotes begin
to call and answer, crying high beyond their echo
all along the valley
What did they say, the animals?

> Happy are the empty
>> for they shall be filled
> Happy are the dead
>> for their eyes see no more
> Happy are the poor in spirit
>> for they will know

Or sing?

> Were you there when
> Everybody knows the
> When peace like
> Nobody knows the

Their voices may still be there matted
in the earth with the September leaves and you
would feel them if you walked there again, your feet

and body bones shiver with their barking, their raw
laughter, their squeals and long carrying sorrow
their aloneness like the moon fading behind
cloud but always somewhere, on the other side
of the earth perhaps and, as it seems, gone but
always somewhere, growing larger or waning but
forever there, more and more, a desperation roaming
up and down the valley like the gigantic moose
a black shift between the silver trees, calling
and then at last hearing a faint answer, you cannot
tell is it sound, is it echo, is it the torque of intense
listening in the harmony whorls of your ear
is it Coyote still and pointing at the sky
like you with mouth fallen open

> softly, silently now the moon
> walks the night in a silver rune

It did not snow the first night, though clouds
trundled noisily up the valley, hesitated, sniffed
over the cliff like an incontinent old man poking
at the world with his cane and cackling heh heh
when he turns over something worse than even he had
imagined. Snow fell the second night, a humming
warmth edging leaves and branches, the blue
metal, the fibreglass modulating into flawless
white and only the black-knotted aspen remained
grey and groaning in their occasional movement, stiffening

And the long knife lies inside
the canopy that has always been more or less
white, lies waiting to be unsheathed, waiting
for an uncle's soft, indelible approach.

there is a sound not like a child or other small animal
alone a sound like people holding each other anyone
whoever may be somehow at hand heads perhaps
bumping knocking please please but there is no
answer a sound groping with fingertips or
sudden fistfuls of clutching and finding
only alone an indestructible sound
like rain like snow like bullets
striking air or some
thing more sensitive
than air a sound
like
like

The telephone shrilled, an explosion in his paralyzed
mind. Hal bumbled to his feet, grabbed at the basement
receiver, dropped it but saw the number and collapsed,
rolled onto his back again while clutching it, jabbed the
right button.

"Dad . . . hello Dad?"

"Miriam . . . how, how . . . hey . . . are you!"

"What's wrong, Dad, what—?"

"Sorry—no—I'm okay, good good, I just swallowed—arrgggh—some coffee wrong . . ." (Why was he lying?) "I'm fine . . . especially now, you, how are you all, you four darlings?"

"A bit late, decaf I hope—please be careful, sweet Dad . . . well, we're all usual here, like usual."

"So. So Michelle's through her friend disaster?"

Miriam's easy laugh rang in his ear, "C'mon, it's two days! You know their 'Forever'! They're in her room studying . . . at least that's what they said, Grade Eight math."

"Good . . . you heard from Emilia, she all right?"

"Just talked on Skype. Has she called you, she didn't say?"

"Not since last week."

"She looks relieved, even on the blurry computer, she's glad she moved to Santiago, such a beautiful city, the Andes she says, and the ESL students are better than in Buenos Aires. Not in English but eager, they want to learn so badly."

"She has friends, in Santiago?"

"Not yet, but she will, soon. I think that's what she's happy about: no one she *has* to be friends with like Leo's family in BA, all their heavy—"

"Yeah, their disappearances, politics—heavy stuff."

"Emilia loves them, you know her, so understanding. But it's too heavy sometimes, and there's nothing to do but listen, especially with the aunts for a year now so she's sort of happy to get away, six months, I can't blame her . . ."

"Good, see something else."

"Chile's as bad as Argentina for memories, it won't last."

"See, better like me to know only one word of Spanish, 'adios' and that's it!"

"German's not such a happy language."

"True—and Low German's hardly better. But I think there's some of you in your lovely daughter —if necessary, she can be a sort of avoider, eh what?"

Miriam's superb laughter again. "Hey! I think she's more an 'evader,' like you!"

"No no, get it right, I'm not so much underhanded as slippery, I *elude* things I want to avoid."

They were both laughing, able as always to feel quickly happy together, momentarily.

"I should never play word games with you!"

"No no, you should, words play real good, especially on the phone."

"I know, and you always know more than enough for a comeback."

"Yeah," said Hal, suddenly heavy as guilt.

"Dad? Something wrong?"

The Orange Downfill, he had to . . . "Nothing's wrong," he lied quickly. "Still alive, it's enough."

"Da-ad!"

"Sorry."

They were both silent; waiting. Finally Miriam said, "I saw in the *Sun* today Edmonton got its standard end-of-April snow."

"Yeah . . . today it's melting."

"It's not even raining here. Why don't you get in your fast Celica and come out, walk around English Bay, Stanley

Park a few days? Michelle would love it, evenings getting longer and everything's lush green, there's no snow in Jasper or the Coquihalla."

"Well . . ."

"You promise, but you haven't come . . . it's months."

Confess something. "I went into the basement, I opened two Gabe boxes."

Silence.

"I haven't touched those boxes since Yo and I took them down . . ."

Silence lengthened, then Miriam murmured, "'85. Everything stops."

"And starts—you and Leo, soon your lovely kids."

"That's not why you opened them."

"No. I only got into two, all the paper—not his things—his two diaries and the notebooks and I suddenly thought—"

"Before Frankfurt or after?"

"Both, '84 and '85, and his number three notebook, that's the same time, longer thoughts and everything dated, a pocket notebook too and there's quite a few loose pages and—" Hal stopped himself, then continued quickly before Miriam could ask the obvious question, "Yeah, he writes quite a lot, daily stuff, also lists of definitions and has discussions with himself about God the Father, the Creator, and his problems with him, and word prayers and anger—but nothing about Jesus. Not a word. And I can't remember ever talking with Gabe about Jesus either, no memory at all. All the times we talked, isn't that strange?"

"Of course you talked about Jesus, you even taught his Sunday School class a whole year. You certainly talked about Jesus."

"That was when he was little, six or seven . . ."

"Sure, but you did after too—"

"Yes, I know we did, but I can't remember! Not one exact thing I could say, now. And then I thought of Norman, he was in Gabe's Sunday School class too, how he . . . how he was gone . . . he was even younger, twenty . . . remember?"

"Yes," Miriam said faintly. "In his locked room. Right above his parents' bedroom."

"Gabe and I were doing fall cleanup at the cabin when Yo phoned and told us, and then we went down to the creek, we looked at the beaver dams, they weren't very high that autumn. We talked, I remember, we sat on a log . . ."

"It must have been something okay, Gabe was so strong at Norman's funeral. He was even a pallbearer."

"I know I know, we sat on the log-jam above the beaver pond, that one in the bend where you see the cabin on the cliff, but I can't remember . . . not one word."

"Why," Miriam's voice so gentle, "why does it matter?"

"Oh I guess we must have talked about life and death— we'd all been through both grandpas and one grandma dying, open coffins, good Mennonite face-to-face funerals, older people okay, but his friend and age, from his church Young People, I just . . . I hope I didn't talk about God too much, that we talked about Jesus . . ."

"Dad, you would have."

"I just hope to hell I—excuse me!—I didn't say Norm's death was God's will."

"You would never!"

"I don't know . . . then . . . I remember once arguing at a funeral there was no such thing as 'accident.' After a car crash."

"Did you call the crash 'God's will'?"

"No no, I think I said, 'a law of nature,' like Thomas Hardy's 'convergence of the twain.'"

"Didn't Hardy mean something different? Like 'inevitable destiny'—'fate'? You never talked like that to us kids."

"I guess . . . I hope not," Hal said, hopelessly.

"No! You talked about laws of nature and our decisions, us deciding what we did, not *fate*."

"You remember it that way?"

"I do, Dad."

"Good. But in Gabe's last years of desperate writing—it really is . . . reading it now it's sometimes more than desperate—heavy heavy Holy God is there a lot, a Creator who made us whatever we are, he calls himself a 'fool' so often, or 'shy,' 'sick'—'So here I am, God, the sensitive fool you made, me! I never asked to be . . .' But he never mentions Jesus, not once."

"Listen," Miriam's voice changed quick and strong, "Gabe talked about Jesus to me that last summer, I remember it, about Jesus and the two thieves."

"What?"

"On the cross, the two thieves."

Hal can only grunt, his surprise staggering him. He stretched out completely on the floor, away from the rustling paper and with his eyes closed: seeing his tall daughter's beautiful face leaning into the telephone, her voice murmuring gradually into happiness,

"It must have been August because we were in Leo's apartment, 80th Avenue, drinking coffee, Leo was out working and Gabe told me he was reading the Gospels and he noticed—"

"August '85? Gabe was reading the Gospels?"

"Yes! And he said all three Synoptics say there are two thieves crucified with Jesus, and Matthew and Mark say both reviled Jesus when they were nailed there but Luke says one thief did not revile. He defended Jesus and that's a big difference, Gabe said, but it's two against one, no, actually *three* against one because John's Gospel mentions the two thieves too but no defense either, three to one, so why, he said, do we believe Luke?"

Hal sang quietly, "'Jesus, remember me, when you come into your kingdom, Jesus, remember . . .'"

"Yes!" Miriam exclaimed, "our communion song! The thief's prayer on the cross, in Luke, yes."

"That last August?"

"In Leo's apartment, it had to be right at the end . . . August."

"I just read his two diaries and the third notebook, and you know before July '85 there's all these names of movies— he went sometimes to two a day—sometimes a quick fact, 'lunch with Oleg,' 'drink with . . .' stuff like that, and about every week notes of weeping and anger and 'God, please have some mercy' . . . and then there's nothing at all in the notebook and nothing daily in the diaries, no movies and all the dates ignored, it's all just overwritten down and side-ways with rage, despair, his mind seems made up, no debate or discussion, and he's just sorry for the person who finds him but everything seems deci—"

"Dad, I've never read them."

"Sweetheart," Hal said.

They were silent. Breathing as they could; good he was lying flat, stretched out. He had never even thought that Miriam might not . . . okay, young Dennis not, nor Leo, but Yo had packed them away after he had seen her reading them, again, and until now he'd simply assumed that Miriam long ago had . . . why? We all live alone, Hal thought, beyond comprehension alone within whatever secrets we cannot forget. Years of talk, so much secret. This small plastic in my hand and our words—they mirror some thoughts if we dare to speak a few out loud—our words pass each other somewhere, like spirits flung from space satellites and there was a time when I was so happy to simply believe heaven was up on high, Jesus seated at God's right hand singing "in the sky, Lord, in the sky," where the circle would forever be unbroken in that better land awaitin' and all the dead who had been saved from everlasting hell by accepting Jesus Christ as their personal Saviour and Lord forever and ever were with him watching me. And I was so scared at them seeing me every single minute and also so happy at never ever being alone, not even on the Wapiti road allowance walking home in the dark and Deacon Block's farm dogs came roaring out of the black trees at their corner but they knew me instantly and I could pat them on the head, especially Felix jumping so huge and black, his long tongue almost knocked me over there in the wagon track soft as dust.

"Dad?"

"I'm here."

"At the phone in the kitchen . . . did you bring them up, the diaries?"

"I'm in the basement," and then, before he thought, "You do know about Ailsa."

"Yes," Miriam said quickly. Then, "Is there much about her?"

"Enough."

After some time she said, "I will read them."

Hal's mind leaped sideways, 'No rush, it's only twenty-five years,' but luckily that stuck in his throat. He offered, more sensibly,

"He expected us to read them. Once he writes 'Hi' on a blank date that August—like he's greeting a reader, and other times he seems really angry, 'Quit reading this trying to find clues who I am!' But . . . really they're . . . his words, to us. "

"He wanted us to read them."

"Yes."

"Yes," Miriam said, barely audible. "He could have destroyed them."

"Who knows what all he destroyed, he planned every-thing so . . . but this he didn't destroy, no."

"All the papers he left, I will."

"Okay," Hal said, steady again. He took a long breath, but Miriam was silent. "So-o," he said finally. "Three to one, what did you say: Why believe Luke?"

"Oh . . . I remember I was surprised, then. Gabe never talked Bible with me, not really, not after his year in Bible College. That's probably why I remember, it's so different."

"From your usual Edmonton talk?"

"Yes . . . that last August he was so . . . silent . . . heavy . . . but sometimes he seemed really happy too and we'd get into it like we used to in college when I'd go visit him in his room full of books and posters, and his guitar he was always strumming—"

"I know I know, that beautiful picture Yo took of you together stretched out on his dorm bed and laughing—"

"Yes! Like that! In college, like we all always argued at home around the supper table, and we got into the textual arguments again about the Gospels, the 'oral witness' argument, and the 'date of composition' problem."

"That they were written long after, from stories people told about Jesus?"

"Yeah, at least thirty, fifty years after he died, but Gabe said Luke has that careful introduction about writing an 'orderly account from eyewitnesses,' like a classic Greek historian's investigation. And all four Gospels do agree, there were two thieves—"

"But only Luke says one supported Jesus, he didn't revile him."

"Yes." ˙

"So what did Gabe think?"

"I'd never noticed the Gospels there were different— Gabe asked the question."

"Why, do you think?"

"I don't know. I've thought about it . . . I don't know."

"Of course you don't, but what do you think?"

Miriam's laugh, "Dad! You old prof!"

"No no, I'm trying to be a *histor*, a wise Greek who gathers stories—"

"Like Luke? Are you gathering stories about Gabriel? To write down?"

"No . . . yes . . . not write. Think. Stories, so I can think his life, over. I haven't talked to anyone for so long about him, just you now—" Dennis's phone call flashed across his mind, but no, leave that for the moment—"nothing about him for so long, and now you just told me a story I've never heard! Twenty-five years after. Look, all of a sudden I want to know his stories, for myself . . . those he left us, to think . . ."

But Miriam's continued silence pressured him into more: "His written words are often so much the same, just a movie name, or a bit of music, or book read—but more his one-track obsessions too, and anger, rage, it's despair, endless, obsessive despair."

"About Ailsa."

She had said it, so he could respond.

"All the way through, yes, that's the—that's one big one. At least whenever he wrote—but he had so much other life, I know that! There are glimpses of it—and I remember the last summer how often he came home, after NFT he had no steady job but then he got Unemployment Insurance and he was looking for jobs, he applied—jobs were really tough in '85, but there was a picture-framing job he thought—and he'd come for supper and Yo and he and I we talked, and I remember he yelled a lot, out of the blue, anything, I can't remember exactly why—but we talked and he had quite a few friends, not church much but NFT and university and you and Leo came back from Ecuador and we were planning your wedding at the cabin, he too, and he always saw his philosophy friend Oleg . . ."

"But he writes about Ailsa?"

"Yes. One strand, all the way through, of his sadness *is* always Ailsa, but at the end, in the last two months it seems like it's not much her anymore either, he doesn't even write the goddamn initial of her name, he's just one black hole of anger and overwhelming despair!"

Into his burst of rage Miriam spoke quietly, "There was more, to his life, lots more, but he could live that part out with us. The writing was secret. He was always so controlled, polite, but it was often a 'don't bother me' polite that—"

"Evasion—"

"Yeah, but more secrets, you know, we all have them! Maybe Gabe, alone with that notebook, then he could write the stuff he never could say, to anyone. His depression."

"I hate that word, it's so fucking small!"

"Yeah. Like 'ash' is so fucking small for the tree outside your window."

Her sudden curse echoing his shattered his rage.

"I'm sorry."

After a time she said, "Listen, we did discuss the two thieves, Gabe and I, ideas flying all over—about the oral eyewitness stories written down years later, memories changing as you keep telling them to different people—"

"That's why I'm reading what he wrote, what he's thinking that minute he wrote it . . ."

"Yeah, exactly, and how some people at the crucifixion would have heard just voices yelling from the two crosses, in horrible pain or cursing, who could understand what—and how loud was it? Doctors say when you're crucified you have terrible difficulty breathing, hanging like that you can only breathe at the top of your lungs and you actually choke to death, on air you can't get out—"

"So who knows how loud or clear they were yelling at each other?"

"Sure. Some heard reviling, some rebuttal, prayer, and then someone heard and understood Jesus's really quiet promise—all four versions could have eyewitnesses."

Eyewitnesses! He had seen the Orange Downfill. He should tell—no, the weight for Miriam now, how could he confess to her the disaster he had started: she could do nothing from Vancouver and he who could had done nothing—he flipped into facetiousness:

"Eyewitness . . . the Bible is 'The Word of God,' every syllable true!"

And Miriam did laugh a little at the old joke. "I know, especially in English translation—no, only in holy Luther, right? Well, they could all be true, four little bits of The Big True. As they say, God only knows . . . four bits of 'true' isn't so bad."

Only one flitting pass of orange is worse.

"Dad? There is something wrong."

"I . . . tell me, what did Gabe say about Luke. You remember?"

"He liked the second thief in Luke, he liked him."

"Not 'If you're God's Son, you get us off here'?"

"No no, the other one."

"Why?"

"I don't know why! I can't actually remember, exactly, what he said. I've thought about that so often, and maybe . . . maybe I just want him . . ."

Hal said it: "'Jesus, remember me.'"

Perhaps Miriam was crying. Hal could never quite tell, on the telephone; she had practiced that as a teenager, he had sometimes noticed the phone at her ear and tears running down her cheeks but her voice steady, steady—but he could hear it, yes. He was tormenting his only daughter.

"Mir, forgive me. I'm being stupid, too much . . . stuff here . . . look, if I can find Gabe's Bible, I haven't yet, maybe he marked that story—sweetheart, it's marvellous you told me this, and I'm sorry. Please."

"You could come to Vancouver, Dad, a few days? Away from so long alone."

"Well . . ."

"You promise but don't come, Leo was saying just yesterday. Not since Mom. It's so good to talk but there's a lot we never say on the phone. And we haven't remembered this together."

"Never dared," he said, evading again.

"That's the word, 'dare.' If we sat face to face and deliberately . . ."

"It's been long."

"Yes. Twenty-five years long enough."

"What about Denn?"

"With him too, of course, but even just us two starting with Gabe, starting—and Leo. He has memories too, a lot."

"I will come," Hal said quickly, momentarily meaning it and feeling good. "Soon, real soon. I'll call in two days, this time, at most three. I promise."

"I want to tell you," Miriam said, "I pray that, every night."

Every life is lived in secret. "'Jesus, remember me.'"

"Yes."

"Pray it for me too?"

"I will. Sorry to talk so late—goodnight, beloved Dad."

"Goodnight, darling daughter."

Dial tone. *Kyrie. Kyrie eleison.*

Nearly midnight of an unending day. But he had to search for it, he could not think to stop, not the first GABRIEL box, not the second, the third box on the shelf, below bundles of cards and sympathy letters, below some photocopied pages there lay the blue Holy Bible, Revised Standard Version.

Hal did not remember how unbelievably used it looked. The blue cloth cover a maze of grey rubbing tracks, every edge worn down and open, raw to the glued press of tan cardboard, every inch of both front and back covers, their corners worn round, blue cloth curling back bare off the worn cardboard. And the spines double-taped in wide black binding tape, both the outside spines and the inside line of the front flyleaf; the flyleaf where small Gabe had practiced writing his full name in cursive, twice, as if taking full possession above the

TO: Gabriel Wiens, from his mother and father, Jan. 28, 1968

His seventh birthday, already half through Grade 2 . . . Seventeen-and-a-half years of reading, wearing the cover raw, down into layered, separating cardboard. The stack of pale-blue-edged pages soft as old cloth.

And dog-eared, tiny tears from much fingering, colour pictures—"Jerusalem from Mt. of Olives," "In The Wilderness"—and many pencil marks as he riffled; a grey square around 1 Samuel 3: "Now the boy Samuel was ministering . . ."; Jeremiah 10: "They are both stupid and . . ." not heavy marks, brief underlines, dozens of them; Habakkuk 3: "The mountains saw thee, and writhed . . ."; and then a thick pencil line under Matthew 4: "Then Jesus was led up by the Spirit into the wilderness to be tempted by the devil. And he"—no Luke, the thief on the cross, Luke—he was riffling swiftly, the pages years ago fingered so soft they still fell open quick and flat: chapter 23, verse . . . 39: "One of the criminals who were hanged railed at him . . .";

But there was not a pencil nor pen mark, not anywhere in the entire paragraph. Not anywhere on the two crowded pages, nothing—but then he saw something . . . possibly . . . in verse 42. He lifted the book, angled it up at the ceiling light . . . there. A faint, almost invisible pencil stroke between two small words:

And he / said, "Jesus, remember me when you come in your kingly power."

Remember me. He. Said. On the cross.

And then Hal noticed: the paperclipped pages under which Gabriel's blue Bible had been lying. The pages were covered with Hal's own handwriting. From that unbearable September, scribbled tight, words twisted: photocopied sheets of Hal's personal 1985 Daily Appointments book.

Photocopied? He had never . . . had Yo made them? Had she read his cryptic notations, and then copied and deliberately placed them in Gabriel's boxes as well? Hal knew he never—who else could have? Here they were: all his 1985 diary words. O Yo, stone facts.

Monday September 9
awoke 2:30 a.m., read diaries, papers till 6 when Yo woke Oh why didn't I see—clothes for coffin / funer. arrangements and cremat. details / plan funeral   talked of obit—started working on it—all relatives both sides arrive, Yo's mom, all my bro.+ sist. even ancient David. Talk/ talk/people everywhere—I'm trying to quote my beloved son: he has left/given me too much to condense: make it clean, true / some grace, grace / first U Eng Lit class: evening, George will go, cancel

Tuesday September 10
His frozen face   hands   only the coffin body suit / shirt / tie   white satin lid open in lobby, shut in church—some grace for him at funeral. Ps. 51—also Allegri's *Miserere Mei*, 3 min. on intercom / choir: Children of . . . / obit just possible to hear Herbert read / after in church hall a wash of sorrow: who was I crying with? Church, university, business, people of a lifetime. Yo beside me but soon

separated: hundreds crying, everyone crying with/for/ over Clara dreamed G dead the night before he was found Wanda's praying hand on my head   Mike's contorted face Joan holding and holding me, "He was so beautiful when he was vulnerable" you should know—seemed hrs.   and evening useless talk, house full of bro. and sis. and sudden crying and

Wednesday September 11

Drove to crematorium with Herbert: "you're not going there alone" 9 a.m. Same closed coffin on dolly / last frozen look, then screwed tight. Older man explained calcination—6 hrs. at 1800 degrees, flames in oven like Dachau we saw '76 / he shoved it in on rollers, clamped door, pulled switch, roar / in parking lot we watched black smoke from chimney boil into blue sky / does hell smoke / all relatives except Yo's mom left: really tough for them too how to behave, how (not) to think where (they think) he certainly is now. After funeral last night one explosion, me at bro David's old preacher-death plat- itudes, "Shut up, you understand nothing, not one god- damn thing!" Walked ravine with Yo / worried when Miriam didn't come back for hours / Whitemud Ravine alone. Drove Denn to HSch today noon, got him p.m.

Thursday, September 12

Yo took her mom with car to airport, me Denn in pickup to HSch, then to U—tried to work for 2 hrs but couldn't, had to walk home 1 1/2 hrs. Talked with Yo   got pickup from U she drove it   3:30 to downtown chapel, small container of "remains" + to fun. home for clothes G wore in pickup. Drove car to Aspen cabin / walked where he parked   snow gone, began to rain, small birch all around, close, mud tracks where Dave plowed out. Made a circle in cabin   Yo, Dennis, Ailsa, Colin, Grant, Miriam, Leo, Rick and Lorrine, Holda and Dave, Big Ed, Joan, me / little Rick crying, grdma. Holda carried him / couldn't sing but some talk of happy Gabe, how he worked, built so much of cabin, read "Einsamkeit" and "Beatitudes"   Dave and Yo prayed all walked down path into valley. Cold rain, Yo holding jar, I holding onto her. Chunky ash calcified: all took turns, poured them in rapids below beaver dam / some sank grey as gravel, some drifted away toward N Sask River, ocean. Back to Edm. / at Grant and Joan's / listened to Bach / what? Wake up soon, horrible dream   who said that

Friday September 13
Drove Denn to HSch, then univ, tried to work on lectures, George came, then Shirley, always with her own long depression   such good colleagues, only a few dare come and talk, most avoid you in the hall.   BK phoned from Calgary, he's so caring, understands so well tho nothing actually helps   in class mostly useless   wrote snatches of things about G's death   try to think clear and logical, why   there is far too much too far beyond thinking / immoveable

Saturday September 14
Apparently Dave went to Aspen Creek, all day alone / we have to get rid of pickup, can't stand being in it, seeing

that canopy parked by our house. To G's neat apt. all his familiar stuff, lifetime of gifts   On neat bed, quilt-blanket Grandma sewed him   cutlery so careful in drawers, kitchen—o—Fred helps carry furniture out to pickup, tells Yo it's okay, he'll clean up, he's already moved out, not staying there / cried / hauled away / reading more G papers—too many   Evening with Yo/Denn to Jubilee Aud. Tickets to Mendelsohn's *Elijah* / intermission and there's John in lobby crowd, his young wife brutal cancer, curled tight in stomach "like a baby" he says making a fist, maybe one more week   beauty of music rips you apart, especially Widow's dead son / If with all your heart ye truly seek / Then, then shall the righteous shine as the sun

Sunday September 15
To church, no talk, away quick. p.m. walk river valley woods along NSask. with Joan and Grant and kids   beautiful fall colours, turning cold in sunlight   Dennis and Colin clowning, yelling a bit on the river path, Ailsa too. Yo nor I can look at her   never she at us   what does she think   can she ever have a clue   please God never

Monday September 16
Worked, managed one lit class, students silent. TC came to office, PhD student, talked about death of her baby—she's all alone. p.m. went with Yo looked at a silver caravan, almost made a deal. Dave left work, came to U, we walked bush trail down, sat on edge of NSask, watched water. Dave said: About time for the ashes. We're all exhausted.

Three areas of G's life: images/music/words. And all the love he gave and got—nothing enough to hold him   kept him less than empty

Tuesday September 17
Boxes of letters, cards, more letters in mail, at home and U. So easy to open, such good people, good   Got pickup regist. from RCMP and traded it + loan from bank for caravan   Evening with Miriam and Leo   wedding impossible this weekend but nothing will ever change, why wait? So next week Sat. 28. Mir looks pale as a spirit / talked into morning   told/retold all we all saw but didn't see, why couldn't—had we?

(3 days blank)

Saturday September 21
Wedding/Mir & Leo   NO
   To Aspen Creek   new caravan drives silent as a ghost yellow fall leaves falling in small rain   walked woods, dug up potatoes, carrots by myself. The everlasting life of relentless earth forever there. Got pickup bedding from town RCMP— very bad (both) that evening / all boxes, furniture stacked in home garage now, all his "stuff" he collected, made, loved

Sunday September 22
(blank)

Monday September 23
Dreadful day   a bit of work routine

(4 days blank)

Saturday September 28 across Sunday September 29
A.m. arrivals, p.m. <u>Wedding at Aspen Creek</u> lovely, in
semi-circles of (funeral) friends, lovely music, loving
words. All poplars golden now in brilliant sunlight.
Miriam's ethereal beauty   Leo's Latino band music so
lifting heartbeat ceremony (Herbert has to do it all, life,
death) and pictures and eating. Gabe could have enjoyed
some of it. Bits of laughter   sudden hidden weeping

Words crammed together, or blank gaps. 1985 endured.
But photocopies do end.

Abruptly Hal's overwhelming basement concentration
split, exhaustion slugged him. He sagged among the boxes,
the pages fell, but he found himself still clutching Gabriel's
black-taped blue Bible and his hands opened it instinctively,
his mother said the Bible always has a verse gift from
God—and in the middle you're sure to hit either Isaiah or
Jeremiah—there it was, Lamentations 3—with two verses
on facing pages underlined so heavily not even his burning
eyes could miss them:

> The Lord is good to those who wait for him,
>   to the soul that seeks him.

O yeah.
And again:

Thou hast seen the wrong done to me, O God;
　　　judge thou my cause.

Judge, O judge . . . always the God Almighty judge.

　And then, in mercy, the indelible prayer of his childhood came to him, singing on the memory of sweet Yo's midnight piano:

> *Muede bin ich, geh zu Ruh,*
> 　Tired am I, go to rest,
> *Schliesse meine Aueglein zu;*
> 　Close my little eyes;
> *Vater, moeg das Auge dein*
> 　Father, may your eye
> *Ueber meinem Bette sein.*
> 　Watch over my bed.

Sunrise burned in the slats of his living room windows. Staggering a little Hal reached his front door, twisted the bolt lock and pulled the door open: the *Edmonton Journal* lay as usual on the doormat and, holding onto the door grip, he stooped carefully—a khaki parka hood beside the newspaper. And a human body. Stretched out the length of the porch to the edge of the steps; on its left side, knees slightly bent and booted feet—a hole worn open in one toe—boots stacked neatly right on left. No head visible, hood pulled over tight, fur edge worn to fruzz and khaki gleaming with grime, sleeves crumpled empty—no arms?—they bulged the parka at the stomach. Was he breathing?

Never before. Not in twenty-three years.

The body moved. Twisted over onto its back and the jean legs kicked out, the hood opened to half a bristly face: coarse hair, black but trimmed, and tan skin, a thin bent nose with its tip still hidden in stubby fur. The eye was shut. A car swished by on the street; the sunlight was bright as ice on the strip of skin between parka and jeans, the narrow track of hair above the navel.

Hal lifted the newspaper and closed the door softly; turned the bolt. The house hummed with freshness, warmth. Never before.

His night on the basement floor dazed him, his body as saturated as aching stone. What is to be done?

He dropped the paper on the couch and swayed across the room between furniture, grabbed for the railing to hoist himself up the stairs, steady, swing the right arm in rhythm. Inside the second floor closet, below the bedding shelves he found the box, and inside it the Hudson's Bay point blanket Gabriel had bought the first winter he worked and often slept alone in the Aspen Creek cabin. Canadian boreal forest, he said, you sleep under HBC wool. Later, Yo could not let it go. Finally she and Hal slept together under it every winter, until her heels grew too tender for its weight: the full four-point blanket, white with four broad stripes of indigo, yellow, red, green, queen size thick and heavy. Brought from England to trade for fur since 1799. He felt the wool against his bristly face as he walked step by careful step back down into the living room; for a moment he could hug this comfort tight.

The weight Plains Cree Chief Big Bear felt hanging over his body when they forced him to sit on a stool with his ankles chained, surrounded him with four policemen and took his picture. Prince Albert, North-West Territories: 491 river miles down the North Saskatchewan from Edmonton. July 4, 1885.

He unlocked the front door again and pulled it open.

The man lay breathing in the crisp, ironic sunlight. His midriff still bare. Hal spread the heavy blanket gently over

him, carefully covered his boots. The point blanket drap-
ing Big Bear had only one stripe. What colour had it been?
The man's legs twitched, but his eye did not open.

Here's the archives' photo, Gabe said. Red for sure.

That afternoon Hal and Owl hunted the Strathcona, Mill
Creek and Cloverdale banks of the North Saskatchewan
River valley. All the places Owl knew, and some they were
told about by people they met, and some they discovered
together. They began with the high arch of stones layered on
the ground beneath the concrete Saskatchewan Drive bridge
across 106A Street ravine. The stones were too massive to
move by hand, but they found shapes among them where
people had nested high up beneath the roadbed, behind the
concrete arches, crumpled cardboard in cradles of rocks as it
seemed levered into hollows for human shapes to curl or
stretch out. Also discarded grocery carts, knapsacks and torn
garbage bags and bright ripped polyester jackets, gnawed rib
and chicken bones. It was possible a couple, or a tiny colony,
of people had lived there dry and close under the ceaseless
traffic before winter, though not yet after.

Hal was breathing hard, all this walking, climbing, scram-
bling through snow patches with the air snipping cold in
his nostrils. Such a beautiful spring day; so empty. A winding strip of boreal forest through the centre of his city;
naked of any leaf. He had walked the manicured park
paths so often, but this wildness, he realized, he had never
truly seen; living high on the riverbanks, he had always,
simply, looked over it.

A long valley ridge of snowy spruce and wind-shattered brush; farther below them they could see the disintegrating gape of Queen Elizabeth Pool through masses of bare trees standing, trees leaning and smashed against each other. And suddenly, on the ridge, they came upon a grey plastic mound. A valley resident lay inside between layers of canvas and sleeping bags and blankets, grizzlied and alert, a pot steamed on the three-stone firepit just inside his shelter. He never lived under bridges, he said, snow's nothing you gotta stay clear of that, too much noise under streets, bridges shiver in traffic you can't sleep, sleep is the last thing and the best thing and only thing you got, you feel them bridges sing at night from cars running them all day long, stay away from bridges. Okay, orange. Why should he tell them anything anyway?

Owl said mildly, "Because we're looking."

"So look. It's no shit to me."

"*Hiy hiy, keyam.*"

Walking the narrow track of melting snow in the draw below the ridge, Hal had not recognized a possible human shelter among the grey brush. Only if you knew what you were looking at, like Owl.

They climbed up stairs to 99th Street and ordered coffee in a shop they had never entered together. They rested at a table along the front window. On the sidewalk outside was the usual city garbage can, and a broad-shouldered man in a thin blue jacket bent there, looking into it. He reached far down, his left hand came up with a paper cup, his body straightened, he tilted his head back and poured the contents into his mouth. Hal could see his bristly

Adam's apple move. The man dropped the cup back into the can, but in the same motion bent down even farther, and after a moment his hand came up holding a half-eaten apple. No, Hal thought, not—the gnawed edges of the apple were rank brown. The man's right hand took the apple between its thumb and forefinger, in his left hand a knife appeared, a long blade flicked and he began to chip away brown bits, they fell into the gaping can, the man turning the apple and paying no attention to the pedestrians staring at his quick skill. When the apple was trimmed to white, he lifted it to his mouth and began to eat, bite by thoughtful bite. He ate it down to the thinnest core.

Through the window Hal and Owl watched him together, drinking their coffee.

~

The point blanket, carefully folded to reveal its stripes, lay beside the doormat on the front porch. Hal shoved his arms under and lifted it to his face. He thought he smelled wood smoke. He raised his head, sniffed—cars swishing past all day on 104th Street—he bent to the blanket again. Perhaps.

No Miriam or Dennis numbers on the phone; but other messages:

"Hey Hal, it's John, missed you at Coffee and Conversation yesterday. Hope the Papaschase land-steal talk last week—or the full moon, ha!—wasn't too much for you! Call when you can or—"

Work on your Sunday sermon, John.

Ben's voice: "I got a genealogy for that Isaak Wiens, third cousin twice removed but there's a *Rundschau* entry I can't read, of course, when will you—"

Maybe never—bumble it out with your computer translator.

"Hal . . . Al at Double Cup, you're where? Becca says she hasn't seen you in four—"

Becca we agreed, don't lie.

Nothing police yet, good! so forget it, leave it all, especially phone, computer, e-mail—in what was life now there was always maybe later, sometime—he poked the speaker off. Tired. Exhausted actually. But good exhausted, the sharp air of valley walking, the good body ache and right hip no worse than usual and he felt no need for food, already eating forever for seventy-five years, who needs it? He poured a glass of cherry juice, drank it slowly and beneath his feet he felt the basement, waiting. All day it had sifted through his mind, always there, even when he was concentrating on some rotten log not to stumble over the basement like an irrepressible song reeled through his head, he had not been able to shake it, tramp it into the snow-spongy mud, discard it in any of the numberless city garbage cans. So . . . okay . . . only skim, touch here, there, just enough to sleep deep tonight, all that back and leg work, arms swinging, just skim . . .

GABE'S SPIRAL NOTEBOOK (1), *the first page*

Oct/81   *Great Expectations* "Mrs. Joe is a very clean house . . .

Skip.

June / 82   W. L. Morton cliché "The American Fathers . . ."

No.

Nov 11 / 82   Went to see *Mephisto*, all sound seems
dubbed . . .

No.

"*Tess*   Feb 15 / 83 - moving and complex tragedy of one of
the most delightful and loveable heroines in all literature . . .
    Powerful music: Gregorio Allegri's *Miserere* . . ."

That's where that soul-wrenching requiem began? And
suddenly there folded in the notebook, between 1983 pages,
a single sheet written in Yo's distinctive angles:

Jan 1, 1977

Dear Mom + Dad,

If you ever read this its because
I never woke up this morning and because
I never wanted to. It's not your fault, you
guys were great giving me all that stuff,
"material goods." But in my case, I'm in
love with a girl I'll never get too meet, just
read about. She means everything to me
but I'll never get to touch her, kiss her,

talk to her. And also because my life is a
total waste, you guys have a right
to get mad at me like you do so this way I'll end
all my problems, my very large problems.
Don't let Dennis turn out like me, he's
really a great kid, and Miriam's wonderful too.
She goes good with life, I don't.
So good by, hopefully . . . maybe some
day we'll meet in heaven . . . some of us.

Love, Gabriel Wiens

New Year's Day 1977. Hal scrabbled to remember: "total waste" on the verge of sixteen years of—that Romanian gymnast Comaneci . . . Nadia, the Montreal '76 Summer Olympics. Born the same year as Gabriel: on the TV screen her perfect child figure dancing light as fire on the high beam and the gym floor; perfect 10s no one had ever scored before, and Gabriel's staring fascination that neither Yo nor he grasped—not even after the letter. Yo found it, and together, as always with each of the kids, they asked Gabe about it—the kitchen in Riverbend, the three of them around the table where they all ate, every day, and Gabriel yelled at them for snooping—but it was addressed to them!—and stamped upstairs to his room and tore it up and flushed the shreds down the toilet. But Yo had already copied it just in case—and on the other side too:

Jan 3, 1977

Dear Mom + Dad,

You guys call me a brat and
yet don't even know what I'm going through.
And I'll never talk to you about it because
I can't. I just wish I could talk to her. Right
now the only person I can talk too is god but
he does not seem to be listening or he just does
not care, he can be anything / too me he's deaf

Love Gabe

"Love Gabe." Yes. And Yo so deeply disturbed she copied . . . but Hal—the exact memory of his flippant words
suddenly stabbed him—"Ach, puppy love"—puppy . . . o
forgive me—on the brink of sixteen talking "too deaf
god." Too deaf indeed.

SPIRAL NOTEBOOK (1): *January 28, 1983*

"We want to touch, and a culture that has placed a 'taboo
on tenderness' leaves us stroking our dogs and cats . . . we
are starved for the laying on of hands."

Feb. 18, 1983

Interesting to note the types of movies I have seen in
the recent past. One type I have obviously pursued is
the little girl film, *Cat People*, then *Christiane F.* and lastly
Beau Pere. They all have blatant, exploitative parts,
however there is much more that I like, not just the
child-woman parts, it's the dream-like quality, the

camera moves in a dreamy-drugged atmosphere, so lyrical, beautiful

To dream, yes . . .

Sunday, Feb. 27, 1983
Lunch at church. Sat beside joking Grant, Ailsa off at the kid's table (Denn, Colin, Joanne etc), sad eyes that don't meet mine when I dare glance . . .

Ailsa at eleven. Slender as a tiny Romanian gymnast.

March 13, 1983
How can one go from complete happiness to complete despair in less than 8 hours. Perhaps because neither moment is "complete"—at church I saw A watch Mir put her purse around my neck, then hand me her books so she (Mir) could put her coat on. I held the books like girls do, folded tight against my chest. A was watching me and laughed; I was putting on a show for her, the closest I can get—One should not have any great expectations about life—esp. possible romantic love. Perhaps I am just reveling in my despair; it is something I love and hate at the same time.

If you are reading this, which no one but myself should be, forgive me. We are all just human and even my confessions are not all that true. Can anyone be objective when feelings are so

Even your private written "confessions are not all that true"?

March 21, 1983
> The joy I had at Aspen Creek at Christmas and New
> Year's did not last . . . The only thing that lasts is the
> long sleep. I weep
>   If this book just sits and no one knows it exists, it does
> not matter what I've written

O, it does matter. Particularly because you did not destroy it: you left it for us to read.

July 3, 1983
> World Universiade, Gymnastics, here at UofA. Nadia C.
> was back in Canada, so close I could have walked up and
> spoken to her! She's coach of the Romanian team, sitting
> there on their bench. She looked exactly the same. I felt
> rather indifferent, considering that during Montreal
> Olympics 1976 I developed an enormous crush, in fact it
> was the first one to overtake me. Despite her, this time
> gymnastics was humdrum, until I discovered a CCCP,
> #169, Elena Veselova. The smallest Soviet, always off by
> herself, alone, always looking sad. Took pictures, close
> with zoom. To do all that her perfect body must feel hard
> as   just a little girl chewing her fingernails

No.

July 18, 1983

I've been looking at pictures of myself from grade 3 or 4, I've noticed that I am a cute little kid. For a few years then, just after the crew cut, just before the awkward adolescent years I looked really cute. Then I noticed I had the same kinds of feelings towards this "Gabriel" that I have towards young girls. I think if I had met me when I was that age I would have liked myself.

However he is me. Can it be that these girls are just extensions of myself (ie. my love for myself), or rather a love for the forever unattainable / changeable of what once was . . . what really makes up a person's soul . . . what?

August 20, 1983

Looking at this notebook I get the impression that I am not getting anywhere. In my next book—I should just stop with this one, start again, clean—in my next notebook I should write more openly . . . get into a routine of writing, 15 minutes every day is certainly enough to tell what little I have to say

It is a quarter after 2 in the morning and I cannot sleep. I'm ridiculous, the silly desires that occupy my mind are such trivial stuff. I know from years past all things will pass, even slender little A (my feeling for) will go. I wish I could arrive someplace really real but looking at my past, I will never get anywhere, can't run anywhere   what to do   I can't even have the patience to write down my   too bad for the reader

Gabriel: no more. I need sleep, tomorrow Owl will pull me even farther into the forest ravines towards the University, I'll be limping by then, the High Level Bridge, the unending river—and here's a folded letter.

The one from Kathleen, October 29, 1985. Impossible to forget . . . impossible.

Dear Hal and Yo—

Bob told me that one of your kids had died + I wanted to let you know that I'm thinking of you. It's always hard to deal with the death of someone close, and suicide is a form of death that leaves a lot of guilt behind. People that I know have died that way, although never close friends, and one always wonders what could have been changed or done differently. I don't know if my brother ever told you—he wouldn't— but I tried to kill myself when I was 24, and I've been suicidal since then once, this past year. My experience is that it's a very internalized kind of solution to what seems like an unbreakable continuum. In my case a lot of my feelings had to do with anger and power, but by the time I was actually planning what I was going to do, I was so far inside my self that I really don't think anything or anyone outside me would have made much difference. The second time, this year (it seems decades ago), I recognized what was going on + I could take steps to deal with it, but I wouldn't have had that recognition without the first experience. What I think I'm trying to say is that once that solution becomes attractive, it's hard to get out from under it, even if you love your family + your friends, and your son may have just not had the experience to handle it, to resist the attraction. My brother felt that to choose your country place could have been an expression of anger towards you, but I don't think so. I think it was a choice of security and reassurance, for support in the face of a major unknown, an experience that was still really frightening even once chosen and fixated on.

Oh, grief and regret are a hard, slow process always. Please take care of yourselves, and take heart: don't lose that wonderful warmth I felt in your home the one time I was there. This is an awkward letter, because I don't really know you well, and tragedy is so difficult to approach in our culture. And mourning. All people can say is time will help you get over it—please, I'm not trying to say that!—but please accept my best wishes, my hope for good in the future.

—*Kathleen*

You met us once, Kathleen, and such a letter. Blessed are you, wherever you may be.

And my beloved son: you left your Spiral Notebook (1) a third blank, and started Spiral Notebook (2) after you stopped your studies at the University of Alberta. But the school's motto, *Quaecumque Vera*: "Whatsoever things are true," remained there on the cover. Did the second notebook move help you to get somewhere "truer"?

SPIRAL NOTEBOOK (2): *August 21, 1983*

Aspen: creek, running into North Sask. River west of
Edm;

a translation of the Cree name for the tree, wapus
ahtik: whiteskin (Tyrrell)

Flip, flip to the middle.

January 1, 1984

New Year's eve/day party at cabin: A has grown.
Changed. She is no longer the silent little girl tagging
after D & C, the child who will not sing after one false
start. At the cabin she stated frankly, catching my eye for
a second in the crowd, 'Why not, be different!' Yes, she is.
We all change. Even memories

one generation passes away and another generation comes

but the earth abides forever

Good. Flip.

Friday March 16, 1984

it is 12:30 in the morning, waste time reading my notes
over the years till my laundry is finished in spin cycle.
My feelings go back a long way . . . not very coherent . . .
my feelings so often dictate what little I do. I want to
have reason before passion as my motto, and yet how
can I help it, I see her lovely face and I'm gone   awww
Laundry rough spin in the middle of the empty night.

Next page.

April 14, 1984

> carol: - a song of joy or mirth
>> - a popular song or ballad of religious
>> joy
>> - to sing, esp. in a joyful manner—

> Whom then will you cry to, heart?
>> Your path more and more lonely
> dragging on toward the future,
>> toward what is already lost

Flip.

June 16, 1984

I've had one beer too many. Denn and parents are touring
Europe beyond The Wall and I sit alone in our family
house. It's not that it's so bad; just I want to be happy, but
for some reason I can't. Anything that happens I feel as
loss. My sole success is nothing. Digging my own hole. If
only I could cover myself up . . .

Then, as a ghostly shadow, haunt that 50s house I
know like the inside of my hand, into the entrance, up
the stairs and into the doorless kitchen with all the
cupboard plates and cups exposed into the living room
I see out as they see in into the bedroom where I set up
the bed frame and turn each bolt tight with a wrench,
there is a cut in the headboard and I point at it with my
screwdriver and she nods, This is the bed I've slept in

all my life, and I carry the floppy mattress in past the
dresser with the Garfield bank and brushes and everything already neatly arranged on it, such a lovely thing
to struggle with and lay it down for her into the base
of the bed beside the chair which holds the person
holding the MJ poster, the person whose slender body
will lie asleep on this mattress I lay down for many
more . . .

What can you do with beauty. You can look it in the
eye. What can you do in the void.   what does it
matter what moves me here, there, anywhere. I can't
even say something, clumsy writer that I am. What is
there to say, leave alone write. Well, I guess that's it
then   Period.

Flip.

July 22, 1984
"why would I want to phone you"

These words are written in your Daily Planner 1984 as well;
same day. Words Ailsa said to you that Sunday? Not you as
a "ghostly shadow," it must have been to physical you, at
church, when you'd been alone at home for two weeks, the
Sunday before the Tuesday you took a taxi to Edmonton
International Airport and flew to Amsterdam. What did
you say to her, in church? Anything? And on that long flight
through night into morning, alone with several hundred
strangers, did you anticipate the despair?—the joy?—of
that Germany meeting our two families had so carefully

planned; where we would be together for a few days without amiable Miriam to divert issues—meet without any
possible distraction or security or evasion of home or
church? No wonder terror struck you in Frankfurt. No
wonder Ailsa's hand reaching for yours crashed you.

Memory like a crab clawing itself out; everything we
did to each other. Over years.

Loving Lord Jesus Christ, have pity on us poor sinners.

You were eighteen, leaning over me, the yellow
chainsaw in my hands, the snarling cutter-bar
Your left arm was pushing the notched aspen to drop
it exactly right. Slowly the whiteskin leaned, leaned
down the July air into a green crash no one heard as
I pulled back and sensed a touch, just barely a steel touch
on flesh, the tanned skin below your left elbow
opened and you made no sound as I screamed

Every contact, for the lover, raises

the question of an answer:

the skin is asked to reply.

In the back seat of the car roaring over gravel we held
each other, your head against my shoulder hard, then
in my lap. I would not let the knotted handkerchief
go, not too tight, not too loose, the right side
of your head on my thigh, the coiled skin of your ear
your tangled hair. The town doctor already waited
in the entrance and you disappeared

I cannot continue to be in love
with an image. Is it that I want to be
someplace that doesn't exist?
On the smooth highway back to Edmonton you
talked, you laughed so amazingly complete with
happiness, your sewn and bandaged arm a commitment
between us, a summer of healing to come
On that road I told you about the worn hills
along the Oldman, brittle grass and sky white
as spring skin

> *October 14, 1984: what I want to do is get myself*
> *together for my Oldman River quest, April 28,*
> *1985. There is no physical space in this world*
> *that I seek; is it in the itch of the mind?*

Always places named, dates detailed, every
word bearing its inevitable past exact
as an artichoke unlayered of each edible
leaf down to that ultimate taste at the core
You considered every word large, you held each
quotation in your hands, unleafing, dipping each
in the acerbic relish of your imagination until it burst
on your palate but it was never enough, this wringing
of words, never exact enough for your taste
always at their core they were elusive, yet you
could not trust yourself to abandon them, and your teeth
sank deeper, deeper into your hunger, you would find that
understanding sweetness, gnaw that ultimate hunger, god
damn it you would

I said, I get obsessive about
things. She said, I know
What did she mean
In the unrelenting spin of a pickup motor among
the whiteskin trees above Aspen Creek
which flows into the North Saskatchewan River
which is later joined by the Sturgeon and Dogrump
and Turtle and Battle Rivers and eventually by the
South Saskatchewan, which has already merged with the Red
Deer and the Bow and your Oldman, and grown together they
wash down the Grand Rapids into Lake Winnipeg fed by
the Red and Assiniboine Rivers which joined each other
where you were born, a blur of crocuses waiting for your
opened eyes, and the last great swamps of the Nelson River
and finally vanish forever in muskeg and
the passage of geography and stone and time ebbing
into Hudson Bay, into the frozen Arctic Ocean, the
colour of your ashes an incarnation of the ice
and the darting fish and seals and belugas
and polar bears and gravelly tundra where caribou
hunch to calve every spring and dawn lightens
the limitless ice, its pressure ridges
rammed into immense castellated islands
by every new-moon surge of the sea
as controllable as your relentless
hunger. Breathing in that steady
motor did you see the coming
thunder of angel wings

who when I scream
would hear

Yo is cleaning, so much dust in a very large
area, as always things have to be clean
always such a desperation of dust, and then
two arms are around her, clasping her so tight
the mop clunks to the floor, such a hard body
pressed against her back, such a powerful hug she
feels instantly who it is. I miss you
so much, she says. And again, Why did you
do it? And again, So much. After breathing for
a time she asks, Are you happy now? She lifts
her hands back to his head, his ears, his hair is short
with a touch of curl and remembering she says, Show
me your hands. The elegant fingers slightly double
jointed and longer than the palms, the lines a map
of prairie rivers she has known since the moment
of his birth.

The second long day of their hunt for the Orange Downfill in the ravines and deeper river valley randomly bent, gouged by glacial water through flat, sprawling Edmonton. April had faded into the first day of May. Warmer afternoon light brightened over them as they trudged up an inclined scar scratched into the south valley cliffs. A century ago it might have been the narrow bed for a cable railway to haul people and goods up and down from John Walter's ferry strung on a cable across the river, but now they had to force their way through its brush, the traffic on Walterdale Hill Road roaring down just beyond deadfall and leafless bush on their right. Cars and buses and vans and pickups . . . remorseless pickups.

Hal's body was dragging slower and lower and Owl kept exact pace with him, both saying nothing. But Yo's piano had begun singing in the valley search, and now words settled gently on the notes:

> . . . when peace like a river attendeth my way,
> when sorrow like sea billows roll,
> whatever my lot . . . whatever my . . .

And abruptly they were out of wet, snowy brush and facing the five-road intersection at the height of 109th Street. Inevitable Edmonton skyline: brilliant sunlight in the bluest air to the thin eastern glaze of oil refineries; around them waiting and surging traffic, pavement and massive machines and stink. They crossed right with the light and walked down, so gently easy now, down, the bent sidewalk to the south-east steel massif anchoring the High Level Bridge: fresh black paint, a commuter cyclist smashed there a year ago.

And grey and black straight ahead, one kilometre of concrete and riveted steel stretched over trees towards the running water against the opposite bank: eighty-five metres high. A staggering depth. The tops of the trees far below here, and that distant, it seemed motionless, snake of grey water blank as mindless fear and thick enough to conceal any thing, slip it beyond imagining under the ice of the Arctic Ocean, truly a Yo song for singing ". . . O my soul it is well, it is well . . ." so step up on the bottom rail, lean out, fold your body forward over the top rail. It is well.

Close your eyes. Bend a little farther, longing pulls you soft, steady, your hands clenched together on the rail, feel it grow, lift the left leg, over, and quick as you can the right and both hands open and gone and well with my soul with my soul

Sometime, somehow, the river would give some of you back, somewhere. Nevertheless.

Gabriel's long body was not broken. It had only one scar.

. . . praise the Lord, praise the Lord O my . . .

Hal said without thinking, "Owl. Listen. He walked across here, over this, hundreds of times. He lived and worked over there almost a year, every time he walked to university or home to us he could have . . . but he never."

The stone Legislature Building loomed on the opposite cliff, the skyline city buildings stretched away east like the blunt spikes and stumps of teeth in the river's dinosaur jaw. But Owl stood looking steadily down the valley, across trees and snow-blotched park and river to the spidery construction cranes tearing at three Edmonton power-station chimneys on the river's edge. Century markers being smashed. Perhaps Owl was trying to discern, at their base, the circle of steel memorial beams leaning over the unnamable, the lost graves of vanished Fort Edmonton. Almost two centuries, probably more. In the world over a million people—the population of Edmonton—killed themselves every year, over four hundred in Alberta, many by falling; the Lions' Gate, the Golden Gate Bridges were two favoured high places, any high bridge, there is a kind of ecstasy in high air—who could walk this narrow grey track and not feel—looking down, down into always more unresisting air. The water that will accept, will vanish, every thing.

"Yes," Owl said, so quickly Hal could barely hear him for traffic swishing just beyond the girders.

"Not this. He refused this."

"Yes," Owl said again. Then: "No smashing his body."

"He's not here in the valley."

"The orange jacket isn't here."

"No."

"You have an idea."

"Not the Orange Downfill I saw on the street, no."

From the trees below the Legislature dome a black flame flared up. A great bird riding up, westward on the steady air. Gradually it lifted higher over the river until it reached the rim of the bridge, then it dipped, and was gone.

Hal said, "We don't need to look here any more."

"Yes," Owl said. He too had watched the raven fly.

They stood together tilted against the southeast pillar clotted with round black rivets. New paint. Endless vehicles streamed past them just beyond the steel, a city bus blasting diesel, a convertible already open to the cold light, a blue Chev pickup. It seemed every particular thing on earth was continuously moving: it seemed any one thing must eventually, inevitably, pass by every one given place and inevitably crash. Or stand tilted and inert.

For once no people from the high-rises along Saskatchewan Drive were walking down the 104th Street sidewalks toward Whyte Avenue. Hal could calmly limp the short blocks—cars roaring around the corner from both directions in bursts of acceleration—move as quickly as he could still push his right leg. He waited inside his neighbour's hedge for a brief break in the traffic, then ducked out and under his apple tree and climbed to the porch— vacant—no bills in the mailbox, of course Saturday—and unlocked his front door fast. The furnace sighed warmth in the floor registers. He locked the door and crossed the living room, not looking at the stacked *Journals* he had not read since Wednesday but he drew the wooden folding cover down over the blank TV as he passed it, and turned towards the kitchen.

CLANG! the door chime banged beside his right ear and his calm exploded—but he choked his shriek.

One: the back door—police!

He collapsed onto the bottom of the staircase to give his heart a chance. Thanks be to God he hadn't set the security alarm when he left: now he wouldn't have been able to get to the back door to code it out, the door-window blinds were always tilted slightly open and it was certainly the police, there was no one else it could be. They would be peering inside for movement. He edged his head around the staircase wall: light through the slats of the back living room window, yes, heavy blue shoulders. Two, they were on the back porch. The glint in the alley beyond the garage must be the black nose of their car.

Just go and unlock the door. Yes it was me, here I am, come in.

He looked at his wristwatch, 4:11:36. He could hear a mutter of talk, their heavy boots, but the backdoor chime did not clang again. The three tubes of the chimes hung on the wall before him crumpled on the stair, the longest swaying gently into motionlessness. They knew whom they needed to find, where he was, they even knew he always used his back door. But today he had come in the front—

Suddenly a pounding. The door was metal but the double lock flimsy enough for official fists:

"Mr. Wiens! Mr. Helmut 'Hal' Wiens!"

He waited. If they had a warrant would they break the

door? He'd have time to get out the front—the single chime
clanged! again—double this time and stunningly louder.

Have mercy on me, a sinner.

4:15:12.

The boots trampled hard. The heavy shoulders and
police ears, hats, were moving, down, off the porch,
bending under the crabapple branches, they were so tall,
huge. He craned farther around the wall, a full minute
and the car started to ease away—City of Edmonton
Police. Quickly he walked to the front side window:
through the blind slats he saw the black and white car
hesitate in the alley, then cross the sidewalk and turn
south into the traffic on 104th Street.

There is a crack in everything, that's how the night gets
in. Especially into a conscience.

By the sofa Gabriel's blue worn Bible lay open on the
footstool where he had left it. He had begun to tag the
underlinings, here Deuteronomy 28:25:

> The Lord will cause you to be defeated before your
> enemies; you shall go out one way against them, and
> flee seven ways before them . . . your dead body shall
> be food for all birds of the . . . no one to frighten
> them awa—

The phone shrilled in the kitchen, he was there before the
third ring, almost expecting the door chime to clang again
as he lurched past but it didn't and he saw call display: not
Miriam nor Dennis thank God, John, good John, more
friend than pastor, though that too—

He had to leave the house, quick. He grabbed the Celica keys out of the drawer, the phone stopped as it should at eight rings, and before his voice came on he was reaching to code in "Away" security beside the back door. In the kitchen his eight words ended, the answering machine clicked, and:

"Hey Hal, was at Double Cup Thursday, but you were nowhere, though I waited, and yesterday and again today and Becca says she hasn't seen you in five days! What gives, friend? Call, or see—"

He was outside, the double-locked and coded door jerked tight and managed the porch steps carefully unhurried, kicked aside wrinkled winter crabapples still falling from the tree—police boots had splotched a few—unlocking, walking into his garage. Hal's last Papaschase treaty discussion with John over coffee had splintered away into talking about evil, again, why all this endless heavy in-your-face violence and evil when the world is endlessly beautiful and every human being everywhere on earth—except maybe a few psychotics—people love to laugh, long to be happy and to give and receive goodness, why—the heft of the Bible in his left hand—and Jesus insists God the Creator is good to everyone and everything and some of the world's most passionate god-lovers are often the most horrible haters. The black-butted car key in his hand sizzled like John's alphabet game through his head—the word-reversal game they sometimes played and bumbled into tough ideas, two and three letter words were easy, "pin" and "nip," or "god" and "dog," but it got trickier with four letters or more: the first two-thirds of "evolve" was "love," "diaper" the mirror of "repaid," "live" reversed was "evil"!—a mere accident of living in English, turn "evil" around and you get "live." Therefore language logic implied evil = dead?

Not funny, but they both laughed aloud at that turn. Why had they ever left their ancestral Low German? It could only be spoken, spelled however you wished and thus avoid anything; everything.

Facts: the things already done, acts that could never be undone; especially not by silly game. Are we what we remember? The city of Edmonton sprawled over land filched from the Cree, a rich part of it now classy Southgate Mall and Ainlay High School and prestigious suburbs on a place stolen from Papaschase people by deceitful Whites and sold to . . . ugggh—as Gabe would write—he was a good one to dig for others' blame, guilt . . . and the cemetery on the Two Hills—

Watch it! Traffic now, the more the better, his beloved ancient Celica faded grey and low and hard to see in traffic, stickshift quick as any rabbit. Anywhere but south, snort across 104th, left into Gateway Boulevard, right at Saskatchewan Drive, he had done evil running into the traffic on Whyte. Whatever the Orange Downfill was, the fact of his act injured innocent people and that guilt he would have to face, Saskatchewan Drive and immediately spin tight left full circle down into Queen Elizabeth Park Road, the burden of his thoughtless body reaction, he was swallowed in the triple stream of traffic crawling down the valley incline he and Owl had crossed and re-crossed down toward Walterdale Bridge: stay inside the moving stream, just get out of the city. He mainly drove the Camry, they might not know the Celica—of course they had instantly found both registrations on their patrol computer, but a small car was harder to spot, if he was important enough to try to spot in five-o'clock traffic. How much evil had he done running into a red light on Whyte, he should at least have looked in the newspaper, was he a criminal? Nothing ultimate—nobody dead or seriously—surely not, the police were too slow finding him, but enough thoughtless disaster, injury to be sue—millions beyond insurance? Oh easy, money buried and forgot everything in today's world, only pay and pay and you're wiped clean, no need to be forgiven, no revenge necessary, money piled on money heals every pain completely. But how much did he have for all the healing? Relatively little—his monthly pension and the house, blessed be Yo who insisted they buy up Miriam's and Dennis's huge Vancouver and Toronto mortgages— "What's the point of money in banks at 1.1 percent and the kids pay 5 on hundreds of thousands? Why wait till we're dead? Let's help each other now, especially about stupid money!"

Two mortgages of stupid money reduced their savings neatly—a third was never needed. Only a memorial niche in the Cemetery of the Two Hills. Overlooking the Papaschase theft.

It wasn't as easy as money.

It was a fact: he *saw* that Orange Downfill pass on the sidewalk. His eye and motion memory could not lie. That flowing curly hair. That easy turn of head and long body unforgettable. Had that left arm been bare as it swung into the right "Walk" signal he would have seen a white scar below the elbow: a touch of teen skin once opened, no extensor carpi radialis longus, no brachioradialis cut, a shallow flesh line only, but nonetheless more than horrible when ripped by a chainsaw in his two hands.

Careless or deliberate, it was evil.

Hal had been driving on instinct, very carefully, sixty years of experience, cooling a little and mind slowing as it completed its relentless repeating circle once again. He recognized the familiar route, no thought necessary: he was already past Stony Plain Road and headed south, needing now to round right off 170th Street into the shifty lanes west on Whitemud Drive. Just ahead, beyond the last of the green lights timed perfectly at speed limit, the freeway narrowed into hummocked Highway 628 bordering the Enoch Cree Nation. No evasions possible here, no road-allowance gravel south, only straight ahead lurch and pot-holes, overgrown ditches, rusted barbed wire. For minutes the Celica bumped alone on the gouged blacktop, nothing ahead or behind, such aspen forest and willowed fields of rural Alberta around him an evening white-tail might suddenly leap across—in the rear-view mirror a blue roof, a huge pickup, loomed out of the highway behind him. He slowed steadily to seventy and in seconds it was thudding past him, the mountain of Enoch garbage tires rising beyond the poplars slightly tinged with green as it roared by—RAM 3500 Heavy Duty Cast Iron Turbo Diesel 4x4, Quad Cab—good, marvellous Alberta, with any luck it would swing south at Highway 60 ahead of him.

But it was gone when Hal pulled into the STOP; blasting north. No super-male muscle to run interference for him. Five klicks below speed through the Enoch townsite, Watch for Pedestrians.

Dad, there's so many old cars rusting in their yards
Every ten years they bring in a crusher, they'll be gone
I don't want to play baseball, the coach just subs me when
    the game is lost
I'll talk to that stupid coach
No! I don't want to play at all
We just bought you the glove
Give it to Spud, he needs a better one
Nobody can think only of others, why would a good
    Creator make such lousy self-centred me me mes, always
    nothing but me
We made the rink and a nice net and now you're sitting on
    the snow bank
I got a penalty, two minutes for cross-checking
What's cross-checking
You use your stick, both hands like this, knock a guy down
    from behind
I make a mess of things, all the time
What's in a mess? Your university courses
I can't finish them, they're so
Why don't you finish? You're plenty smart—just write the
    essays, let me check over
No. I can't finish, I just make a mess
You didn't make a mess working on the cabin
That's boards and logs and ceilings and paint, that's Big Ed

It's you too! He shows you how and you do it, neat, it's very
    good

Everybody's just me me

Look at Jesus, he wasn't just me me me me all the time

Oh yeah, he just talked and talked stories, about sheep and
    goats, you right, you left

Hey! About sons and flowers too, birds, looking for lost sheep

Yeah, farming

You know what I'm talking about

So okay, he starved in a desert and fed 5000, okay, and got
    crucified quick

What's the matter, Gabe . . . please, what

It's no good, Dad. I love the Creek, sure . . . but nothing's
    any good

Had he and Gabriel ever said . . . yes, of course they had.
More. They had talked for hours, for days, all the years, son
and father they had been together! If only he had more
memory, he needed *re-memory,* wider memory recall of the
memories he had already scrambled through thousands
of time—where were they, *more*? Driving this highway to
Aspen Creek with Gabe twelve years at least once, often
twice a week: almost like commuting, so forever and he
could find only tiny, bare scraps, here and there, splinters
when he needed so much more. And sometimes, like now
watching the trees pass, he had nowhere to believe his
memory. Only the diary, the notebook scrawls . . . and the
bandage, the Oldman river-hills and floodplains stories to
re-member. A quarter of a century basically dis-membered.
Was heaven a continuous ogle of total virtual recall,

complete to coughs and glares and twitches and all simultaneous thoughts and stubborn silences? Too much inane facticity, even for eternal God.

Orange Downfill. Ineradicable.

But this land always was; now; had been for the decades they passed through/over it, wherever they looked it always was here. Always again. With Highway 627 gradually bending its open fields into knolls and valley muskegs and tight copses of poplar shimmering faintly spring green at a distance, rocky and twisted. No open Leduc County loam here thick as black cream over swamps of oil. Abruptly he felt unburdened, felt as enormously safe as only he could in a car flying smooth between these remaining bluffs of parkland forest, calm. But the tiny white comfort at Brightbank Corner was gone, a county road bulldozed through the cliff where the church once stood, its gaunt spire and door and two arrow-peaked windows looking south, a beautifully tiny classic church that had delighted them all the moment they saw it, he remembered how Miriam had shouted "Look!" and then Yo, and he hit the brakes and wheeled their brown '72 Ford around on the gravel, as it was then, and drove back and up into the small yard where they could almost see the hitching rail wide enough for three teams of horses, maybe four. The church was gone, the high bluff now heaped with crashed and uncontrollable sprouting poplars.

Nevertheless the coming river hills: the long hills, climbing south up and up where the highway notched into the sky and then quickly folded down to the North Saskatchewan River with only grazing cattle to nuzzle

over them, Herefords and cross-breed Angus: distance
spread between earth and cloudless evening with the sun
down on the right edge of the sky, the world quiet like
drinking a glass of warm milk your sister has just given
you with almost a smile. Over the last long hill, sweeping
up and there it loomed, the immense fortress of Genesee
Power Plant—a plant indeed, relentlessly growing—on the
southern horizon, its two giant chimneys half blazing in
the level light and stuck against a sudden tower of thunder
clouds, its steel power cables lines of light scooping into
the valley and across the river. Beyond the highway incline
in the far west he could see the smoke of Keephills Power
chimneys, farther still the horizon glaze of Sundance
Power. This magnificent land enduring everything human
beings could do to it: millennia of gathering and hunting,
a century of farming, now drilled for oil, torn open deep
for coal. Suffering people.

Then he was across the river and up, curving long till the
raw-ribbed ridges of open-pit coal were flying on either
side: coal lay everywhere below Alberta like an invitation
to hell and celebration. All you needed for electricity was
enough oil to tear the coal out of the ground and crush it
blazing into a furnace.

I heard a leaf fall when I died

Who said that?

And then it was
I could not see to see

When?

Straight snow-flecked gravel south to the notched Pigeon Lake Hills. Emmanuel Lobitski still cultivated the earth his great-grandfather from Bessarabia had home-steaded, and at the moment his fields were too close to Aspen Creek to be ripped open for the next human exploita-tion. Thirty years ago the Alberta Government had prom-ised there would be no more strip-mining within two miles of running water; a promise that could be changed in a legal instant. Hal drove slowly, his lights off, past the farm-house, past the seven oil donkeys pumping steadily on either side of the road allowance; Manny and Belinda and their children and cows and calves and hay and grain were long accustomed to that spin and sucking. And here at the T-intersection stood the No Through Traffic sign. Beside bare mottled trees which the Alberta Government declared were Hal and Yo's—he had words on a piece of paper that declared it, the oil and coal companies believed it—the tips of the trees a shimmer of green. Patches of May snow on the forest floor. DEAD END.

Hal pulled in tight under the spruce and aspen behind the cabin. Even if someone at the road saw his track in occasional snow and heaved the locked gate off its hinges and drove down the triple-bend driveway, they would not see the dark Celica unless they walked around the cabin. He lifted the Bible off the passenger seat, hoisted himself out and closed the door. He breathed sharp, fresh spring. Listened.

He heard the aspen groan. No frogs, no valley coyote song and echo. But the creek, the chuckle of melted snow far below in the rapids.

He did not walk to the edge of the cliff to look down at the ragged path of water gleaming in evening light, down at possible vees of beaver swimming upstream. Nor the path to the shed, behind which they had after cut away the towering aspen and young birch to clear a small meadow for playing thoughtless games, for a narrow garden where every spring the tips of carefully planted saskatoon bushes were gnawed by hungry moose into stark, flowerless brush—but with the single birch they left growing at the spot, bushy now and tall, at least twenty-five feet. No need for even a glance; it was axed in his memory.

Goodbye then. The pickup is serviced, both tanks filled with gas, there is all the time in the world to drive the five hundred kilometres to the Oldman River. But you will not drive there, to park where you can be found only by strangers. You come here: to be found by the ones you love, who love you. Too bad, Dad, you're in Montreal. I love you. Okay Dad, goodbye then.

Hal was walking towards the front door of the cabin. Along the wall, each golden Douglas fir log grooved, notched and stacked and holding its place. The pale aspen hovered over him like ceiling columns branching into the high darkness of a cathedral nave, thin snow muffled his steps, he felt himself walking through the wilderness of this world with a book in his hand and a great burden upon his back.

At the corner of the cabin the setting sun burst between the black western trees: flamed orange to red against burning clouds.

And, suddenly, there were bats flitting over him, here, there, an instant flutter of black that flopped into darkness, chirring like tiny sprockets, darted one instant there and gone and here and gone again, such twitching swoops of summer! Gabriel said, Must be nice to be a bat, the sounds of darkness help you see. But it was too early, too cold for mosquitoes . . . yet it seemed the benevolent bats were there over him, for this instant.

He stood listening to the flaming sky. What is to be done?

Hope is the thing with feathers
    That perches in the soul
And sings the tune without the words
    And never

Through the bars of trees the sun burned into the horizon. Last fall, after Yo's funeral, Dennis and Emma walked there at the turn of the road; so tall, so slight against the last light.

Bats have no feathers. But they do sing their own song. What shall I do.

He sits in the armchair beside the wood heater. Thick warmth from the fire he has laid wraps him like a feather blanket: his mother beside him sewing, Margret rustling above them in her space under the rafters, Thom's big body bent to the muted radio. Hal can hear them all over the static snarking in the small log room, ". . . the Shadow knows what evil lurks in . . ." and the laugh sinister, a radio program he is not allowed to listen to—a mutter of spring thunder coming—the carded layers of wool his mother has laid out on cloth held in a wooden frame that fills the living space as she sews the quilt for a mission auction, sewing she sings:

Schlop, Kliena, schlop.
　　Sleep, little one, sleep.
Buete senn de Schohp,
　　Outside are the sheep,
De Schohp mett witte Woll;
　　The sheep with their white wool;
Nu drintj dien Bukje voll.
　　Now drink your tummy full.

Seventy-five years of his singing memory. Human song must have begun with the howl of lament; which became prayer; which became hope. O Living God, let your mercy shine on us pitiful sinners.

Gabriel's blue Bible lies in his lap. His fingers touch a tab and there opening is Jesus, Matthew chapter 4, four heavy underlines in half a column:

Jesus was led up by the Spirit into the wilderness to be
　　tempted by the devil
And he fasted forty days and forty nights and afterward
　　he was hungry

All these I will give you if you fall down and worship me
God and him only shall you serve
and behold, angels came

The Spirit leads Jesus straight to the devil: the Tempter, the Accuser. Forty days and forty nights and he is most certainly hungry. Well, twenty-four years and seven months and ten or eleven days: how hungry are you then? What if you live searching what is written and filmed and sung and preached for years and face the Tempter, the Accuser every day and every day you starve? Why are the angels who come to you always, only, a terror?

But you know a possible place,
a place of security in the face of an experience
still frightening even once chosen

He unhooks the heater door, wide, and lays in three more splits of aspen. He watches the fire run, leap higher along the raw edges, cower and leap everywhere again into innumerable vanishing and reliving colours, spires and falls and flows of light. Gradually, steadily, the tracks of its running waft upward into the chimney, down to the floor of livid grey ash. This is what remains. In fire we confess our ashes.

His unanswerable questions list themselves like blessed Yo writing herself reminders on the scrap paper pads she bundles together with paper clips:

Why am I alone?

How can I confess?

Why don't I look in the basement storage for the Orange Downfill?

Why didn't I ask Owl to come with me?

How could you become so fearless as to plan that small truck ending?

Why do I try to freeze Yo in the final order of our house?

Why do I refuse to have a cellphone?

How could you lay your body down like that?

Why do I not visit Dennis or Miriam?

How could you imagine we could ever get over this?

Why did you come

The questions mirror themselves, he is surrounded, wherever he turns they repeat themselves into endless distance. Like the small ceremony held here with that urn. Thursday, September 12, 1985. Such a small container to contain all this.

Who am I to doubt fire and smoke and ash?

When will I confess and ask forgiveness for the evil I have done?

Gabe, you had such unimaginable strength to come here to park among the trees. Why couldn't you use that strength to

And from his staring incomprehension of the flames before him, of the open book in his lap, he gradually recognizes a pencil touch in the margin at the bottom corner of the page. The third verse of Matthew chapter 5:

Blessed are the poor in spirit, for theirs is the kingdom
   of heaven.

The burning wood in the heater collapses with a soft crush. From where he sits, without lifting his eyes from the words he can feel the shadows deepen beyond the stacked log archway into the living room. He sat here, in this body-molded armchair, the evening after they poured the ashes on the rapids and he raised his glance and saw Gabriel leaning against the left corner of the arch. Watching them all huddled around the heater. The round butt of a log haloed his head perfectly. Hal jerked erect: in the living room there was only darkness.

There is no need to look up, not now. He contemplates the message of the pencil touch. Night wind whistles in the chimney. He listens, yearning for a piano, and he hears the words of a letter that once came to him from Edmonton Prison, from a woman or a man he can never recall he had visited there:

For many of us, our families have deliberately
forgotten the sound of our names
But you know God does hear
the cry of the poor

Does he know? It may be he is not poor enough. Not yet.
Was Gabriel?
He waits.

RUDY WIEBE's novels, stories and non-fiction stand at the forefront of Canadian literature. He is widely published internationally and has won the Governor General's Literary Award for Fiction twice, for *The Temptations of Big Bear* and *A Discovery of Strangers*. *Stolen Life: The Journey of a Cree Woman*, which Wiebe co-authored with Yvonne Johnson, was awarded the Writers' Trust Non-Fiction Prize, among numerous others. His memoir, *Of This Earth: A Mennonite Boyhood in the Boreal Forest*, won the Charles Taylor Prize for Literary Non-Fiction and was a national bestseller. He is an Officer of the Order of Canada and lives in Edmonton with his wife, Tena.

A NOTE ABOUT THE TYPE

Come Back is set in Monotype Dante, a modern font family designed by Giovanni Mardersteig in the late 1940s. Based on the classic book faces of Bembo and Centaur, Dante features an italic, which harmonizes extremely well with its roman partner. The digital version of Dante was issued in 1993, in three weights and including a set of titling capitals.